W[illegible]EN BEC[illegible]ES NOW

SORREL FARM BOOK 3

SARA MADDERSON

For my wonderful husband, Chris.

This isn't the first time I've had to make this point to you, but I promise this isn't autobiographical!

I love you.

Because of you

I never stray too far from the sidewalk

Because of you

I learned to play on the safe side so I don't get hurt

— Kelly Clarkson

1

2019

When Clara Winters heard she'd have to photograph Alex Molloy, she nearly threw up. And today's the day she has to meet him, and the nausea that's been building inside her for the past couple of weeks is threatening to come to a head. Evelyn, the commercial director of Sorrel Farm and therefore her boss when she's freelancing at the farm, had an enormous smile on her face when she asked Clara.

Presumably she figured, quite reasonably, that Clara would be ecstatic to cover the upcoming wellness conference. It was a huge focus for the farm, and Clara knew Evelyn intended it to be an annual event from now on. Add to that the fact that it was being headlined by Alex Molloy, online fitness guru, virtual personal trainer to millions and national treasure, and Evelyn would, of course, be forgiven for thinking that any red-blooded female would jump at the opportunity.

Clara had been freelancing here for a few months, but she didn't know Evelyn that well. That said, she knew instantly she'd have to come clean. Even if she didn't want to, she could see from Evelyn's confused reactions that her own face must be quite a picture.

She played for time. 'Ohhhh.' She drew the word out as much as possible. 'Thank you—but I'm—I'm not sure I'm the right person for the job.'

Evelyn's face fell. 'Of course you are. You're basically our in-house photographer these days. We don't want anyone else. Alex is bringing his own YouTube team to video it all, but that was his only stipulation. He's happy for us to provide the photographer. I thought you'd jump at the chance! He's very—*charming*.' She smiled mischievously.

That was an understatement. He was nothing short of beautiful. Another chance to buy time. 'Do you know him?' she asked Evelyn.

'Yes, for years, through Seb. Seb's headlining it with him.'

Seb was Seb Macleod, Evelyn's ex-husband, and an even bigger draw than Alex. He and Evelyn were a power-couple in London until last year, when he came out as gay. The way Evelyn explained it, she fled down here to find solace at Sorrel Farm with her great friends Jess and Zoe, the founders. She was now engaged to Angus Rutherford, the farm manager here.

Evelyn had been nothing but delightful since Clara arrived. She was a glossy beauty, her chestnut hair always immaculately blow-dried. Clara wasn't really into fashion, but even she could appreciate Evelyn's designer wardrobe. The day she sprung this bombshell on her, she was wearing a snug navy and red polo neck with interlocking Gucci Gs across the bust. She looked ready to hit the ski slopes. She'd thrown as much extra work as possible Clara's way, for which she was incredibly grateful. Clara was supposed to be here to photograph Zoe, who was head-chef and co-founder, and her delicious food for a new Sorrel Farm cook book Evelyn was spearheading. This request to cover the conference was a coup, and Clara knew it. It was crunch time.

'The thing is.' She looked at Evelyn. 'The thing is—I know Alex, too. I suppose you haven't mentioned my name to him?'

'I had no idea!' Evelyn was naturally effusive about everything. She clasped her hands together. 'How fabulous. How do you guys know each other? No, I just told him we had a wonderful in-house photographer who could document the conference beautifully.'

'Well.' *Shit.* 'This is very awkward—I'd like to keep it between us, if possible. We used to go out, actually. At school.'

There. She'd said it; she'd admitted the truth out loud, and some pressure instantly left her body. But she couldn't rest easy yet. Evelyn's eyes widened in disbelief. It was almost comical.

'You went *out* with him? At school? Wow!'

She knew what Evelyn was thinking. She was doing mental maths. Alex's improbable success story was well known. It had been trotted out on a million morning TV shows and inspirational podcasts and *Daily Mail* articles. Not that she followed any of them. She could absorb every tiny detail of his life like a starving person if she gave herself the smallest opening, but it would be categorically unhelpful. She was in a different place now. She had a husband and two beautiful children, and obsessing over someone from a past life served no purpose whatsoever.

'But he has a pretty troubled past, no?' Evelyn continued. 'Was that—were you around for all that?'

The question she knew she'd ask. 'He has a very *tragic* past. And yes, I was, unfortunately.'

Silence. She could imagine the workings of Evelyn's brain as she looked at Clara with fresh eyes: with pity and not a small amount of curiosity.

'Jesus. I'm so sorry, Clara.' Evelyn put her hand over Clara's, and the sympathetic gesture made her eyes prick. 'I can't even imagine. I had no idea—we'll find someone else, if you like. I understand why you might want to stay well clear.'

It had been twenty-one years. Twenty-one bloody years since she'd had any contact with him whatsoever. Twenty-one years since his life and hers changed forever in a moment. Every major life decision she'd made since then had been coloured by Alex Molloy. It was time to lay the ghost.

'I'll do it,' she told Evelyn.

IT WAS ALL VERY WELL to agree to shoot Alex in a moment of defiance and exhaustion and heightened emotion, but now she has to see the guy. She has to put one foot in front of the other like a normal person, and walk up to him in the flesh, and look him in those ridiculous eyes that could always see into her soul, and actually *talk* to him about coverage and content and social media opportunities. Good lord. She really thinks she might puke. Her mouth fills with saliva and she turns from the bathroom mirror and spits into the loo. Ugh.

She told Evelyn there was no way she could face him in a meeting full of people; she couldn't say hi and shake his hand (or hug him. Oh God, would she have to *hug* him?) in front of Evelyn and Sadie, her PR manager, and whoever was there from Alex' entourage (at that, she imagined him strolling down an LA boulevard in wraparound shades with a crowd of people running alongside him, and nearly giggled. She must be delirious). No, she needed to do this alone, and she absolutely, one hundred percent, had to make sure that Alex wasn't blindsided by this, that he knew who she was. She gave Evelyn her maiden name. He might not recognise Clara Winters, she explained (who knew if he'd ever thought about her at all in the past two decades, while he was busy making his millions and building his personal brand). But he should hopefully remember Clara Fiori. Evelyn should make one million percent certain that he's happy to go ahead with her. With his Clara. With his *angel*.

At the thought of the old nickname, she stiffens and doubles down on her efforts to make herself look as good as possible. She's got to be carrying at least an extra two stone since she was with him. That would be depressing enough, if she didn't think about the fact that his flawless body is now a national treasure in its own right. At least she's still got her boobs. He always loved her boobs. She shakes her head, an attempt to clear an ancient, but strangely vivid, image of them sitting on her bed. He's leaning back against her pink velvet headboard, and she's straddling him, topless. His head is bent to her chest, and she cradles it in her arms, marvelling at the miracles that occur every second under his clean-shaven scalp, her long hair falling over both of them. They're like Mark Wahlberg and Kate Moss. They're probably as young and gorgeous as Mark and Kate. With bigger boobs. *Unhelpful. Get a grip.*

She's chosen a snug v-neck jumper that shows off her assets. Why she feels the need to showcase them to a man who's not her husband, she doesn't want to ponder too much. She's rejected the idea of jeans—her mum jeans today are too depressingly far from those tight little 501s he would have known—in favour of a floaty skirt. She adds a belt. Cinching is my friend, she tells herself. It's going to have to do. Her hair's still as long as it used to be. Her eyes are still as huge and brown. And her boobs are… not looking half bad, thanks to her bra's gravity-defying engineering. Everything else has gone downhill, but there's not much she can do about that. Thank God for Spanx.

It's time to have the most surreal experience of her life: well, of the life she's forged since Alex Molloy disappeared from it, anyway.

2

2019

He can't believe he's agreed to this. He can't believe he's agreed to let Clara Fiori in once more, after twenty-one years of keeping his head down, focusing on getting through the days and pulling himself up, millimetre by millimetre, from the fucking cesspit he made of his life. It's still not a life; it's an existence. On the outside, it's a gilded existence, but the people who perceive it like that are measuring the wrong things: fame, impact, money—and probably his Body Mass Index. In terms of things that matter, he's putting on a poor fucking show.

He sits in a quiet corner of the Oast House at Sorrel Farm. A patch of weak January sunlight makes it through the skeletal trees outside and hits the side of his face. He squints and smiles to himself. Sunlight. That's not something to ever take for granted. Especially not at this time of year. Maybe it's a sign that today will go okay. He slips his fingers inside the open neck of his shirt and briefly touches the silver crucifix that sits against his chest.

She's due in five minutes. When Evelyn messaged him about Clara, he couldn't believe his eyes.

Our photographer's happy to cover the event, she wrote, *but I hadn't realised you two know each other. Her name's Clara Fiori. She wanted me to check with you if you're OK to go ahead. If so, I'd suggest you two catch up first on the remit before we brief the broader team.*

What were the chances? He knew from Fr Pat that she'd stayed in Kent, but he thought she was a museum curator or something—not a photographer, anyway. He stared at the message and scratched the side of his nose. This was bad. He should make a polite excuse, request another photographer. He'd managed without seeing her for long enough. But he found himself typing back *Of course—great to have her on board* and *An initial chat with her makes sense; can you set it up via Trish?* and some other bullshit that didn't make it sound as though he was falling apart at the mere idea of seeing her.

And suddenly, now, there she is: an angel, made flesh. He has the advantage over her; he sees her as soon as she comes into the Oast House on the far side. He recognises her posture, her gait, immediately. It's the same ramrod-straight-backed walk that used to send him wild in the school corridors. She's curvier than she was before, when she was just a slip of a girl. The curves suit her. They really suit her. The next thing he notices is that her hair is *exactly* the same. Fuck, that chocolate coloured hair. He's dreamt of that hair a million times, wound around his hand like a satin snake, tendrils teasing his stomach, his chest, when she was astride him... It shimmers around her as she walks across the sunlit room. And then she spots him, and twenty-one years disappear like a wisp of ash up a chimney—*whoosh*—and then and now converge.

Instantly, she slows down; her walk becomes more hesitant. He can't blame her. He's in pieces. He stands up, shoves his hands in his pockets. As she comes closer, a smile passes across her face. An *I can't believe it* smile. He's right there with her. It's too fucking weird, this. Presumably, she has no more idea of how to act in this situation than he does. He planned to be warm but cool: friendly, but in control. But it's his smile that takes control and hijacks his face as his eyes move over her in wonder. That she's been out there, living and breathing and seemingly flourishing for all these years, and is now *here*, in front of him, seems too herculean a concept for his brain to compute. And she's beautiful. So, so beautiful. She makes everyone else in this place look ordinary. It was the same at school. She's never lost that power.

She stops and smiles, her eyes darting to and away from his face. Shy. Sad. Uncertain. 'Hi, Alex. Long time, no see.'

Now she's here, there's only one conceivable course of action. He opens his arms, and she stumbles into them. He folds them around her and squeezes, more tightly than he's planned. 'Hello, angel,' he says.

3

1997

Before he approached her on the way home from school, she'd never spoken to him. Obviously not. She had no idea he even knew she existed. There were one hundred and eighty pupils in their year-group, and they were in different forms. But she knew who he was. Everybody did. He was Alex Molloy: deadly focused on the football pitch and a waste of space off it. That was what she'd heard a teacher say about him, anyway. They only shared one GCSE subject class: Chemistry. She was in the top set for Maths and French. He didn't fool around during Chemistry; he just never volunteered any answers. When the teacher singled him out, his answers were monosyllabic but usually correct, so she observed idly that the *waste of space* label was unfair. Other than that, she knew he lived on the Jubilee estate, that his brother was far worse news than he was, that he smoked and sometimes drank with Matt Foster and some other Jubilee boys behind the science block, and that he was quite honestly the most beautiful human being she'd ever set eyes on.

She didn't think about him, though. Not really. He may

as well have come from a different planet. Even though he was in fifth year, he hooked up with girls from the lower and upper sixth. She didn't hook up with anyone. She was at St Winifred's to learn. That was what her parents had always told her. Plus, she was scared of boys.

She kept her head down and worked really, really hard in lessons, and her small cluster of good girlfriends did the same. After school, she'd go straight to her parents' restaurant in Otford, Casa Valentina. Valentina was her mum's name, and they'd run it since long before she was born. After she'd helped them with the food prep for the evening shift and nicked an early bite for herself, she'd head home and do her homework. She didn't mind being alone in the house. It helped her focus. She was taking an extra GCSE: ten, instead of the obligatory nine, because she couldn't choose between Latin and German. So she had a lot to keep her busy.

And then one day, a few weeks before Christmas, she was walking to the restaurant and she heard her name called behind her. *Clara.* She knew exactly who was saying it, and she'd never heard anything so wonderful, even though he said it in a Kent accent and not with the melodic Italian flourish that her parents gave it. When he said it, this weird little thrill ran down her inner arms and around her stomach. She stopped and turned around. And there he was.

He came towards her with his hands in his pockets, and she always remembered after that how fully he held eye contact with her. His eyes were the most improbable pale green, in miraculous contrast to the velvety coffee colour of his skin, and his shaved head made them stand out even more. And he just looked at her with those eyes and stopped in front of her, and asked if he could walk her to her parents' restaurant.

He didn't seem nervous or embarrassed. She was too shocked to ask him how he even knew about her parents' restaurant. She just stood there, trying to figure out what on earth he was playing at, bothering to walk her back. She looked around to see if it was a joke, to see if Matt Foster or some other dick was lurking and waiting to laugh at her, but she couldn't see anyone. And so she just asked him, *why?*

His answer was the most wonderful thing she'd ever heard. Even more wonderful than when he'd said her name. *Because I'd like to. Because you're the most beautiful girl I've ever seen.* The most amazing thing about the whole thing was that he never broke eye contact. He just watched her with those green eyes when he said it. He didn't twitch or fidget; he didn't even smile. He didn't even seem embarrassed, though she was dying inside with embarrassment for him, even while she was dying inside from the miraculous thrill of those words coming from that mouth, and those eyes focused solely, intently on her.

And so she said *okay*, because what else are you supposed to say when a boy who looks like him says that to you? And so they walked.

He found her again the next day, in the same place, a few steps out of the school gates. And the next. And after the weekend, he stood at the gates and waited for her to come past. And that afternoon, he took her hand right after they left school, and he held it *all the way* to the restaurant. Neither of them could stop grinning. And the following week, he led her very gently by the hand into a quiet side street near the restaurant. It was good that it was winter, because it was already dark, but she could see the question in his green eyes when he stood there with her, and put his arms around her. And then he kissed her.

She'd been so nervous—sick with nerves—thinking about what it would be like to kiss someone finally, to kiss *him*, but as soon as she felt the miraculous pressure of his lips on hers, she forgot to wonder or think about anything. His tongue was so soft, far softer than she'd imagined it would be, and he moved his hand to the back of her head and stroked her hair gently, carefully, and all of these new, heavenly sensations together made her brain feel as if it were filled with prosecco.

At the end of January, they celebrated the end of their mock exams in her single bed, together in her silent house as her parents worked the evening shift at the restaurant.

By the end of February, she couldn't remember the person she'd been before he spoke her name outside the school gates. She wasn't a whole person anymore; she was one half of him. She couldn't function unless as much surface area of her skin as humanly possible was pressed to his skin. She couldn't breathe unless he was inside her. She couldn't conceive of life without the miracle of Alex Molloy wrapped around her. If this was what addiction was, she was a goner.

4

2019

She's expecting a brief, cursory embrace, but it lasts a few long seconds. It's a proper, committed hug and she reciprocates by putting her arms awkwardly around his back, gripping her phone in one hand and her notebook in the other.

He's bigger now. He was lean and sinewy as a boy, almost balletic on the football pitch, but now he's more solid, broader in the shoulders and across the chest, and she'd put money on the increased girth being pure muscle, unlike her own slow, squishy spread through her thirties. The oddest thing is that he smells the same. Of course he does, and yet... The Lynx is gone, replaced with some heavenly, expensive-smelling cologne, but the scent of his neck when he pulls her into his arms almost knocks her sideways. Her brain can just about compute how it feels to *see* him, but her sense of smell has acted like a stealth portal, propelling her instantly, cruelly, back to her narrow bed and to perfect happiness, the likes of which she's never known beyond the four walls of her childhood bedroom.

He releases her suddenly and pulls back, his face

wearing an expression that she suspects is similar to hers, before he grins at her. He's had his teeth done: they're perfectly straight and very white. His smile lights up his face. She always thought he had one of the most transformative smiles she'd ever seen on anyone. He still has it. He is so bloody gorgeous that she just wants to gape.

'Have a seat.' He gestures at the chair opposite his and she shrugs the rucksack off her back and sits.

'Coffee?' He beckons over a server who's been hovering nearby. He's authoritative but polite, and she has to remind herself not to stare. This easy comfort in his own skin is so different from his twitchiness as a mixed-race kid whose dad bailed on him and who hailed from one of the most notorious sink estates in North Kent. He told her many times that the only time he felt being himself was enough was when he with her. He was more than enough for her; it was an overwhelming, incessant barrage of blessings when she was with him.

Said overwhelm must show on her face, for he settles into his chair after they've ordered and throws up his hands. 'I mean, where the fuck do we start?'

She laughs, grateful for his having broken the tension. 'Hard to know. I guess firstly... how are you? You look—great. Are you?'

'Yeah, I'm good.' He nods his head. 'Really good, actually. Turns out, exercise is a lifesaver.'

'I wouldn't know,' she says drily, 'as you can see. But I'll take your word for it.'

His eyes move down her body. 'Don't say that. You're perfect. You always were.'

Her skin pricks. 'Not sure about that. But clearly you've conquered the world of working out. It's been amazing, seeing what you've achieved.'

'It's good fun. But I haven't done it for the—profile. It just worked for me. Got me through a lot of shit. So if I can help other people get healthy and work through their own shit, then… It's good to feel like you're doing something useful. I was at St Winnie's a few weeks ago, y'know?'

'No way! That must have been surreal. What were you doing there?'

'Tom—Mr Evans—got me in to talk at a school assembly. It was seriously weird. They've built a posh new hall, but otherwise it felt exactly the same. Can you imagine they actually let me back through those school gates again, after all the shit that went down?'

Their eyes meet, and she senses the sadness behind his jokey tone. She manages a small smile. 'I'm sure they were thrilled to have you there—there must have been great excitement. But I didn't know you stayed in touch with Mr Evans?'

'Yep. Him and Fr Pat—they were both really great to me. I couldn't have got through it without them.' He drops his eyes to his lap. 'I still see Tom once a month for a kickabout and a beer. We're good mates. He got me my first job, y'know? After I… he got me working as a trainee PT at his mate's gym in the East End; that's how it all started.'

She feels an overwhelming rush of gratitude for these two men who likely saved Alex, who stood by him when no one else would. There's so much unsaid, it would take years to say it. Instead, she stirs the cappuccino that's just arrived. 'It makes me happy that you two are still in touch. He was always your biggest fan; he thought you were going to be the next Alan Shearer.'

'Yeah, well, he was wrong there. Maybe if I'd spent less time pissing about with Matt Foster and those twats. But he's a great guy. He still teaches PE; he's got a couple of years left until retirement. But enough about me. What about you? I heard you got married?'

'I did.' She resists an odd urge to hide her left hand under her thigh. 'How did you hear that?'

'Fr Pat.'

'Of course.' Her parents still see him every Sunday when they go to Mass at St Winifred's church, next to the school.

'Is he a good guy?' There's a funny, tight look on Alex's face.

'Who?'

'Your husband.'

She starts. 'Oh. Yeah. He's... nice. He's a good guy.'

'Jesus.' His tone is dry. 'Please, don't gush too much over the poor fucker.'

She tries to think of something that will explain her decision to marry Jeremy, but she can't think of anything that wouldn't be hurtful to Alex, because Jeremy is the absolute antithesis of him in every way.

'We've got twins,' she says instead. 'A boy and a girl. Charlie and Violet. They're eleven.' She can't help but smile at the thought of them, and he mirrors her smile.

'Twins. Fuck.'

'You can say that again. It was an experience. But they're amazing now.'

'You didn't give them Italian names?'

'No.' Definitely not. 'Jeremy wouldn't have... He's very British.'

'I see.' He looks like he wants to ask more, but instead he takes a sip of his espresso. 'Tell me about them.'

'Well, they've just started at secondary school, and the difference between them is hilarious. They are night and day. Violet spends all evening doing her homework. She even gets up early to do it before school, and Charlie just wants to play computer games every hour God sends.'

He erupts into laughter. It's such a gorgeous sight—head thrown back, eyes crinkling to nothing, white teeth on full display—that it warms every inch of her skin. He rubs his clean-shaven scalp with one hand, and she can't help but notice that his beautifully pressed blue shirt strains across his biceps as he does so.

'Sorry.' He puts his hand down and attempts to pull himself together. 'It's just that Violet sounds *exactly* like a girl I used to know. The apple doesn't fall far from the tree, does it?'

It would be a throwaway comment, except that he says it so softly and looks at her with so much memory and affection in his eyes that she can do nothing but stare back at him. It's not fair. She has no idea what to do with these feelings, these memories, with the enormous burden of twenty-one years of zero closure—of precisely the opposite, in fact—weighing her down, suffocating her. Twenty-one years of no contact and no answers and no way to heal from the fact that she fell off a figurative cliff, that day in 1998, and she's been stumbling along ever since, trying to exist with no real tools to help her do so. It's as if she fell off an actual cliff and they left her to heal with no scans, no splints, no plaster casts or traction or physio or painkillers. That's how catastrophic the damage felt.

All the emotions washing through her must be flickering on her face. He told her that, years ago: he told her he could read every thought she had, and that the expressiveness of her face was one of the things he loved most about her. It seems he hasn't lost his psychic powers where she's concerned, for he leans over and grabs her hand. He puts it between his two warm, dry hands and just presses down, and something about this hand sandwich, or whatever it is, feels so bloody reassuring and heavenly that she wishes she could just lie down on the pretty rug. She could sleep for a million years if Alex Molloy were there to hold her hand like this.

'I'm so sorry, angel,' he says, and his words are slow and quiet and deliberate. She has no idea how far back that *sorry* goes, how all-encompassing it is, but she suspects it doesn't go far or wide enough.

'It's ok.' Her voice sounds flat, like Violet's after she's been told off.

'It's not ok. And—I know how much there is to talk about. Another time, maybe? If we're both feeling up to it.'

She's exhausted at the mere thought of dismantling the vast mountain of shit that lies between them.

'I'm fine. Honestly. And yes, maybe we can chat another time, but right now I'd love to hear all about the conference.' She almost believes it.

~

HE COULD KICK himself for putting that expression on her face. If there was anyone on the planet, other than his mum, whom he'd do anything not to hurt, it would be Clara, and yet he's hurt her more than he can begin to imagine. It's not okay. She's married, she's a mum, she's an extraordinary human being, and from now on he's going to make sure that he does nothing to upset her and everything to make her life as easy and joyful as it deserves to be.

They cover off the rest of the family chat pretty quickly. Her parents are still running Casa Valentina and doing well. Her older sisters are married, and it sounds like they've produced lots of kids like good Italian Catholic girls. He tells her his mum is thriving. Thank God they totalled Jubilee a few years back, because she would never have left of her own accord. It's now a giant retail park with an Asda and a Cineworld. By then, he had enough cash in the bank to buy her a nice apartment and she's lived there happily, refusing his pleas to let him buy her a bigger place with a garden. His older brother, Connor, runs his website for him. He laughs at the look of surprise on her face. Connor was a piece of work when she knew him.

When Clara talks about her kids, she gets this look on her face: dreamy and blissful. He can't articulate what that look does to him, beyond igniting a fearful mix of deep pride that she's clearly as good a mother as he always knew she would be, and an aching emptiness that he's played no part whatsoever in this aspect of her life. The kids sound like proper little characters. Maybe, if he and she can build some semblance of friendship out of the pathetic ashes of their relationship, he can meet her kids one day.

They don't talk too much more about his career, his success. It's too fucking weird. She tells him what a shock she got the first time she saw him on TV. He can't even imagine what that must have been like for her, having his mug pop up on the TV and in the press from time to time. She says she's so proud of him, and so pleased everything has worked out well for him. She doesn't know the half of it, but there's a light of fondness in her eyes when she says it that makes his chest ache.

They move onto the conference. She pulls her laptop out of her rucksack and shows him some of the shots she's done for the farm. They're quite simply beautiful: like the photographic equivalent of fine art. They're sensual and alluring, whether she's captured the mist rising off the fields on a winter's morning, or the lustre of winter fruit and vegetables in a still-life. They give him goosebumps. She's taken some shots of a beautiful chef who she explains is Zoe. He hasn't met Zoe or Jess yet, though he's heard a lot about them from Evelyn.

'These are fucking incredible,' he tells her as they scroll through, their heads bent together. 'I can think of so much I'd love your help with content-wise, far beyond the conference.' He'd also like to commission some local landscapes for his new gaff, but he'll raise that prospect another time.

'Oh.' She blushes and sits back, pulling away from him. 'You don't need to do that. I'm not even really a proper photographer. I'm self-taught—'

'Bollocks.' He glares at her. 'This is me you're talking to, angel. I know you inside and out—' He stops, horrified, and she freezes.

'Jesus Christ.' He rubs one hand across his face and holds the other one up. 'I'm so sorry. I did not intend that *pun*. Let's move on.' His face has heated up, and he glances up to see hers has too, but she's laughing, thank fuck.

He pushes on. 'What I mean is: I know how talented you are, and I know that everything you put your mind to, you do well. I remember your GSCE Art coursework. It was stunning. You have a great eye and a great talent, and I know an opportunity when I see one. This isn't me trying to do a good deed, for fuck's sake. I'd like to work with you.'

She meets his eye and hers glint with mischief. 'Well. You do kind of owe me, for, you know, ruining my life. So I'm happy to take your charity.'

As they have a laugh and she packs up her stuff, he allows himself to watch her unashamedly. She tucks her hair behind her ear and he recalls having seen her do that a million times before. Diamonds glint in her ears now, rather than the tiny gold studs she used to wear. He remembers everything. Whatever comment she made earlier about her lack of fitness is utter bullshit; her curves are perfect: womanly and seductive. She has some snug sweater on that dips at the front and shows off a hint of plump, golden cleavage that makes him want to bury his head in it, the way he used to. Fuck.

His first impressions were correct. She's even more beautiful than she used to be. He wouldn't have thought that was possible. The flawless gloss of youth has faded, but she's grown into her bone structure and her dark eyes are huge, and more deep set than before, above her cheekbones. She's an absolute pleasure to look at. And she has a refined manner that was always there, even at St Winnie's, but now it's more polished. She's grown into the woman he's always known she would be. She's done herself proud.

She mentioned in passing that her husband is a lawyer. *Jeremy*: what a wanky name. Clearly they're comfortable, judging from the diamonds and the elegant little Rolex kissing her wrist. But she hasn't said much else about him, which is odd. Perhaps she realises the awkwardness of discussing her husband with him; perhaps it's something more. There's absolutely nothing in that expressive face when she mentions him. Fuck all emotion or love. Interesting.

They stand to say goodbye.

'Are you just down here for the day?' She wrestles her rucksack back onto her shoulders and he tries to keep his eyes on her face as she arches her back.

'Nope. I moved down here a few months ago—I bought a place in Hildenborough. But they're putting in a new extension for my fitness studio, so I'm living in the stables here for a few weeks. They're letting me shoot my workout videos in the gym here.'

She raises her eyebrows. 'Nice.'

'Yeah, it is. It's a far cry from the Jubilee.' He grins and she reciprocates. He thought it would be nice to stay here and support Evelyn, but Sorrel Farm is spectacular. The stables make up the farm's largest and most expensive suite; they're more like a beautiful duplex with their own gardens out back. They must be gorgeous in summer. He'll be sorry to move out of here, excited though he is about the new pad. He has a feeling the stables' decor would appeal to Clara's feminine, romantic tastes, but to invite her over so soon would be creepy. He should keep this to professional interaction, with the possibility of a quiet, slow-blooming friendship to hope for.

She goes to hug him goodbye and there's an awkward moment where he goes in for a double kiss and she holds firm in the hug. Their noses brush before he realises his error. Thankfully, she laughs it off.

'Alex Molloy, doing the double kiss thing. I never thought I'd see the day.'

He laughs, runs his hand over his scalp. 'Tell me about it. I've turned into a pretentious wanker.'

'Not yet,' she says. 'But I'll let you know if you do.'

Just before she turns to go, he whispers in the vicinity of her ear: 'I'm glad you didn't cut your hair.'

5

2019

She floats to school for pickup, and when she gets the kids home, she floats around the kitchen. She's wrapped in a bubble of supreme wellbeing. She can't quite articulate it, but at least part of it seems to be due to the relief of seeing him well and happy. It's as if she's woken from a nightmare only to realise it's not real. She's carried an ache for years, that he's been out there in the world without her, clawing himself up from the nadir. And although she's had a few years to acquaint herself with the idea that he's successful and actually famous, it's not the same as seeing him for herself. She can finally breathe easy; she can put down some of the burden she's been carrying all this time.

It's not just relief, of course. She's giddy with the effect that an hour in his presence has had on her. Her pleasure at seeing him and being the focus of his attention is absolute. She can't remember the last time she felt this alive. She expected to feel curious (understatement), heartbroken for how much they've both suffered, overwhelmed, and impressed by the success he's had. She was resigned to the fact that there'd likely be a physical attraction on her part (understatement). She tried very hard not to think about whether they'd still have any kind of connection.

The conversation was lovely, but they kept the topics fairly safe: they both seemed in agreement that opening up old wounds would not be the way to go over coffee. Besides, they've both moved on. She's got Jeremy and the kids and he's got fame and fortune (thankfully he didn't mention any significant female in his life). So it wasn't the depth of their conversation that has her walking on air now. It was just *him*. Looking at him, drinking him in, allowing her eyes to travel all over him earlier was just so bloody *pleasurable* (not that that makes her any different from any housewife in Britain, in that respect). Basking in his smile and his interest gave her a natural high that was magic.

Seeing him today was a watershed. She's spent years and years imagining this moment. It used to be all she thought about. When would she see him? How would he look? How would he be, in himself, and with her? And then out of the blue, Evelyn served him up to her and *poof*, there he was. That face. Dear God, that face, *finally* in front of her. All she ever wanted, for so long, was to see him again, and it's happened, long after she gave up on the possibility of that wish coming true. He's back in her life, in some way, and she got to lay her eyes on him again, and put her arms around him, and just be with him.

And, if she's completely honest with herself, the whole episode has dredged up memory after memory. Intimate memories that she hasn't allowed herself to think about for years. Perfect little vignettes that have been floating to the surface of her brain since she inhaled him. He's up there with Violet and Charlie as the best smell she's ever smelt. So many of his mannerisms are the same, from the way he rubs his head when he's thinking, to the way his hand goes to his crucifix every few minutes. That crucifix was the only thing his pathetic Irish dad left him before he bailed on Carmen and her boys when Alex was just a baby. That he still wears it breaks her heart a little.

The memories that have had the audacity to bubble up in her brain and seemingly turn her blood to champagne this afternoon are, in no particular order: the weight of him on top of her; the sight of him under her; that sharp intake of air from him the first time she allowed him inside her; the perfect curve of his pecs (she bets they're even more perfectly curved now); the look in his eyes that first time he said her name outside school; his long, slim fingers on her stomach (still long, still slim); his shouts of laughter as she stripped off an item of his clothing for every chemistry question he got wrong and stripped off an item of her own clothing for every one he got one right (it was amazing how effective a teaching strategy that was); the jam doughnuts he bought her from Gregg's on Friday afternoons, and the loving care he took when licking the sugar crumbs from the corners of her mouth.

So basically, she's screwed. Screwed and—antsy. A moment later, she redefines the feeling. She's horny. Good lord. She's never, ever horny at four-thirty in the afternoon. It's all these thoughts of carefree teenage romps. They never had time for their relationship to lose its heat. The guillotine fell right in the middle of their story. Aside from today, all the time she's ever spent with him has had crazy lust, and adoration, and probably unhealthy co-dependence, front and centre. She's programmed to think of ripping his clothes off whenever she's with him; she has no other reference point. No wonder she found it impossible to talk websites and wellness today; her subconscious unleashed itself as soon as she smelt him.

He exists outside of her normal life of school run and home-making and photography and trying to be a decent wife. He exists in a parallel world that's just the two of them, and it's as if every moment, every touch, that they invested in each other in the distant past has served to provide so much commonality that they could quite easily just pick up where they left off, in a bedroom, on a bed, clothes and phones and laptops and all other intrusive paraphernalia cast aside. It's almost as if she has the right to desire that, to expect it, to demand it from him. It's her due. As she told him, he owes her. That was only half a joke.

She has no coping mechanisms for dealing with her sex hormones in the middle of the afternoon, so she gets to work chopping onions and mincing garlic and simmering tomatoes for dinner. Violet stuck the Les Mis soundtrack on when they got in (the movie version, which Clara finds quite underwhelming compared to the original West End version), and she finds herself singing *On my Own* at full pelt, with not a small amount of emotion, when her daughter re-enters the kitchen.

'No offence, Mum'—she pops a grape into her mouth—'but you really don't have the vocal range for that song.'

There's nothing like the brutal honesty of a child to burst your bubble. Clara was quite involved in the performance, actually.

'Thanks a lot.' She pulls Violet's plump plait. 'No snacking before supper.'

Violet shrugs. 'You have a nice voice. Just... I don't think you're a soprano. It's best to work within your limits.'

They make faces at each other.

'Have you done your homework?'

'Obviously. Charlie's playing Fortnite, though. I heard him yelling at Noah on his headset.'

At least, she reflects as she bolts up the stairs, parenting offers a convenient distraction from inappropriate sexual thoughts about inappropriate exes.

SHE HAS A DILEMMA AT SUPPER. She's never mentioned Alex to Jeremy. He knows the basics, and at some point she probably called Alex by his first name, but at no point since Alex Molloy shot to fame has she ever connected the dots for him. She's confident he's never had sufficient interest in Alex's story, as told in the press, for it to sound familiar.

It's seven-thirty: too late for the kids to be eating on a school night, but Jeremy insists on a couple of family suppers a week and he was late back from the City this evening. He's already railed about the incompetence of South Eastern Trains, so it would be churlish of her to make him feel any worse, but Charlie's wilting and Violet's quieter than normal.

She takes a breath. 'I met Alex Molloy today,' she tells the table. 'He's doing a wellness conference at Sorrel Farm in a couple of weeks, and they've asked me to take photos on the day.'

'That sounds nice, darling.' Jeremy reaches for more broccoli. 'This little photography hobby is really coming on, isn't it?'

She keeps her tone even. 'I'd like to think it's more than a hobby. But yes, it's a coup for me.'

'What's he like? Molloy? He looks like a bit of a thug.'

She stays very still in an attempt to shrug off the most

bizarrely strong inclination to throw the bowl of broccoli at her husband.

'He's not a thug.'

'You can't say someone looks like a thug just because they're mixed race, Daddy.' Charlie's mouth is a horrified O. 'That's massively racist.'

Violet pipes up. 'He's on the *Sunday Times* Rich List.'

Jeremy blinks at her. 'How on earth do you know that?'

'I remember seeing it last year. I was looking it up to see how many parents from school I could find in it.'

There's so much wrong with this statement that Clara doesn't know where to start.

'Is he really, really strong?' Charlie asks. 'We've done a few of his keep-fit videos in PE when it's raining and we have to stay in the hall.'

'I doubt your mother asked him to drop and give her fifty push-ups.' Jeremy's tone is dry.

'Daddy's right. We just had a nice coffee and a—work chat. He seems very—impressive.' *He was strong, even when he was eighteen. He could flip me over like I weighed nothing. And he's built like a brick shit-house now, so I can only imagine...* Jesus. She squirms in her seat.

Jeremy stares at her. 'You alright?'

'I'm fine. Violet, stop shoving that broccoli around your plate.'

'I don't like the stalks.'

'Just eat the birds in the trees, then.' It's unbelievable that they're still negotiating this shit, eleven years on. And yet, she'd put money on the fact that they eat the exact same thing at school without batting an eyelid.

'How many weeks till skiing?' Charlie asks. He pops a whole broccoli floret into his mouth and smirks at Violet.

'We are off in'—Jeremy consults his watch—'three months. Three months yesterday, in fact.'

They're going to Val d'Isere at Easter for some late-season skiing. Clara finds skiing holidays to be a horrifying waste of money, but Jeremy skied every winter as a child and is adamant that the kids learn. Heaven forbid one of them should be unmasked as a sub-par skier by Inigo or Tallulah or one of their over-privileged little school friends.

'It's going to be awesome!' Charlie shouts. 'Can we go to the dry ski-slope for some practices?'

'That's my man,' Jeremy says. 'Great idea. Mummy can book it up.' He turns to her. 'He's right, you know. Time for us to start getting some practice in so we don't crash and burn. You might want to think about some squats.' He pats her thigh under the table.

She turns to him, mouth slack in disbelief. She's always so careful not to project any negative body issues onto the kids, especially Violet. What a wanky thing for him to say. It's not that he can talk—he never works out. She thinks back to Alex's words from earlier. *You're perfect.* This coming from the most famous personal trainer in the country. Jeremy can stuff his squats up his—

She looks at the kids' excited faces and sucks down her anger. It's not really Jeremy's fault. To give him credit, he's always been exactly who she knew he would be. He hasn't changed a bit. She married him because he was the precise opposite of Alex. She could read him like a book, and he's never done anything to alter her opinion of him.

She met him a year into her very, very junior job at the National Gallery. She'd graduated from her Art History degree at Bristol the year before, to the enormous relief of her parents, given everything that had gone down. She was doing an evening shift at the Sainsbury Wing, helping to host a corporate viewing for Clifford Chance of the Titian exhibition. She'd written her undergraduate dissertation on the Venetian school; a Titian exhibition was a dream come true for her.

Jeremy was there with clients. After she'd (very enthusiastically) extolled the virtues of *Bacchus and Ariadne*, he asked her out. He took her to J Sheekey's after work one night. He was fair-haired and patrician and handsome and successful and ambitious and consistent and very, very sexy. Above all, he was stable. He was precisely what she needed and deserved in life, and she knew he'd never disappoint her. And she was right. She looks around the table at their beautiful marble kitchen and her happy children, neat as pins in the smart uniform of their lovely day school, excited about their ski trip, and she gives thanks for this picture of stability that's such a given that her children don't even think to question it.

She thinks of Alex's adolescence: that tiny, if immaculate, flat on the eight floor of Jubilee's Elizabeth block; Carmen's double shifts and night shifts and weekend shifts to provide for Alex and Connor; the ghost of his long-vanished dad that still haunted all of them for as long as she knew him. But against all odds, he's come good; he's more successful, by an enormous margin, than anyone else she knows from school.

Before today, the final words she ever spoke to Alex were: *Why don't you go home, sober up, and fulfil your fucking potential? It's such a fucking waste.*

They've haunted her for twenty-one years, but not as much as his letter to her a few weeks later—the letter that still sits upstairs, tucked in a box in a dark corner of her shoe closet.

This is the last time your going to hear from me.

You need to forget I exist.

I need to do this shit by myself, babe.

Don't write, I won't write back.

Don't visit, I won't show.

I fucked up. I fucked up so badly + I'm a worthless piece of scum.

I never deserved you.

Your far far better off without me.

Your an angel.

I'll love you forever.

She read it a million times, noted the pressure the biro made on the thin paper. She sniffed it a million times, as if by picking up the smell of prison on it, she could get one step closer to even beginning to understand how he must be suffering in there. She served every day of that sentence right there with him.

6

1998

Making her come for the first time was the single greatest achievement of his life. She didn't even know what it was, really—not in practice. The first few times they'd had sex, he'd been in ecstasy. He'd shagged a few girls before her, but this wasn't shagging. The experience of being inside her was the first time he even came close to believing in God. After the first time, she seemed to like it too. She started asking him for it, and when he was inside her and her legs were wrapped around him, the look in her eyes was so *much* that he could hardly cope with it. He could tell their closeness meant as much to her as it did to him, that the slide of his skin against hers felt so fucking right to her too. He knew because she told him.

But he could tell it wasn't *as* good for her. He believed her that she liked it, but he wanted to show her how good it could be. She wasn't really interested, though. She said being close to him like this was enough for her. She didn't know what coming was, really, because she'd never come, even by herself. He'd tried to persuade her to let him go down on her a couple of times, but she went all weird and stiff and said it would make her feel uncomfortable, so he dropped it. When he'd briefly gone out with Sam Carter from the Upper Sixth, she'd shown him exactly how to make her come with his fingers. She knew a lot more than him, and she knew exactly what she wanted.

One evening, when they were back at Clara's house, he told her he wanted to give her a present. *You don't know what you're missing*, he said. *It's not fair that the guy gets to feel like this and not the girl.*

It's fine, she says. *I just want to be with you.*

I'm not leaving here till I've given you your present, he said.

And he went to work. He laid her on her back and sucked her nipples softly, then harder, one at a time. She was so beautiful. He still couldn't believe that he got to lie here like this with her and stroke her stomach and put his head between her boobs and actually put his dick inside her. He couldn't believe she was there waiting for him every day after school. He thought she'd get tired of him, that she'd see through him. But she didn't seem to.

He'd spent a lot of time on her boobs since they'd started messing around together, but he'd been mainly touching them for *him*. He couldn't leave them alone. Tonight, it was for her. After a while, her breathing started to change and she made a couple of tiny noises in the back of her throat that made even more blood rush to his dick. He prayed very hard that he wouldn't disgrace himself before he made her come. He ran his fingers lightly down over the soft, soft skin of her stomach and gave the underside of her thigh a little tug with his hand to show her she should pull up her legs. He grabbed the lube he bought for the first time they had sex, and squeezed out a bit. Then he put his finger on her, just like Sam showed him. She rewarded him with another little noise that sounded like she was enjoying it.

Sam had shown him how to rub softly and slowly. She'd demonstrated with her finger on his inner arm. *See if I press down hard*, she'd said, *you can't feel much? But if I tickle it really softly, it feels a lot nicer*. He says a silent prayer of thanks to Sam as he recreated this move. He stroked her very, very softly and very slowly. *How's that feel?* he asked.

Mmm, she replied. *It's lovely*. She shifted, and stretched her legs open more, which he took as an encouraging sign.

She had her eyes closed, and he was lying next to her, propped up on one elbow. It meant he could bend his head and suck on her nearest nipple, but it also meant he had a front-row seat for the changes that were happening on her beautiful face. He could do this all night, forever. As he stroked her, her breathing sped up and her mouth opened. She made those tiny moans every time she breathed out, and they started to get louder. They were the best noises he'd ever heard in his life.

He scooted up onto his knees and clambered round to kneel between her legs. He tentatively put a finger from his other hand inside her, and she was so wet that he practically came himself, right there. He increased the pace of his strokes; he could feel her filling up with blood right under his finger pad. He stared at her in amazement as she squeezed her eyes shut and opened her mouth wider and pushed herself against his hands. Her head went back and she scrabbled at the mattress with one of her hands, before going rigid and shuddering, back arched, and her cries the loudest they'd been.

This was the best thing he'd ever, ever seen. She opened

her eyes and gave him this exhausted, smiling *look* that he knew meant: *Holy shit—I get it now. I see what you were talking about*. There was no going back. He'd never unrolled a condom so fast. He was addicted, and by the look on her face, so was she.

7

2019

He sits in the Oast House, in a patch of sunlight. That obsession with sunlight has never left him since being banged up in a cell eighteen hours a day at the young offenders' institute. He tries simultaneously to make himself as inconspicuous as possible under his baseball cap—there are far too many women in here doing coffee mornings—and to keep an eye out for Clara. She mentioned she's usually at the farm on Wednesdays. He feels like a teenager again.

It reminds him of the times he'd spend his free periods in Lower Sixth in the library, trying not to arouse the suspicion of the librarian (he'd never set foot in the place before he got together with Clara). As soon as she arrived, they'd head off into a dark corner by the science books and shamelessly feel each other up. Once, they got a bit carried away and sent some books flying, and he had to make a run for it. The librarian would never have suspected Clara on her own.

Too many memories have been surfacing, these past few days. They've been well preserved; he thought about her every fucking waking and sleeping moment when he was inside, though he tucked her away into a sacred and private place in his memory when he got out and had to go about building a life for himself. But this past week, since their coffee, the memories have gently pushed their way to the surface, as if reminding him there's no point or need to keep them quashed. Having her back in his life again is a miracle, though he's done enough work on himself to know he needs to maintain careful boundaries. All suffering is caused by desire. Plus, she's married.

She rewards his patience by turning up and settling herself by a window near the kitchen. He waits a moment and, mentally kicking his self-imposed boundaries to the kerb, skulks over, cap pulled down. Smiles to himself that he gets to do this, after so fucking long. It feels miraculous. He hovers behind her, taking a moment to enjoy the glossiness of her hair and the delicate curve of her jaw, before leaning over and uttering a soft *hi*. She jumps, looks up at him, and giggles.

'You scared me!'

'Sorry. I feel like we're back in the library at school.'

She giggles again, but her eyes flash across his face and he knows she's remembering too.

'This is a bit more glamorous, thankfully.' Her tone is light.

He straightens up and shoves his hands in his pockets. 'Are you here to work?'

'Yep. I'm doing some editing. Zoe and I shot some dishes yesterday for the book.'

'I was wondering if I could pick your artistic brain. Connor sent me the mock-up of our new site design. I'd love your opinion.'

'Sure.' She looks around. 'Where are you sitting? D'you want to bring your stuff over?'

'Actually… any chance you fancy coming back to The Stables with me? It's a bit more private.'

She raises her eyebrows, and he adds hastily: 'Not like that. It's just—I sound like a wanker, but I don't want to be recognised. It's a bit busy in here.'

'Oh. Of course. That must be annoying for you.' Her posture is less comfortable, and he feels like a dick for even referring to his celebrity status.

'It's fine,' he says. 'I can't complain. But we'll get more done if we don't have anyone bothering us.'

He helps her pack up her stuff, and they head out of the Oast House. The trees are bare and there's still a touch of frost on the lawns, but it's a beautiful, clear day. They make small-talk on the short walk, before he throws open the door of The Stables and gestures.

'Go for it.'

As she steps through the threshold, her face lights up. 'Oh my God! It's stunning!'

The entire ground floor is open plan and airy, with large windows and blonde wood floors. In front of them is a cluster of sofas and armchairs in muted chintz and rich velvet; at the far end a large kitchen designed around a marble island. Light pours in from a huge picture window at the kitchen end, which is double height with vaulted ceilings. The wood-burning stove's not lit, but thanks to the underfloor heating and the sunlight, it's extremely cosy. He'll never get used to being able to afford places like this, but it turns out he has a soft spot for extreme luxury. Two years on a thin plastic mattress will do that for you.

'I'm not sure why you bother going to the Oast House, if you've got this place.' She struggles out of her coat and scarf and he takes them from her.

'I was lying in wait for you. I was hoping to bump into you.'

She glances at him and he smiles as if to say, *I'm serious.*

'Don't worry. I want you purely for your artistic eye. Coffee?'

When he's made the coffee, they settle on a large velvet sofa and he puts his laptop on the coffee table in front of them.

She takes a sip. 'This is delicious.'

'Says the girl whose parents make the best coffee in the world. I didn't even like it before I met you.'

'We turned you into an honorary Italian.' Her eyes are soft.

'You did that. Sadly, my pizza days are behind me.' He pats his stomach. These days, he cycles between keto and paleo. 'I miss your mum's *biscotti*, though. Fuck, they were good.'

'She still makes them. I'll steal some for you some next time I'm at the restaurant.'

He groans. 'Heaven. Just don't tell them they're for me. They wouldn't approve.'

'My parents never blamed you, Alex. They were really fond of you. They were devastated, for you, as well as for me.'

His throat constricts painfully as he recalls Vincenzo and Valentina, the kindest, warmest people and the most adoring parents. Of course they were. They had the world's most incredible daughter. Some of his happiest (non-sexual) memories of his relationship with Clara originated in the kitchens of Casa Valentina after school.

'Well.' It's hard to speak, all of a sudden. 'I'm just sorry I let you all down. You'll never know how sorry.' He clears his throat. 'But I'll take any *biscotti* you can swipe.'

She shifts. 'Right,' she says brightly. 'Let's see this website, then.'

IT'S hard to believe Connor's put this together. It's beautiful. The dynamic links aren't live yet, but she's able to play around with each of the main pages. It's video heavy; the footage is gorgeously shot. There are plenty of videos of Alex, and it's beyond weird to watch them while he sits there beside her. The first content box on the home page is a slickly edited montage of Alex doing an impressive array of squats, planks and other moves whose names she doesn't know, but which showcase his physical prowess. He's in a sleeveless top that's like a second skin, and shorts. He's so physically beautiful, it's astonishing. As soon as this is live, she'll watch this on a loop in the privacy of her bedroom. She stares dreamily at the video.

'Sorry,' he says. 'That's all a bit wanky.'

'No, it's not.' She looks over at him. 'It's beautiful. I mean —the video—it's been done really well.' She returns her focus to the screen and flicks through. She grimaces.

'What?' He's onto her. She must remember he can read her face. 'Tell me the truth. There are too many people on my payroll who only tell me what they think I want to hear. Spill it, Fiori.'

She smiles at the sound of her maiden name. Her eyes are on a Before and After section, a grid of men and women in their underwear before and after working with Alex, presumably. The differences between the two shots of each person are staggering, and yet...

'I said spill it.' He nudges her with his shoulder.

'What would you say your mission is?'

'It's Be Well and Whole. My original goal was to make people well and whole through physical fitness. As the brand grows, though, we're making the message far more holistic, to incorporate mental health, nutrition, mindfulness… that's why the conference is going to be so great. It gives me a chance to pull all these strands together.'

'Hmm.' She flicks back through the web pages.

'What gives? There are links on the main menu for all those buckets, see? We'll build out the content as we go.'

'It's not so much the content, exactly; it's more the—overall vibe. It's gorgeous, but it's intimidating. If I stumbled on this, I'd be so freaked out by you on the homepage doing handstands and stuff, and all those awful before and after photos, that I'd run for the hills. It just feels very… clinical. Like your only goal is to give people perfect bodies. It's quite intense.'

He stares. 'I see what you're getting at, but it's supposed to be results-oriented. To get people to sign up for my premium monthly training programme, they want to see that big results are achievable. I need to show them the return they'll get on their investment.'

'I get that. And it really is impressive. I just wonder if you could add in a bit of extra humanity. When I do my weekly Pilates class, I feel great afterwards, even if my body doesn't look like *that*. I'm glowing. I've got colour in my cheeks. I feel thrilled with myself. Maybe you can show more of that. Not on models or athletes, but on real people. If you can capture that chemical high or whatever it is—'

'An endorphin rush.'

'Exactly. If you can show that, that might go some way to motivating people like me who are scared shitless by seeing perfect gym bodies. It offers me something that will be good for *me*, not that looks like it's for another race of people entirely.'

When she looks over to gauge his reaction, he's watching her, shaking his head.

'Well, well, well. I knew it. I knew Clara Fiori would come up trumps. You're totally right. And it should be you, taking those photos you've just described. You know what we need. Will you come and shoot one of my classes at the farm, if my pupils are happy?'

She'd love to. She knows exactly what his site needs. 'Okay. If you're sure.' She gives him a little smile.

His own smile is growing more wistful. 'You know, if this was Chemistry revision, you'd be taking off your top around now.'

She can't believe he's had the balls to bring that up. 'I think you'll find I only took my clothes off when *you* got something right. From where I'm sitting, you got this wrong. Even though it's a lovely site.'

'In that case, you should be taking an item of *my* clothing off, if I remember right.'

'Nice try.' She shakes her head and tries to keep her voice even. The problem is, they spent practically every waking moment outside of school fucking, so it's impossible to play the *do you remember* game without it turning dirty very, very quickly. She returns to the screen and pulls up the homepage again. The loop of Alex working out starts up. He's doing a plank, and he has some phrase tattooed down the inside of his upper arm. She cocks her head to try to read it.

'What does that tattoo say?' She points to the screen and looks at him. He stares back and says nothing, but his face has gone all funny. 'Alex?'

There's a pause. 'I'll show you,' he says, and pulls his

sweater off over his head. He holds up the arm furthest from her. He's in a snug, soft-looking white t-shirt that shows off his caramel skin, and it cuffs right above his bicep and skims over his pecs with a perfection that makes her mouth water. She focuses on the tattoo. It's blue-black, blotchy and badly executed. She reads it aloud.

'*FULFIL... YOUR... FUCKING...* Oh. *POTENTIAL.*'

She pulls back as if she's been slapped.

'Ring a bell?' His voice is soft. Her gaze moves to his face; he's looking at her. Searching.

'What I said to you. In our fight. Right before you walked out and—' Her heart is breaking. She's never forgiven herself for saying that to him, and setting in motion a series of events that ruined both their lives and so many others. Her horror must show, for he grabs her hand.

'Listen to me, angel. They're the best words you could have said to me. I got them inked on as soon as I got out. They've brought me here. I could never have come this far if I hadn't known that the most amazing girl I've ever known believed I had something to offer, somewhere inside me. I've looked at this every day for nearly twenty years and it's spurred me on, even when things were really, *really* fucking bad. You did that for me.'

She puts out her hand and strokes the soft, paler skin of his inner arm. Her fingertips move against the words he's, unbeknown to her all this time, had immortalised on his flesh, and the dam bursts. Tears roll down her cheeks and her ability to keep up this polite veneer of friendship shatters.

'Oh, *God*,' she cries. 'I can't bear it. I can't bear any of it... it's not fair, Alex. We didn't have our time. It's not *fair*, for God's sake.'

He pulls her head into the crook of his neck, his arms

around her instantly, and as she struggles to catch her breath between sobs, she inhales great, shameless gulps of his skin.

'I know it's not fair, angel.' His voice is in her ear as he strokes her hair away from her face and rubs her back. 'None of it was fair to you. None of it.'

She just has time to consider whether she's making an embarrassing scene and his hug is born purely out of guilt and sympathy, when he pulls her back slightly and moves his head so he can kiss her, and instantly, just like that, they're in a rhythm that every muscle in her body remembers and which makes the past twenty-one years feel irrelevant. As their lips move and their tongues slide, he pulls her hair back and she can feel him winding it around his hand like a rope, just the way he used to. He uses it to tug her head back slightly, away from him, and when they make eye contact, there's a slight question in his. He's offering her an out with his gorgeous eyes. But the problem is, Jeremy doesn't exist right now because she's seventeen and madly in love with the boy—man—she's kissing, and nothing else in the universe matters except for his mouth and his hands and the heat and closeness of him against her. She pulls him back in to her mouth.

There's an inevitability about this kiss. She's hyper-present. He's the most perfect combination of everything her senses have ever wanted. The faint scratch of his stubble against her chin. The soft exhale of his breath, which she breathes in, greedily, so she can get more of him inside her body. The flawless softness of his lips, which haven't changed one single bit. The tingling in her scalp when he pulls her hair back with the most delicious amount of pressure. Kissing him is alchemy. Alchemy that hasn't changed at all in two decades. It's been frozen in time, waiting for them, and all they needed to do was put their mouths together.

She's reminded of the passage of time in the most pleasurable way when she gets her hands on this new version of his body. He's bigger, broader, more *everything* than he was before. Her hands stroke down his pecs, they glide along the sharp ridge of his triceps; they roam greedily over his back and shoulders. She manages to get one hand under the hem of his t-shirt and strikes gold: skin. She traces a line along his spine with her fingernails and he groans a little. The sound is catnip to her, and she pulls him closer. He can never, ever be close enough. Her mind and body are partying like crazy. Every cell, every atom shouts *I remember this*!

It seems he's finding this trip down memory lane equally gratifying. He still has one hand entwined in her hair and the other one has worked its way up under her sweater and is cupping her right boob. His thumb finds a nipple and rubs through her bra and suddenly this very adolescent make-out session is so real that she thinks she may actually physically die if she doesn't get all of him. She moans into his mouth and he jolts and lowers her down onto the sofa and she pulls him on top of her, covering herself with his delicious weight. She can feel how hard he is through his jeans and her skirt, and she moves a little against him. Dry humping is seriously, seriously underrated.

He hoists himself onto his elbows and smiles down at her and he's quite honestly the best sight she's ever seen. He's perfection. His lips are wet and swollen from kissing her and his beautiful, mesmerising eyes reflect twenty-one years of memory and heartbreak and adoration.

'I've missed you.' He's still the master of unbroken eye contact while declaring his feelings.

'I've missed you, too.' Understatement. They both smile wryly at the inadequacy of the words.

'Our bodies haven't forgotten.'

'They certainly have not,' she agrees.

He lowers his face towards her, eyes open, his long eyelashes fluttering. She arches her head back and takes his kiss like the greedy, wanton temptress she's somehow morphed into since sitting down on this sofa with this man.

Her phone rings. *Mummy, pick up! Mummy, pick up!*

He springs back. 'Fuck. What's that?'

Shit. It's the kids' school. The only number she will categorically take a call from, no matter what she's in the middle of—hence, the thoughtfully recorded bespoke ring-tone, courtesy of Charlie.

She reaches over to the table for the phone as he gets off her and sits upright.

'Hello, Mrs Winters,' says a cheery voice. 'It's Susan from the school office. Everything's fine with Charlie and Violet, it's just that Charlie's thrown up in the lunch queue, I'm afraid. Can you come and pick him up from the office as soon as possible?'

8

1998

Her parents took a while, but they warmed up to Alex. They weren't convinced a boyfriend would do anything for her grades, but they relaxed after she scored straight A-stars across all ten subjects in her GCSE mocks. After a while, they got used to him turning up at the restaurant every afternoon with their daughter and they put him to work as if he was any other member of the family. Her middle sister, Maria, who was at uni in London, pitched in some afternoons too.

She had to admit, he played it perfectly. He was respectful to her folks and adoring towards her, without giving them the slightest suggestion that he was banging their daughter's brains out every evening after they left the restaurant. He wasn't vocal at school, unless it was with her, but in the warm and crowded kitchen of Casa Valentina, he opened up to them while learning how to knead gnocchi, and mince onions, celery and carrots for *soffritto* and machine-slice the *prosciutto*, while sipping on espresso and stealing Mum's *biscotti*. Her parents grew fond of him. And

Maria never tired of teasing him, because he took it like a pro.

Mum became worried that he wasn't spending enough time with his own mother, though he always explained how long and exhausting her office cleaning shifts were. More and more often, Mum would pack him off with tupperwares of lasagne or risotto or *parmigiana melanzane* so his mum got a square meal between working and sleeping. His main windows with his mum were late in the evening, after he'd left her house and before his mum either got to sleep or went back out for a night shift. He didn't talk about his home life much, and he never complained, but it made her so happy to see him warming up to life at the restaurant, fighting back when Maria teased him and nipping out for a roll-up behind the back door with the chefs.

He scraped through his mocks, but then his grades started to improve. He had no choice but to study more: she told him in no uncertain terms that she wasn't going to mess up her GCSEs for him, and she'd study with or without him. He came to the library with her at lunchtimes and she'd reward him with a snog or a grope somewhere private once they'd done their studies. He even came to sit next to her in Chemistry, in the front row, smiling smugly at their teacher's shocked expression. He spent every minute of school that he could next to her. He got a lot of shit from Matt Foster and the other boys he hung out with, but he didn't seem to care. He told her he was so proud of being her boyfriend that he wanted everyone in school to know they were together, and he didn't want to waste a minute with her.

He told her he loved her so much that he could never imagine loving anyone else ever again, and he was going to nail his GCSEs so he could stay on at St Winnie's and do his A Levels with her. He told her she was like an angel to him, that he'd never known someone so good and pure, that she lit up the world and he could feel himself becoming a better person just by being with her.

She said it all back to him. She knew he meant it, but honestly, it felt as if he was her guardian angel, too. He breathed life into her and he showed her a world of deep and beautiful emotion that, until then, had only existed for her in books. She was entirely, marvellously cocooned in his love and his company filled her with wonder and with security. She never understood why so many girls at school cried over boys and played games. Alex had never played a single game with her since he said her name that day. He was steadfast and serious, and she knew their love was unshakeable. He was the best person she knew.

After they took him away, all that love and support and security and awe and wonder was gone in a flash, and she simply didn't know what to do with the pain. She didn't know what was worse: the physical agony of not having him there, or the knowledge that he was suffering, and she couldn't get to him. He'd never needed an angel more than where he was now, and she couldn't help him. She thought the pain might kill her, and she was terrified it would kill him.

9

2019

She drags herself away from him like a lovesick teenager, which, of course, is the exact role she's been acting out here. He kisses her as he helps her on with her coat; he tugs her hair gently out from under the collar; they stumble together to the door in an awkward dance. And then she lays her head against his chest and sighs as he rubs her back over her coat.

They don't say much. There's so much to say, it's pointless to say anything at all. In any case, those few minutes on the sofa have said it all better than she ever could with words.

'I hope he doesn't barf in your car.'

She rolls her eyes. 'Talk about back to reality.'

'He's lucky to have you.'

He kisses her again, and smoothes her hair, and she makes a wistful grimace of regret before floating back across the resort to the staff carpark. She takes the back roads to Sevenoaks in a kind of daze. If there was a breathalyser test for being drunk on emotions, she'd flunk it. She's drugged up to the eyeballs on him. How could he *taste* the exact same as he used to? That feeling of his hands pulling on her hair did things to her that she couldn't even... all she knows is they make magic together.

But by the time she steers the car into the leafy parking area of the kids' school, she's spinning out. The sweetly familiar location jolts her squarely back into the real world where she's a wife and a mother. She steps heavily down from the car and trudges across the tarmac. This wonderful school is the centre of her children's world. *She* is the centre of her children's world—she, and Jeremy, and school are supposed to be the constants in their lives, their safe places. Stability. That's what it always comes down to. She saw what a lack of stability did to Alex, and she's always sworn her kids will know nothing of that. Her job is to be boringly consistent for them, and that does not include getting it on with hot, famous, physically perfect exes with criminal records.

Charlie's waiting for her in the office, looking forlorn. It's revoltingly stifling, and she tugs at her coat buttons as she signs him out. It says something for her emotional state that the sight of him slumped in the plastic chair almost moves her to tears.

'Are you ok, sweetie?' She pulls him in for a hug and inhales the top of his head, before wondering belatedly if she smells of Alex.

'You'll have to keep him away from school for forty-eight hours to make sure he's not infectious,' Susan reminds her.

Perfect. Just what she needs.

As they thank Susan and exit the building, she says, 'What happened at lunch?'

'I'm not sick, Mum.' He wriggles free of her.

'But Susan says you threw up.'

'I did. But it was just water. Me and Noah and Otto were

playing a game to see who could neck the most water. I necked a whole pint really quickly in the queue and then I *literally*'—he gesticulates, his hand making an arc—'vommed the whole thing back up again. It was so gross. But actually it was quite cool, too.'

'Oh, for God's sake. What a stupid thing to do.' All sympathy vanishes instantly. She's seething. She and Alex were interrupted for *this*. She'll call the school when she gets home and explain the situation; hopefully they'll let him go back in tomorrow.

She marches him back to the car and gives him her phone. 'Here. Play some maths games.' It's a cheap parenting trick, but she needs time to think. Now she knows Charlie isn't ill, her knee-jerk reaction of guilt and catastrophizing begins to recede. No great harm has been done. It was a one-off. It won't happen again, and nobody needs to know. Their brief moment of connection was inevitable, for Christ's sake! Look at how much they've both suffered; look at how brutally they were wrenched apart, when they were just kids! This is closure. It's a fitting end for a tragic story; it's their reward for all the pain and uncertainty and longing they've suffered. That's the way to think of it. A reward. God knows she deserves it; they both do. And now she can draw a line under him, wrap a neat little bow around their story.

At home, the front door resists her efforts to push it open and she squeezes an arm through the crack and scrabbles around on the doormat for the pile of post that's blocking its passage. The culprit: a chunky local magazine with a smouldering photo of Alex on the cover, announcing the upcoming Sorrel Farm 'wellness summit'. Nice coverage for Evelyn. A kick in the teeth for her. In the hallway, she stands and stares at the photo. It's beautifully lit, with deep shadows. His eyes burn into hers. If she didn't know him, she'd assume they were Photoshopped. That green is ridiculous. But she can confidently say, having drowned in them from millimetres away this morning, that they're exactly like that in real life. IRL, as the twins would say.

She sets Charlie up at the kitchen island with a laptop and a sandwich (she'll take his word for it that there is not a jot wrong with his stomach) and logs him into his school portal.

'I'll be back in a minute,' she tells him and scurries upstairs. Kneeling on her dressing room floor, she unearths an ancient shoebox and takes out Alex's infamous final letter. She allows herself a moment to wallow. It's just her, in her room, and she needs some space to process all this. She sits back and leans her head against the wall.

The boy who wrote this impassioned letter to her is the same man who kissed her (understatement) earlier and told her he'd missed her. The very same. Twenty years feels like everything and nothing at all. In that moment, on that sofa with him, her then and now converged, and it was clear nothing had changed. Who is she trying to kid? This isn't closure; it's creation. It's the recommencement of something that never, ever stopped being. She smoothes the thin prison paper over her thigh.

I'll love you forever.

It's not hard to imagine his mental state when he wrote this: anguished, scared shitless, lonely, heartbroken, and totally fucking failed by the justice system. But she knows what she saw in his eyes this morning. It wasn't just desire; it was recognition. Homecoming. She'll warrant he saw the same in hers. They're the love of each other's lives. Time hasn't changed anything.

Her game of mental ping pong continues all bloody afternoon. Jeremy is home early for once, and the sight of him is enough to jolt her back to her senses. She loves her husband. She loves this man who's committed his life to her and given her two beautiful children and all the stability and constancy she could ever require. He retires to the study to log in remotely and she brings him a cold beer and a bowl of crisps. His smile of surprise and thanks is lovely. It's everything she needs. He grabs her hand and kisses it in an uncharacteristically tender gesture and she squeezes his hand back. She is loved; she is appreciated; she is safe. She is *married*! She should not have to remind herself of that! That phone call was fate. Someone up there prompted Charlie to down a pint of water and puke it up right as she was about to make a colossal mistake. That cannot be a coincidence.

She's twitchy over supper, overwhelmed by the enormity of what she did today.

'You seem stressed, darling.' Jeremy leans over and rubs her shoulder. 'Why don't you have a nice hot bath?'

In the bath with a glass of wine, her inner devil's advocate kicks in with another counter-argument. It's as if her brain houses two opposing, overly well-prepped university debate teams. It's bloody exhausting. It's probably to do with her being naked, but she can't help but wonder what would have happened if the school hadn't called at that moment, if Charlie had chosen tomorrow to pull his stunt. They would have had sex; she knows they would. They were both completely committed to that kiss and to each other. Ancient, deep-rooted muscle memory would have worked against them, and continuing their reunion, garment by garment and body part by body part, would have been the most natural thing in the world. Their enthusiastic experimentation of old showed them how well they fitted together in every position. He would have been inside her immediately and effortlessly (far more effortlessly, now her pelvic floor is shot to pieces from carrying twins—she clenches it at the thought) and it would have been bloody amazing—so good that she wouldn't—couldn't—have had the slightest regret.

She lies back and admits one should-be-shameful thought to herself. Deep down, despite her usual female guilt and her confusion over such an intense indiscretion earlier, she doesn't regret the kiss at all. She can't. It was by the far the most exciting thing that's happened to her in... God knows. Exciting is the wrong word; it's too superficial. It was life-affirming in the sense that it reminded her she's not just a robot—a top-of-the-range Mum-Bot 3000 who never, ever malfunctions—but a woman who's alive and powerful and sexual and not just capable of *being* all those things but *owning* them.

Hell, yeah! When she was wrapped around Alex, she wasn't a wife or a mother but Clara, and she was precisely what he wanted. It's taken someone who knows her past version of herself to remind her how much more she can be, if she dares to look for it and claim it.

And speaking of claims, she and Alex have such an enormous, all-encompassing prior claim on each other that it pretty much supersedes any other commitments, even marriage! If she were Anne Boleyn, and her righteous king found out about her and Alex's past shenanigans, they'd both be done for treason. They were practically betrothed; they were promised to each other. Today was the natural expression of affection (understatement) between two star-crossed lovers reunited.

Before she can compare herself grandiosely to any more tragic heroines of bygone years, factual or fictional, and be overcome by her own dramatic abilities, she pulls herself out of the bath. Wrapped in her robe, glass in one hand, she lies on her bed and types *Alex Molloy* into the *Mail Online*'s search bar. The findings are less a rabbit-hole than a tunnel to the earth's core. Holy shit. She's avoided as many of these articles as she can in the past, but he's been photographed with *so* many women: entrepreneurs; models (come on, Alex; show some originality); fitness instructors who are also, apparently, YouTube stars; soap stars. He's been a busy boy.

She puts down the wineglass. She feels sick to her stomach. Of course he has access to any woman he wants. Of course he makes use of that access. She doesn't doubt that his words and actions were sincere earlier, but they were in the heat of the moment. She was emotional; he was emotional; they have so much history together and she fleetingly took him back to his younger self, when he wasn't famous and she was the girl for him and she was the only person in the world who really, really saw him. Today was a heady and wonderful outlet for all that old passion and heartbreak, but she's a decent-looking mother of two from Sevenoaks. Nothing more. For a brief, dangerous moment, they confused their pasts with their presents. He needed her then, when he was a disenfranchised boy; he doesn't need her now that he has the world at his feet.

10

1998

When Clara told him that her parents would close the restaurant down for the month of August and go to Italy for four weeks, as they apparently did every summer, he couldn't believe it. He could not compute the concept of spending that much time apart from her. He kept expecting her to say she'd changed her mind, or her parents had agreed to let her stay at home, or the trip was off. But, although she was hysterical at the thought of leaving him, the trip went ahead.

They broke up from school a week before she left and spent as much time together as her parents would allow. They got the train up to London and did stupid touristy stuff together. They watched the Changing of the Guard and hired pedalos in Hyde Park, pedalling into the middle of the Serpentine and eating the sandwiches they'd brought with them. She was a fucking useless pedaller, and he had to do all the work, but he couldn't give a shit. They kissed and kissed and kissed on those hard plastic seats while the pedalo went round in lazy circles.

And then she was gone, and life turned grey in an

instant. She said she'd write but not to get too excited about letters because she'd probably be back before the letters turned up. She said she'd use up all her pocket money on phone calls to him, and she was as good as her word. He made her describe what she could see. She told him the payphone was on a narrow cobbled side street off the main square, and that above her hung rows and rows of laundry between the apartment buildings, and that the air smelt of seafood cooking in oil, and that everything was bathed in golden light. He imagined her there, sitting on a kerb in a sundress, her hair freshly washed and loose, her skin smelling of sunshine. It was like she was on a different planet.

He was bored. That was the problem. This year, his whole world had revolved around Clara. He'd only got his homework done because of her. It was school and football and Clara, nothing else. He'd have tried skipping football, but there was no way Mr Evans would go for that. Now there was fuck all going on. No school. No football matches. And no Clara. He thought he might go insane, stuck on the estate for a whole fucking month.

Mum was still working crazy hours, so he tried his hands at cooking: some basic pasta dishes he'd learnt at Casa Valentina, but that didn't take up too much time. He needed to work. He needed some spending money. Connor was on holidays too; he was supposed to be doing a GNVQ in Health and Social Care at a sixth form college, which was ironic as Alex hadn't seen him show much care for him or Mum or anyone else recently. Weirdly, the only person he'd seen Connor show any respect to was Clara. He couldn't quite say why, but she had a kind of self-belief that he suspected Connor found intimidating. Anyway, Connor was always polite to Clara.

He spent a week helping Mr Evans out with teaching little kids basic football skills at a summer camp, which was more fun than he expected. He got paid to goof about and show them how to dribble. Most of them were good kids; a lot of them were from the estate. There were a couple of real naturals; it was fucking depressing to think they'd probably never get any proper opportunities to see what they were capable of.

You're a good teacher, Mr Evans told him. *You should think about teaching as a profession. I'd support you.* He laughed it off; that meant uni and he didn't see that happening. He needed to start earning after his A Levels and pull his weight.

Then Connor offered him and Matt Foster the chance to get in on a gig he and some friends had going on. It was basically being a runner for a couple of the dealers on the estate. It was just pot, and the money was decent for not much work, so they said yes. He gave most of the money to Mum and told her he was still helping Mr Evans out. She was out all day, so she didn't know, anyway. He and Matt spent the rest of the money on beer. It was easy work and they worked out their routes pretty quickly.

When they were quiet, Connor taught him how to drive Mum's car round the estate. It was a shitty little Fiesta, but he got the hang of it easily. They never left the estate, though. He wasn't stupid. After about a week, the dealers offered them a pay rise if they got involved with some of the harder stuff: mainly coke and E. They said yes, obviously. It was all pretty routine, and it made no difference to him what they were delivering.

Finally, Clara came back, a week before term started. He realised that just as he'd never thought she'd go in the first place, he hadn't really expected her to come back. He'd had a month of readjusting to the monotony of life on the estate, and she was this vision who seemed too good to be true. But she did come back, and she was so golden and gorgeous and her hair was all lightened, and they were both horny as fuck. She had to help her folks get the restaurant ready for reopening, but whenever she could, she slipped home and called him and he came over so he could be beside her and inside her and drown in the smell and taste of her. He couldn't get enough of her; he couldn't believe she was here in the flesh.

He didn't want to let her go, not even for a second, but the money from the running was too good to turn down. So, once school restarted, he stopped going back to the restaurant with her and he'd go hang out at the estate for a few hours, and then he'd head back over to hers after dark. He told her he and Connor had started doing food shops for some of the older residents, and she believed him. There were a couple of times where he and Connor and Matt and some of Connor's mates would kick back with a few beers or vodka and an E, and on those nights he didn't go see her. She was so innocent that he didn't reckon she'd even realise he was high if she saw him, but he didn't want to take any chances. If she found out he was on drugs, and helping to deal drugs, she would go fucking mental.

11

2019

Clara has agreed to come and shoot today's workout session. He wasn't sure she would, but Connor loves her idea for website imagery, and Evelyn is thrilled at the idea of offering a spontaneous Alex Molloy class to their members, so they've agreed to do it immediately, before the run-up to the conference gets too crazy.

It's been two days since he kissed her, and he's going crazy. The trappings of the life he's built for himself have felt pretty good up until now, but the moment he put his arms around her on that sofa, everything fell away and the only thing—person—that mattered to him was right there in front of him, in his arms. He doesn't know how many hours he spent fantasising about her when he was inside, but nothing could have prepared him for the feeling of utter rightness that's come over him in her presence two decades later.

He's speculated in the past whether they would have made it work if he'd kept himself clean and hadn't been locked up. It was so real to them both, but they were both awash with hormones and their relationship existed in a tiny bubble of school life. He's seen the world now; he knows how vast it is and how many opportunities there are out there and how much people can change (he, thank fuck, being an example of that). But he's always believed that what they had was more than a teenage infatuation; that they had something special. He's been careful to keep his flings light since then, and his therapist tells him he has some pretty obvious, and apparently fucked-up, reasons for doing that.

The truth is, that kiss vindicated all his beliefs. It's all still there. The magic. The connection. The attraction. None of it has gone away; time has done nothing to weaken it. Einstein would say that in another plane of potential, they've been living happily together all this time.

And yet, he can't deny the glaring problem. She's moved on. She's married. He can tell she's a great mum from the way she talks about her kids. He could have told anyone she'd make a great mum. She's a good person who's built a life for herself, and he has no fucking right to mess that up for her.

He's kept his WhatsApps to her neutral, in case her husband sees them.

Thanks for agreeing to shoot this morning's workout. Looking forward to it.

Her response:

Sure. I'm afraid I'll have Charlie with me. He's still off school. I've told him you and I have just met.

He's not sure what he was expecting: obviously not full disclosure to her family of his and her mutual past, but he'd have expected her to mention that they were at school together, or something. Obviously not. Well, he has no intention of ratting her out to her kid.

They show up around twenty minutes before the class starts. Jesus. He's the spit of her. He's a good-looking boy—lanky, with her huge brown eyes and floppy brown hair. He stares at Alex with undisguised enthusiasm, and Alex suppresses an inner air punch. Yes. First objective accomplished—get him onside.

'Hi, Clara.' He and Clara exchange a glance loaded with a mixture of emotions, before he turns his attention to Charlie. 'You must be Charlie. Good to meet you, mate. How you doing?'

He holds up his hand for a high five, which Charlie reciprocates.

'I'm good.' He's still staring at Alex like he's a creature in a zoo. 'You're the first famous person I've met IRL.'

Alex laughs out loud at wonder in the poor kid's tone as well as Clara's look of mortification. 'Hope I don't let you down, mate. I heard you puked up a pint of water and got yourself a couple of days off school. Man, I wish I'd known that trick when I was your age. I'm impressed.' He catches Clara's warning look and adds hastily: 'Your mum mentioned it when we were setting up this session. She didn't want me to think you were infectious.'

Charlie grins delightedly. 'Thanks. It was cool. Mum's cross, though. Is it true you were in prison?'

'Charlie!' Clara exclaims. 'That's incredibly rude!'

You've got to love the lack of filter kids have. He puts up his hand to stop her blocking the poor lad.

'Hey. It's ok.' He shakes his head at her and turns back to Charlie. 'It was a young offenders' institute, but yeah. I did two years. I did something very bad, even though it wasn't intentional, and I ruined a lot of people's lives. So I deserved to be banged up. I don't recommend it. You want to keep yourself out of trouble and stay away from those places.'

'Was it really, really scary in there?' Charlie's eyes are saucers. It's so weird, seeing Clara's eyes on this kid.

'It was horrible, mate. I cried myself to sleep every night for the first couple of months.' His gaze flicks to Clara and rapidly away again; her distress is evident on her face. 'It was scary, and lonely, and really, really boring. There were just too many angry, bored young guys in there who wanted to cause trouble. It was hell.'

'Wow.' Charlie appears to be struggling to look sympathetic while fighting off the gleeful morbid curiosity. He's probably heard enough for now. Alex slaps him on the shoulder.

'Right. I need to catch up with your mum for a minute—work stuff. Why don't you run over to the Oast House and get yourself a smoothie, and then be back here for eleven if you want to watch?'

He gives Charlie his room key to charge the smoothie and watches him leave. Finally, he's got Clara to himself.

'Hi, angel.' He smiles at her. He feels like he's drugged, like all he's capable of doing is grinning at her like a fucking idiot. He takes her in. She's got more make up on today than she did when he took her by surprise, and her hair is beautifully blow-dried so it bounces over her shoulders. Interesting. She's in what must be her professional photography uniform of all black.

'He likes you.'

He shrugs. 'He likes who he thinks I am; he doesn't know me.'

'Did you really cry yourself to sleep for that long?' Under the makeup, her face is pale and her eyes huge. He wants to pull her to him and kiss her eyelids, but instead he gives her a friendly pat on the arm.

'Don't worry about it. Now's not the time to rehash that

stuff. We're here; that's what matters.' He throws his arms wide and takes in the large, airy studio. It has a vaulted ceiling anchored with light wooden beams, and one side is all glass. The weather can't make up its mind, and watery sunshine illuminates the raindrops on the wall of bi-fold doors. He's worked out in worse locations.

'Ok.' She doesn't look convinced.

'Can I see you again—on your own? I think we should have a chat.'

'It's fine,' she says. 'There's nothing to say—we should never have done that, the other day. I'm married, for God's sake.'

'I'm well aware.' He raises an eyebrow at her. 'But I don't think what happened was nothing. We should talk about it. Clear the air.' He watches her, wishing he could fill his hands with her hair and twist it into a silken rope and tilt her beautiful jaw back and kiss along it. Conflict is written all over her face. He's glad he hasn't lost the ability to read her expressions, and irrationally chuffed that she seems to be struggling with her willpower.

'Please,' he says. He produces his trump card. 'I know you want to talk about what happened—how we left things. I'm all yours. I'll tell you whatever you want to know.'

He has her; he knows it.

'Fine.' She raises her head defiantly. 'But it can wait until after the conference. Neither of us needs the distraction.'

He smiles at her until she relents and smiles back at him, even though it's more of a tight smirk and she rolls her eyes like a sulky schoolgirl. He'll take it. He'll take whatever he can get.

By the time the class attendees dribble into the studio, she's set up in a corner with her camera and Charlie is noisily slurping a smoothie on a plastic chair next to her. Alex is at the door, grinning his megawatt grin and shaking hands with everyone who comes in. The attendees are all Sorrel Farm members who've been offered this very special class in exchange for agreeing to be photographed during it. They requested the admin team ensure there are some men in the class, but it looks female-heavy. Who can blame them? He's good enough to eat, his skin glowing with health although it's January, and his snug t-shirt and shorts showing off every single muscle. He's the best possible advert for his own brand.

Now that she's here with him, in the flesh, her self-control is wavering. It would have been so easy, just now, to give into that lazy, hungry smile he gave her and kiss the curved corner of his lips before sliding her nose and mouth over his jaw and down the slope of his neck. She's tired just from trying to ignore his pull. But it's all very well for him to flirt with her; he's single and carefree. Thank God for Charlie, who's effectively a chaperone today and a reminder that she has a happy family life, and that Alex is not the only force that exists in her world.

Once everyone's in the room and standing by the mats, Alex walks through the plan for the session. It's his signature sequence, he explains—one that his successful tech-entrepreneur clients found so flexible and effective on their travels during the internet boom, one that allowed them to transform their bodies from the privacy of endless hotel rooms because it only requires body weight, no equipment. Of course, he adds, the sequence didn't originate in a swanky penthouse suite, but on the floor of a poky cell at his young offenders' institute.

'I tell you, if I could get fit in a cell, you guys can get fit in your bedrooms or basements or gyms. My old PE teacher and football coach used to visit me, and we'd spend a lot of our time discussing the optimal sequence to give me cardio, strength and fat-burning. In those days, I just wanted to be fast and strong and to find an outlet for all the mental struggles I had while I was inside. Then I refined it over the years as I learnt more about different kinds of fitness, so we'll do some yoga-based stretches at the end to build flexibility.'

He puts on some high-octane pop music, and off they go. Clara is relieved she's not doing the class; she'd make such a fool of herself. They do thirty seconds on each exercise and they have thirty seconds rest in between moves, but the heat builds in the room as Alex takes the class through evil-looking moves like side-planks and press-ups and virtual skipping (no rope; presumably they didn't hand out many skipping ropes in prison to vulnerable young inmates) and chest-to-floor burpees, the last of which has everyone groaning and laughing.

Observing Alex in action, in celebrity fitness instructor mode, is something else. Against all her instincts, she's largely avoided footage of him over the past few years, so today brings home how much he's grown. When he's been with her she's seen plenty of the old Alex—the good parts, anyway—but the boy she knew would never have had this supreme self-assurance in front of strangers. It's awe-inspiring, the extent of the troubles he's had to put behind him to get here. His presence fills the room; everyone hangs on his words; all heads are turned to him.

He keeps up a steady patter of conversation the whole time. God knows how he has the lung capacity to do it. He talks through the correct form for each move while he's doing the reps, demonstrating optional modifications as he goes. Between sets, he focuses on bigging up his pupils, praising their efforts, and reminding them what a good thing it is that they've done for their bodies and their minds today by choosing to come here. Twenty minutes in, he's broken a light sweat, while most people are panting, towelling themselves down and glugging water from their bottles during the brief rest periods.

She prowls around the room. Her objective is candid snaps, capturing those most human experiences of discomfort and determination and the achievement of pushing through one's pain barrier. There are plenty of the usual glamorous Sevenoaks mums here—in fact she recognises a couple from school—with Pilates-honed bodies and glossy highlights. They make the exercises look easy. They're not the people she's after for website content, though she gets a few nice wide-angle shots of the entire class, the light rain beyond the windows providing beautiful, soft natural light. Alex had everyone introduce themselves at the start of the class.

There's a young woman who mentioned that she's struggling to shift her baby weight after giving birth eighteen months ago and wants to make more time for herself. Another woman, who must be late fifties and is in incredible shape, says her motivating factor for keeping fit is building strength and keeping her osteoporosis under control. And a guy who can't be over forty confided that he's been signed off from his work as a trader for stress and is attempting to focus on his mental and physical health and lose some of the excess weight around his middle. He's sweating hard and is bright red, but the catchy pop beats and Alex's star quality are infectious, and the atmosphere is lighthearted. People are working hard, but it's not intimidating or perfection oriented: it's fun.

Clara doesn't want to make anyone self-conscious or invade their privacy, but capturing human vulnerability and triumph is her reason for being here, and showcasing it will allow anyone viewing Alex's website to believe health and fitness is accessible to them. She pads around the room in bare feet. She gets the best candid shots towards the last rep or two of each set. The final seconds of the side plank on fatigued, shaking arms. *Click.* The wobbly, excruciating upward stroke of the last push-up. *Click.* The flopping, flailing limbs and laughter during the millionth jumping jack. *Click.*

The final set before they move to the stretching section is more chest-to-floor burpies, designed to finish everyone off. Briefing them, Alex sounds like a Premier League football manager pepping up his beleaguered team.

'I know you're all knackered. This is the final push. We have J-Lo and Pitbull in the house, for God's sake! Thirty seconds of this can make all the difference to your body. Every time you jump up, I want hands in the air, a huge smile and a loud 'Yes!'. Got it? Ok. Let's do this.' He gestures to Clara. 'Ready? This should be good.'

While *On the Floor* pumps out, twenty exhausted people crouch in time with Alex, kicking their legs back and flopping to their mats in a snake-like move, before hauling themselves up to a jump. Hands fly in the air.

'Yes!' Alex shouts.

'*Yes!*' they chorus.

Thirty seconds. Clara has herself positioned up front near Alex, over to one side. She clicks and captures the exhausted exhilaration as his pupils jump.

There are five seconds left on the large digital clock above Alex.

'One last one!' he yells. 'Come on, party people, *get on the floor with me!*'

They squat. They kick back. They flop. They fight gravity and somehow they peel themselves off their mats. They jump for the final time. *Yes!* She gets a group shot: that priceless moment when they all realise the torture is over, and it didn't beat them: they beat it. This is the shot that should be on the home page.

The atmosphere is infectious. Alex congratulates everyone and invites them to lie down as the playlist switches to yoga music. Clara quietly takes some shots and retreats to the side of the room to wait out the cool-down. Her gaze is on Alex. Even he is out of breath, and she ogles him shamefully as he guides the group into twists and stretches from his mat. He can't see her from where he's lying, so she's free to enjoy the knotted muscles contracting under his clothes and skin as he moves. He's perfect curves everywhere: quads, shoulders, pecs, bum. God, that bum. She should have groped it more the other day. He's still surprisingly flexible for someone so muscular. He always was flexible; he was like an eel in bed. The thought sends a shot of heat to her core and she looks at Charlie, squirms, and crosses her legs.

When the class is over, Alex takes the time to thank each attendee personally as they file out. Then he saunters over to her and puts his hands on his hips. His blue top is soaked with sweat under the arms and in a deep V down his front. He grins at her.

'What d'you reckon? That go ok?'

She puts her hand up. 'Hold that smile.'

She raises her camera to her eye, adjusts the aperture slightly. She can hide behind it and gape freely at his beauty. His skin shimmers with sweat. He's looking directly at her, smiling just for her. His eyes are tropical, bottomless pools of green. She clicks. He's in focus; everything behind him a luminous blur. It's exactly the same as when she looks at him without the camera: he's the only thing she sees. Everything else is muddied, unfocused, when he's in front of her. She knows she'll stare at this photo for a long time when she gets home.

12

1998

Afterwards, she blamed Matt Foster for everything that happened, but she didn't fool herself for a minute. There was only one person to blame, and it was her. She was the one who handled the situation badly and treated the boy she loved terribly. But it was definitely Matt who set events in motion, and it was a very long time before she stopped replaying every move she'd made that day in an endless, pointless attempt to rewrite history.

She knew Alex wouldn't be around to walk her home that afternoon; he'd told her already, at lunch. If only she'd stayed at school and got her homework done in the library. But she headed back to the restaurant as usual, and Matt stopped her just outside the school gates. She could tell he could tell she didn't like him, and she didn't. He was a right dick. He wasted time in class, he was obnoxious to pretty much everyone except Alex, and he made snide, sexual comments to her that made her skin crawl, but he wasn't stupid enough to say anything in front of Alex. She knew Alex would beat him up if she told him.

Leave me alone, Matt, she told him as she stalked off, head down.

Leave me alone, Matt, he parroted in a high-pitched voice. *Don't you ever wonder why your boyfriend's spending less time with you these days? Don't you wonder what he's doing instead of shagging you the whole fucking time?*

Fuck off. She hardly ever swore, even though Alex did, all the time—she couldn't get comfortable with it. But at least even stupid Matt Foster understood those words.

Ooh. The posh girl swears. Where's your boyfriend, then?

He's working. She increased her pace.

Damn right he's working, running E and Charlie around the Jubilee. You knew that, right? You know that's how he could afford to buy you that ring?

She looked down at the silver Claddagh ring he'd given her when she got back from Italy. He'd explained that it was an Irish tradition to give one to the girl you loved, and that if she loved you back, she would wear the ring upside down, so the heart on the ring was pointing inwards, towards her own heart. She looked back up at Matt, who had to be one of the thickest boys in their year, and knew in an instant that he knew everything and she knew nothing.

Fuck off and leave me alone, she told him, and ran all the way home.

~

SHE WAS SO STUPID. *So. Stupid.* Of course he was involved in drugs! He'd been weird ever since she got back: no less loving towards her when they were together, but more withdrawn, more furtive. He spent more time back at the estate, and he told her he was running shopping errands for some of the elderly residents to earn a few quid. He was evasive when she pressed him for more details, and there was this one time last week when he came over and he was just twitchy. He shuffled around her bedroom; he wouldn't just sit down and talk to her, and when she had her head on his chest after they'd had sex, she thought his heart would burst out of his body. He was dealing, and he was doing drugs too. She should have worked it out more quickly, but no one in her group of friends did anything; they hardly even drank. She hadn't known what she was seeing.

He came over a few hours later. She could tell the minute she saw him that he was twitchy again—he had that look in his eye that she'd got used to without recognising what caused it. She could taste beer on his breath when he kissed her. She devoured him for a few minutes, partly because he was irresistible, and partly because she was putting off what she knew would be an unpleasant conversation. Finally, she pulled away.

I know you're doing drugs, and I know you're dealing them, too.

He wouldn't meet her eyes. *That's bollocks. You don't know what you're talking about.*

I know, Alex. Don't lie to me; we don't do that. It's drugs, *for God's sake! How could you be so stupid?*

Look. He brushed his palms down her bare arms and she shivered. *You have no idea what it's like on the estate. Everyone's doing them, ok? It's not a big deal. It's a fact of life, and it's a good way to make some cash.*

He was speaking to her in a slow, cajoling style, as if she was a baby, or stupid, or someone who might blow up on him at any moment.

You don't have to do that, she pleaded. *You can get a job in Spar, after school, if you really need to, or at the restaurant. I can speak to my parents.*

Yeah, for fucking three or four quid an hour. That's not going to cut it, angel. Mum's dead on her feet and she's not bringing in enough. Connor's a waste of fucking space; you know that. This is easy work! It's so easy, it's ridiculous. Trust me.

He kissed her forehead and folded her into his arms and she wanted to die, she loved this boy so much. She couldn't process the strength of her feelings for him and the magic she felt when she was with him and the fierce, desperate need she felt to protect him. He'd had such a crappy life compared to her, and he didn't complain, not really, not as much as she definitely would if she were in his shoes.

Why are you doing them too, though? You don't need them, Alex.

Perk of the job. He laughed into her hair, but it wasn't even remotely funny. She fought a cold, crawling sensation of dread.

You don't need them, she repeated, she begged. *You've seen what they do to people. There are so many zombies on the Jubilee; you always say so. You've even said that about Connor. You were doing so well at school last year. Why would you do this?*

He pulled away from her. *It's no big deal. Just leave it, for fuck's sake.*

I won't leave it. I love you, and I know how much potential you have. I see it every day. But I can tell you're on something right now. What did you take?

Just a line of coke. Just a tiny one, before I came out.

Why would you do that? She drank in his face. She didn't really know what she was looking for, but she could see his pupils were huge. *You're just here, with me. Do you need coke for that? Do you need drugs to make things more interesting?*

Jesus Christ, Clara. What are you, my mum? Get off my fucking back.

He stalked around the room. *Honestly, I'm going to go if you don't give me a break. I didn't come here to get nagged.*

I'm not nagging you. She followed him over to the window and leant her head against his back, her arms reaching around his sides to hug his chest. She inhaled his sweatshirt; he smelt like school and sweat and Lynx, and the fact that he was pissed off with her made her sick with horror. *I just—I think you're amazing. I know you're going to do something great with your life. You have so much potential, Alex. I don't want to see you throw it all away.*

He took her hands and pulled them roughly off him. *Will you stop saying that fucking word?* Potential. *Jesus, you sound like a fucking teacher.*

She'd never seen this side of him, not with her. He swung around to face her, and if she didn't know better, she'd think he hated her.

I'm sorry. She kept her voice steady. *But someone's got to say it to you. Whether you like it or not, you're a smart, talented guy. I know you've been let down in the past, and I won't let you do this to yourself. I'm sorry if you don't like the 'P word', but you've got it. Potential. So why don't you go home, sober up, and fulfil your fucking potential? It's such a fucking waste.*

He crossed to the door, shoving her with his shoulder as he went.

Fuck you, she heard, as her bedroom door slammed behind him.

13

2019

Clara's very quiet at the final meeting ahead of the conference. It's party because she's star-struck. Evelyn's ex-husband, Seb Macleod, has come down for the meeting and watching him and Alex together is both fascinating and a huge turn-on. She despises herself for thinking it, but watching two extremely attractive celebrities doing their alpha-male bromance together is very, very hot.

She has most of Seb's cook books at home—not that she's ever managed to stick to the guidelines in his healthier ones much—but he's even more attractive in the flesh, and if Evelyn wasn't such a strong character, she suspects he'd dominate the meeting. As it is, it's a lively discussion up on the pretty, sunlit mezzanine level of the Oast House. The conference is this weekend and will run over a Saturday and Sunday. Seb is headlining the nutritional aspect of the event and Zoe's here to confirm that the menus she's created for the weekend are in line with the healthy eating message Seb will be pushing. They are, of course—the food line-up sounds mouth-watering, with plenty of slow-cooked, nurturing soups and stews and roasted vegetables to counterbalance the grim mid-winter weather.

There are a few others at the meeting too: Zoe's wife and co-founder, Jess, is here. Clara knows her from various school events over the years and is fond of her; Jess is always a breath of fresh air with her irreverent take on the teachers and school rules. The farm's PR manager, Sadie, a stunning blonde in skinny jeans and a black polo-neck, looks lithe and chic in a way Clara could never, ever pull off. She can't help casting a glance at Alex to see if he reacts to Sadie, but from the banter around the table, it sounds as though Sadie is madly in love with the farm's Finance Director, Ned. Seb mentions that he was down last weekend to cook dinner for them all at Evelyn's home in celebration of Zoe's spectacular *Sunday Times Magazine* cover feature, which Sadie procured for her. In any case, poor Sadie is the butt of much good-natured ribbing from the management team over Ned, but her radiant smile whenever he's mentioned suggests she doesn't mind it too much.

Alex's brother, Connor, is here too this time. It's a seriously freaky moment when she sees him. For years, she blamed him (and Matt Foster) for what happened, but with the twin perspective offered by parenthood and time elapsed, she can sympathise with the struggles Connor must have had as the eldest son of an absentee father and a broken, exhausted mother. She's not privy to how he's spent the past twenty years; all she knows is that now he's a highly skilled web designer with his own digital agency who also acts as a sounding-board for Alex's brand. In any case, she's glad he's got himself together and that his wasn't another life wasted in the fall-out.

He's a good-looking guy—he always was—but next to Alex, he looks positively ordinary. Alex is luminous; she's unsure whether his star quality has emerged as he's acclimatised to his celebrity status, or whether it's the force that's always driven him and allowed him to reach these heights of success. She suspects it's the latter. She's not sure how to greet Connor, but he steps around the table and engulfs her in an enormous bear hug.

'It's Fiori!' He holds her away from him, gripping her upper arms firmly and shooting her an enormous grin. She laughs. It's impossible not to like this new and vastly more good-natured Connor. The last time she saw him, they were both in agonies over Alex.

'Great to see you, darlin',' he whispers.

There are some raised eyebrows around the table. No one except Evelyn knows of her link to Alex.

She gestures vaguely at Alex and Connor. 'I was at school with these guys.'

Seb sits up straighter. 'Fascinating! Tell us more. What was the perfect specimen that is Alex Molloy like at school?'

Clara holds Alex's eyes for a brief, endless moment. 'He was fairly dodgy.' She forces a smile at Seb.

Seb grins. 'Of course he was. We all know you were no angel back then, were you, Molloy?' He elbows Alex in the ribs.

'Right.' Evelyn interrupts. 'Let's get this thing going. Alex, are all your guest speakers confirmed?' She shoots Clara a small, apologetic smile, which she returns gratefully. When she looks back at Alex, she has the impression that he's finding it difficult to tear his eyes away from her to engage with his laptop screen.

The meeting eventually wraps up. Clara can't get out of that room fast enough. As the door to the stables closes behind them, Connor slaps Alex on his shoulder blade.

'You ok, mate?'

'Fuck.' He rubs his scalp, back to front. Connor's unaware of his indiscretion with Clara last week. 'Every time I see her, you know, it has me in bits, man.'

'She's still fucking fit.' Connor grins widely as he sets his laptop on the breakfast bar. 'Jesus, you really did bag yourself the hottest girl in Kent. You were such a jammy bastard.'

'Until I got totally fucking shafted by the justice system and banged up for a first-time offence, you mean?'

'I know, mate.' Connor's expression darkens. 'But look where you are now. You've got it all to play for. The app's been number one in the Apple App Store for a month now; subscriptions are through the roof and you've got Nike and Tag Heuer knocking on your door to supersize your sponsorships. Don't look back. You've left all that shit behind you, man. It's just onwards and upwards, if you keep working like this.'

Alex crosses the room to the resort landline and calls through a lunch order for two chicken salads from the Oast House. When he puts the phone down, he edges back towards Connor and hesitates. He knows what his brother's response will be before he says anything, but it will do him good to hear it says out loud. He could do with having some sense knocked into him.

'You know, man, it's been a real head-fuck, having her back in my life. I think I still feel the same about her; I don't think it's ever really gone away.'

Connor spins around to face him. 'What the fuck? Didn't you tell me she's married?'

'Yeah, she is, but—'

'No. You hear me? *No*. How can you even think about going after a married woman?'

'I wouldn't, obviously, but I'm pretty sure there's still something there in her mind, too.'

'Have you guys talked about it?'

'Not really, but we—we may have kissed the other day, in here.'

'Jesus Christ!' Connor slams his hand against the wall and Alex flinches. 'If you weren't built like a brick shit-house, I'd beat the shit out of you right now. Did you bang her?'

'No.' Unfortunately.

'Well'—Connor's hand hangs uselessly in the air—'stay the fuck away from her. You hear me? I can't believe you could even think about breaking up a marriage after what that slag did to us. You told me she has kids, for fuck's sake. Stay. Away.'

That slag was the woman who lured Dad away when Alex was barely walking and Connor was three. The last Mum had ever heard of him was that he and she had gone up to Newcastle to try their luck up north. Mum didn't talk about him, and she never mentioned the woman by name, but Alex gleaned precious snippets about them over the years. The uncomfortable truth seemed to be that infidelity wasn't Dad's only shortcoming; he was a pretty useless husband and father long before that woman came on the scene. However, he and Connor needed a narrative that neatly explained Dad's reasons for abandoning them all, and it was more convenient and less painful to believe he'd been bewitched into walking away from his young family than it was to accept that they were better off without him.

That said, the institution of marriage has always been sacrosanct in Connor and Alex's book. You don't mess with someone else's relationship. If you do, innocent parties get hurt—kids get hurt, and you don't fucking do that. But it feels different with Clara. It's hard to articulate, but it's as if he has a prior claim that, together with the injustice he and she suffered all those years ago, means he's entitled to do whatever the fuck he likes to get a second chance of making it work with her.

Connor must be a mind-reader, for right at that point, he says:

'You ruined her life once, man. Have some fucking decency and just allow her to live it second time around.'

~

CLARA MAKES a beeline for her best friend Abi's house before she has to pick the twins up. At the island in Abi's vast, spotless kitchen, she puts her head in her hands and groans. 'Ugh.'

'You okay, C?' Abi pats her on the shoulder. She's the coolest mum at school, in mesh yoga pants and a chunky sweater that falls off one shoulder, showing off the intricate straps of a yoga bra. Clara knows that if she asked who the designer is, she wouldn't recognise the name.

She takes a deep inhale. 'I could do with a bit of advice from you, if you're game.'

'Of course.'

The truth is, she has no one else she can confide in, and she's bloody bursting. She's definitely not ready to talk to Mum or Maria about Alex. They'd hit the roof if they thought she was involved with him again, after the years of heartbreak they helped her through. Most of her friends these days are parents from the school her kids have been at since they were four, and they all know Jeremy. She doesn't have anyone who's removed enough from them as a couple, but Abi is always unequivocally Team Clara, even if her husband Rich is golf buddies with Jeremy. Their friendship is tight, but their conversations have never ventured beyond low-grade bitching about their husbands into this uncharted territory.

She takes the plunge. 'I'm shooting a conference at Sorrel Farm this weekend. Alex Molloy and Seb Macleod are headlining it.'

'Shit!' Abi shakes her hand as if she's been burnt. 'You lucky bitch. Can I come and be your assistant? I'll do anything! They're both so hot. Pity Seb's gay, but Alex Molloy... Yes. Please.'

Clara grimaces. 'It's a lot more complicated than that.'

'How so?'

'You know I told you once, over wine, all about my first love, and our tragic ending?'

'Yes.' Abi looks totally confused. 'What's that got to do with anything?'

Clara puts her head in her hands. 'Oh, shit. This is so hard to say.'

'Clara. What the fuck is going on? What am I missing?'

'My first boyfriend, the love of my life, was Alex Molloy. Turns out, the boy did good.'

'Hoooooly fuck!' Abi spins around and doubles over in glee. She jerks her head back up, hair flying back. 'Oh. My. God. Your bad boy boyfriend was *the* Alex Molloy?'

'I'm afraid so.'

'Jesus. I can't even look at you right now, I'm so jealous. My sweet little friend, Clara, who looks like butter wouldn't

melt in her mouth, is telling me that she spent her school-days fucking pretty much the hottest man in this country.'

If she was Abi, she'd be reacting this way, too. From the outside, it must sound like a fairytale rather than a nightmare.

'It's not good, Abs. He was the love of my life. We were *crazy* about each other; we spent every waking hour together. The night he got arrested, we'd had a huge fight because I'd found out he'd been doing drugs. He stormed out of my house and... you know the story. They arrested him, and I never saw him again, until a couple of weeks ago.'

'Shit.' Abi sobers up, puts her hand over Clara's. 'I'm so sorry, C. That must have been devastating for you.'

'Thanks.' She allows herself a moment to enjoy the comforting warmth of her friend's hand. 'It's hard to explain how devastating—it ruined my life, basically. It took me years to get back on track. I've never really got over him, and now he's in my life again... well, it's clear there's a shit-load of unfinished business. He still—affects me far more than he should.'

'How was it—seeing him? It must have been so fucking weird—Jesus. Do you think he feels the same?' Compassion and curiosity compete in Abi's huge eyes.

She swallows. 'It was so weird. I was so nervous. He definitely feels something, because he kissed me last week in his amazing suite in The Stables—he's staying at the farm for a few weeks while his house gets decorated—and let's just say it was like travelling back in time twenty years. God knows how carried away we would have got if school hadn't called to say Charlie'd thrown up in the lunch queue.'

Abi's a picture: disbelief, horror, mirth, empathy.

'You can't make it up. But you kissed him, babe—oh my

God.' She squints at Clara. 'Was it amazing? Tell me it was amazing.'

Clara throws up her hands. 'It was—incredible. It felt so bloody right. I can't explain what it's like to have him back in my life, to see him so safe and well, with my own eyes, after everything he went through. It's a miracle. But'—she shrugs her shoulders—'I'm *married*. I have *kids*. For Christ's sake, what the hell am I doing?'

God knows what Abi will think of her. She and Rich are happily married, and their relationship has always struck Clara as lighthearted and intimate. Abi would be forgiven for assuming the exact same about Clara and Jeremy's relationship.

They're both quiet a moment, then Abi asks:

'I suppose the first question is, do you know what you want at this point? I mean, I assume you and Jeremy were happily married until Alex came along—you guys always seem okay?'

She shrugs. 'I guess I was—I mean, we were fine. You know.'

Abi narrows her eyes.

She presses on.

'I don't know what I want, no. It's such an unfair comparison! I was a different person when I knew Alex; our relationship was totally unlike the one I have with Jeremy. And there's this unbelievable spark with Alex, and attraction, and *so* much emotion, I can't even tell you, but it's so hard to tell whether it's real or just the product of having had zero closure and so many years of wondering what might have been.'

Abi smiles naughtily. 'It doesn't help that the guy's a god. I mean, he's ridiculous. If he came onto me, Rich would be dead in the fucking water. I wouldn't even give him a backwards glance. Or the kids.'

'It is extremely unhelpful,' Clara agrees. 'He was the best-looking guy at our school, but now—holy shit.'

'It sounds to me as though you need some answers, C, if you really haven't spoken to Alex in all these years. That must have taken such a toll on you, to lose him like that, without even a goodbye. You must have had so much grief—I can't even imagine it! And now he's back from the dead, if you like, and you're expected to carry on and deal with him professionally and not question what role he has in your present and your future? I don't bloody well think so.'

Abi's kindness feels like absolution, like a timely and benevolently bestowed gift. Grief is the perfect analogy. She's been grieving for twenty-one years, and Alex's physical appearance has brought with it such a tidal wave of regret and anguish on the one hand, and a flurry of hope and endless possibility on the other, that she's totally ill-equipped to know how to deal with it. She releases a shaky exhale and nods in agreement.

Abi keeps talking. 'I'm sure Alex is feeling the same way. This must be overwhelming for you both—you have so much to catch up on. You're a grown woman, babe. I know what a fab mum you are, but you deserve to be happy. Take this time with Alex to get to know each other again, to talk about your regrets and your emotions, and maybe then you'll make enough space for yourselves to understand what you mean to each other. I'd say you owe it to yourselves to bridge this gap, to really try to understand the journeys you've both been on since you last were together, and maybe then you can make sense of this crazy situation you find yourselves in.'

She stares at Abi. She wasn't expecting such an

outpouring of wisdom. Abi's right, of course. She needs to sit down with Alex, preferably wearing a chastity belt, and talk through twenty years of shit and grief and misunderstanding and regret and torment and what-ifs and unconsummated desire and fuck knows what else, and perhaps then she'll understand whether Alex Molloy is merely a ghost from her past or possibly, terrifyingly, a vision from her future.

14

1998

After Alex left, she paced around the house for a very long time before going to bed and having a spectacularly rubbish night's sleep. The next morning, he wasn't waiting for her outside her house. He always, always walked over from his flat, even though she wasn't on his way to school, and walked her to school. That cold, creeping feeling from their fight last night came over her again. It was a month to go until their first anniversary as a couple, and that fight was the first proper argument they'd had.

She waited five minutes and walked to school alone. Maybe he was ill. Maybe he was hungover. He'd probably carried on drinking after he'd left her. Maybe he'd ODed on drugs! She started to pray. *Please, God, I'll do anything as long as he's okay. Please, make him be okay. I can't live without him.*

They weren't doing any of the same A Level subjects, so she didn't have a chance to work out whether he'd made it to school. But during her free period after lunch, Mrs G—Mrs Gilmore, the deputy head—came and found her in the library and asked her for a word in her office. When they got there, Fr Pat, the school chaplain, was already sitting down. He had a very serious look on his face and she knew, she absolutely knew, that his expression had to do with Alex. Her sick feeling got worse. Oh, God, what if they'd discovered he was peddling drugs and expelled him?

Fr Pat and Mrs G exchanged glances before Mrs G started to speak.

I'm afraid we have some bad news, Clara. I know this will come as a shock to you, but Alex Molloy was arrested in the early hours of this morning.

She didn't expect her to say that—she couldn't really understand what she meant. Did the police find drugs on him after he left her? Oh, God. She stared at their faces to try to understand better. Fr Pat looked on the verge of tears.

Mrs G continued. *It's very serious, I'm afraid. Fr Pat has been down at the station most of the morning, but he hasn't been allowed to see Alex. He had a car crash, you see—*

Alex had a car crash? It must be a mistake.

He doesn't drive—he doesn't even know how to drive. He doesn't have a car!

Another grim look between the two of them.

Is Alex okay? Is he hurt? Maybe Connor was driving?

Not badly, no, as far as we know. He was definitely behind the wheel; as far as we know, he was in his mother's car. His mum called me first thing from the station. But I'm very sorry to tell you that he killed someone—a pedestrian. I know this must be very upsetting for you, Clara—

No no no no no no no no no no no no. She couldn't process what they were saying, that Alex was driving, that he killed someone. He never, ever mentioned to her that he'd learnt to drive. She didn't even know Carmen had a car. And here they were, telling her he was under arrest. It was ridiculous. She thought of the beer she'd tasted when she'd kissed him, of those crazy, massive black pupils. What she wanted more than anything right then was for them to tell her it was all a misunderstanding, that he was fine and sleeping off his hangover at home.

Who did he—Her words sounded strange, like they were coming from deep inside her body but from far away at the same time. She couldn't say it. She tried again. *Who died?*

A young woman, as far as we know. Fr Pat's voice was soft and small and sad.

He killed someone—someone was dead because of Alex. She attempted to comprehend the finality of that concept.

Will he—are they saying he murdered her? The words were sour in her mouth.

Fr Pat sat forward. He'd been the parish priest at St Winnie's since she was a little girl. She'd made her First Holy Communion with him, and her Confirmation. He was reasonably young for a priest, and cool, and even Alex liked him, although they only knew each other from school because Alex's family didn't go to Mass. Clara had stopped going to Mass in the last year, because it felt weird and pointless to go when she was having sex before marriage and was basically facing eternal damnation. But Fr Pat never made a big deal of it; he just said she was always welcome at Mass whenever she felt she needed it.

Not murder, no. They were talking about charging him with causing death by dangerous driving, driving illegally, driving while intoxicated, and possibly possession. They found some small quantities of cocaine on him, I believe.

Fr Pat had aged a decade overnight. His skin looked grey and the skin under his eyes was sagging onto his cheeks. Every word he said made her sick, cold, creeping feeling from last night come back more violently.

What happens now? When I can see him?

Silence. Mrs G reached over and grabbed her hand and held it tightly.

You have to be brave, Clara, she said. *Fr Pat and this school will do everything we can to help Alex. Right now, the government is appointing him a lawyer. But you may not get to see him for a good while. The charges are very serious. They may not let him out anytime soon.*

She lost it then. She pulled her hand away and crossed her arms over her stomach and sat as far forward as possible and rocked back and forwards as if she had the world's worst period pain. Period pains had nothing on this. This was agony. She was aware of the sound of herself balling, howling, and somewhere she was embarrassed by how awful and crazy she sounded, but most of her awareness was taken up by a ball of pain behind her eyes and in her stomach, so great she thought it might kill her.

She was vaguely aware of Mrs G shuffling her chair further towards her and putting her arm around Clara's shoulders, and of Fr Pat standing up and patting her head as if she was a child at Mass who was too young to receive Holy Communion, and saying very gently: *I'll call your mum to come and take you home.*

15

2019

'For the final session of the day, I'm delighted to welcome Je Tsongkhapa to the stage. Je has been in my life for a decade, and through him I've found the strength to live with the enormity of my past wrongdoings. We're going to discuss the healing benefits of radical forgiveness, and Je will then lead us through a short guided meditation to give us the gift of space after what's been an intense day.'

With that, Alex stands aside and welcomes a robed man. He's not Tibetan, but rather an American former felon who left behind a life of drug crime decades ago and found solace through Buddhism. Because Clara's been fully prepped ahead of time, she knows that he took the name of a famous fourteenth century Tibetan monk and has flown in just for a weekend, as a favour to Alex. Clearly, they have some common ground. He opens his arms and gives Alex a warm hug, and Clara clicks dutifully. Her feet are killing her; her decision to wear heels with this black wrap dress, which was based purely on vanity, is coming back to bite her.

There have been so many moments today during this beautiful, thought-provoking and flawlessly executed conference where she's had an inexplicable urge to giggle. It's extremely immature, but every time Alex says something about spirituality or finding himself or meditation or feeling more deeply or practising self-love, she feels like sniggering. It's *such* a leap from the boy she knew and loved to this man. There's nothing laughable about it: the Alex standing up here today is formidable; he's a wonderful testament to human resilience and to the herculean efforts he's made to use the worst of his life experiences as a force for good. But if sixteen-year-old Alex and sixteen-year-old Clara could see him now, they'd have a good laugh.

That said, her eyes have been on him all day. The conference is taking place in a huge temporary structure in a field around the back of the walled garden, because there's nowhere big enough on the farm to hold all the guests. It's like a marquee on steroids: all flawless cream carpet and wispy white fabric wall coverings, with vast urns of eucalyptus and winter berries everywhere. It reminds her of the tents that house the Frieze art fair in Regent's Park (back when she used to go to Frieze, in a previous life). There are sections for break-out sessions, and she gets footage of a yoga class, a paleo cookery masterclass with one of Seb's team, and a breathwork session. The main stage is reserved for the big draws: Alex, Seb and their interviewees.

She watches him in action and she is so bloody proud of him that her heart may burst. What have they done with the Alex Molloy she knew and loved? It's him, and yet it's not. The essence of him is very much still there, but his presence, his poise, his panache—they're honed to a level that she doesn't have the privilege of seeing on anyone often. She caught a glimpse of it as his workout class the other day, but here, in front of four hundred athleisure-clad delegates, he's unleashed. It's clear why he's caught the imagination of so many people on both sides of the pond. His star quality is undeniable.

He and Seb are good foils for each other—Seb's the devastatingly smooth ex-public schoolboy with a sharp wit, and Alex is his grittier counterpart whose down-to-earth take on health is a breath of fresh air. As the press shows it, he's a reformed bad boy with a tough life-story and a highly marketable face and body, who shares his personal transformation so candidly that he can't help but inspire others. Hiding behind her camera lens, she sees him as everyone there sees him while also having the privilege of being familiar with the part he keeps hidden. When she's alone with him, he's exactly as he was—with a few rough edges knocked off.

The session with Je Tsongkhapa is drawing to a close.

'You know, Alex, when you came to Tibet, ten years ago, you were not the man I see before me now.' Je turns to the audience. He hasn't lost his gravelly Texan drawl, but his manner of speaking is so calm, so kind, that is voice is like a shot of tranquilliser. Clara could do with him hosting the kids' tea every evening. Scratch that, she could do with a month in Tibet. She zones back in to what he's saying.

'Alex had built a flourishing personal training business and he was prospering financially, so if you were charting his journey based on purely external factors, you would say he'd been highly successful in putting his troubled past behind him and realising his potential.'

Clara smiles inwardly. There's that word—*potential*. She was a guru before she knew it. Her eyes flick to Alex, but emotion is playing across his face at Je's words.

Je leans forward. 'But Alex was in agony within himself,

because had the biggest lesson of all to learn. That is the acceptance that, while we cannot change our past actions, we are all better than the worst things we have done.' He pauses and nods as he looks around the audience. He's mesmerising. 'We really, really are. Alex came for two weeks and stayed for three months. He left a different man, because he learnt the skill of self-forgiveness. That's not the same as forgetting, or excusing. Above all, we must remain accountable. But Alex learnt to forgive himself and to accept that he was worthy of accepting good things in life. He has opened himself up to life's abundance. And you can too. Let's meditate together on our inherent worthiness, and let's seek the strength and the space to find self-compassion.'

~

AFTER THE MEDITATION, there's a short drinks reception sponsored by some local biodynamic vineyard. Alex is pleased with how the day's gone. The wellness conference format is a well-trodden path for him now; it's a sound way to build connections with current and potential clients and events like this reassure him that there's an increasing number of like-minded people in the world, people who prioritise their mental and physical wellbeing in a dark world.

The last session affected him more than he would have liked. His time at Je's monastery marked a massive turning point in his life, and given what an arse it is to get to Tibet, he's happy to have been able to bring Je here to impart his wisdom. But when he hears him speak about self-forgiveness, it always tears him apart. Je himself is a shining example of the power of radical self-forgiveness, but he was a junkie, not a killer. He may have caused heartbreak to his friends and family, but he hasn't known the indescribably horrifying thud of a human body fatally hitting a car bonnet. Radical self-forgiveness is more like radical self-indulgence when there's one less being on this planet because of you.

The familiar emotion materialises in his throat like bile, and as usual, he shoves it down. He does what he's been doing all day, and looks around for Clara. She's working the crowd, photographing clusters of delegates with their glasses of English sparkling wine or whatever it is they're drinking. He's more of a whisky man: wine has too many carbs. Nevertheless, he accepts a glass from a passing waiter and takes a tentative sip. Hmm. Pretty decent stuff. It's amazing what the UK is producing these days.

He pinches the bridge of his nose. He's knackered. Being 'on' all day is exhausting, which is why he's refused all invitations for dinner this evening. He feels bad, but he'll catch up with Seb and Evelyn tomorrow, once they've got Day Two out of the way. Je's the only person he would have broken his rule for, but thankfully Je's a man after his own heart, and has made it clear he'll be having a quiet evening alone in his cottage on the farm. Alex does the rounds, shaking hands, posing for selfies, autographing people's gym kit and hearing their stories. He loves this stuff, even when he's knackered. He'll never, ever stop being amazed and grateful that people out there, who are mostly far more decent than he is, find his offering valuable. They're why he does this. They're his tribe, and if they can be bothered to show up for him, he can be bothered to do the same for them.

The crowd is thinning out a bit. He looks around for Clara again and makes a beeline for her before anyone can stop him. She looks so fucking gorgeous today. Her hair is in these long, loose waves and she's done something with her eye makeup—he's not sure what, but her eyes look huge and dark and cat-like. She's like a modern-day Sofia Loren; she's wasted behind the camera. Ms Loren would dig that dress; it's a slinky black wrap-type thing that ties at the side and probably comes off like a coat. She's all tits and arse in it, but in the classiest way. She's one of the classiest chicks he's ever known. Her legs are endless in her black stilettos. She always did have knockout legs. He casts his mind back to her in her netball kit, with that tiny little skirt thing she wore, and his balls ache. He realises he doesn't want to be alone this evening. He wants to be with her.

She's thanking a group of women for agreeing to let her photograph them. He edges closer and holds up his finger. She smiles at him and it's open, pure. He knows she's as happy to see him as he is to see her. The women clock him and their eyes open and they thrust their chests out, and suddenly he can't do another minute of chit-chatting with anyone else but her.

He grabs her elbow and turns to the women. 'Hi, there. I'm so sorry, but I need to borrow Clara for a moment. It's a bit of an emergency.'

He leads her out of the bar area, into a breakout room that's now empty.

'What's the emergency?'

'No emergency. But I'm exhausted. You're the only person I can actually be arsed to talk to.'

She pats his arm in a maternal fashion. 'Poor Alex. You must be knackered. I'm exhausted too. These bloody shoes.' She looks down and wiggles her ankles and sighs.

'For what's worth, they're very sexy.'

She frowns at him. 'Professional was the vibe I was going for.'

'Listen.' He rubs his head. 'Do you have to get home just yet?'

She hesitates. 'No.'

'What's that in your voice?'

She relents. 'Jeremy's taken the kids to see his parents in Dorset for the weekend. God forbid he should have to look after them by himself for two days.'

He raises an eyebrow at her tone. Jeremy sounds like an incompetent, ungrateful fucker of a father. But she's off duty this weekend. Interesting. His heart soars, but he keeps his voice steady.

'Will you come and keep me company, back at the stables? Nothing dodgy. I just can't do small talk anymore, but I don't want to be alone.'

'Where's Connor?'

'You're a lot easier on the eye than him. And he's out with some old college mates this evening. Come on, I have nice wine and you can take off your shoes.'

She smiles, and he knows he's hooked her. He takes her hand. 'Let's get out of here.'

16

1998 / 1999

After Alex was arrested, she stopped functioning. The day she found out, Mum and Dad both came to school to get her, and Dad told her later that he'd had to carry her out to the car, because she couldn't walk by herself. She was so hysterical, they got a doctor around and he gave her something to knock her out that night, but they made her go back to school a few days later to finish the term before breaking up for Christmas.

Alex was sent to Cookham Wood Young Offenders' Institute in Rochester, about twenty miles east of Otford. She sought Fr Pat out every day at school, and once they'd broken up she'd walk to the church to have a cup of tea with him and try to glean any information she could. Alex was in custody on remand, and he due to appear in a youth court in the new year for sentencing. Her vocabulary of unwanted new words increased exponentially. As far as she could work out, Fr Pat and Mr Evans and Alex's mum were all visiting him as much as they were allowed, which was once a week.

Her first question was when she could go visit him, and

she listened in absolute horror as Fr Pat explained very gently that Alex didn't want her to visit.

He loves you very much, he says, *and he asked me to tell you he misses you terribly. But you've got to understand, Clara: Alex is going through an enormous trauma right now. He's taken a human life, albeit by accident; he's trying to come to terms with that while having been taken away from his loved ones. He's a strong boy, but he's finding things very difficult and his overwhelming emotions are grief and guilt. He feels responsible for what's happened, and he feels very unworthy of Christ's love and of our love, even though I've assured him he is deeply loved. He has a particularly strong belief at the moment that you are better off without him, so I think the best thing you can do right now, love, is write to him and show him your support that way.*

She went around and saw Carmen a few times over Christmas, and they rocked together in grief and disbelief. She saw Connor there sometimes. He was very angry, very worried about his brother. *Too fucking right*, thought Clara. Connor had got him in with those drug dealers and facilitated his coke habit. When Alex had stormed out of her house that night, he'd met up with Connor on some skanky corner of the estate where they'd drunk more beers and done a few more lines. She'd pieced together the evening's timeline over the course of various hysterical conversations with Connor. Alex was furious with Clara that night, Connor told her, but it was obvious that part of the reason Alex was furious was because he knew everything she'd said to him had been correct.

Alex had decided to work off his aggression with a joyride around the roads surrounding the estate in Carmen's Fiesta, and Connor had left him to it, something he said he'd never, ever forgive himself for. It was after midnight by then, and pretty quiet on the streets (she also found out that she had Connor to thank for teaching Alex to drive while she was in Italy). Alex had made off with the car keys and a can of Stella and that was the last Connor'd heard of him till the police came knocking on the door an hour later. Alex had been doing forty miles per hour and sailed straight through a zebra crossing where Lindsay Smith, a young mum from the estate, had chosen to cross the road on her way home from a night out. Apparently, he never even saw her.

He didn't hit and run. Neighbours heard the noise and the police found Alex crouched over her body, screaming. She was pronounced dead just after the ambulance crews got to the scene.

Lindsay and her partner had a fourteen-month-old baby.

It was all anyone in Otford could talk about. It was all over the press. School became unbearable. She sat her post-Christmas exams in a blur, but she hadn't done a minute of revision over those dreadful holidays, and she just about scraped a pass.

She wasn't even allowed to go to the trial. Carmen went, and Fr Pat went with her for moral support, but Carmen told her Alex had begged Clara to stay away; he was hysterical at the thought of her seeing him like that, she said. So she stayed away and sat between her parents, staring blindly at the TV while she chewed her fingers to pieces. He had a *pro bono* lawyer who Fr Pat said seemed quite good, and who was confident Alex would get away with a suspended sentence given the circumstances: good grades at school, a stable home, the fact that Lindsay's death was a tragic accident and this was a first offence.

They sent him down for two years. The prosecutor was apparently a total shark who made an example of Alex and called out the alcohol and drunk abuse problems on the 'infamous' Jubilee estate. Because he had just turned seventeen, he would serve out his sentence at Cookham Wood, with drug rehabilitation part of the deal, and he could continue his studies there. Apparently, she should be thankful that he wasn't going to an adult prison. Instead, she lost a stone and stopped trying at school, at all.

His letter arrived a couple of weeks after the sentencing.

It was no surprise to anyone when her parents got called into school in June to be told she'd failed the year, and that her choices were to drop out of school or re-take Lower Sixth, but that school would only take her back if she found a way to work through her grief and apply herself properly.

Fr Pat found her on the school grounds a few days later and uncomfortably relayed a verbal message Alex had given him over the phone from prison.

He says you'll know what this means, love. He says, ahem: fulfil your fucking potential. *He says he's begging you to give Lower Sixth another shot.*

17

2019

He pours her a glass of Chablis from the mini-bar and grabs the bottle of Johnny Walker Blue Label. It's his guilty pleasure, and it was the only thing he requested when he moved into his temporary digs.

'You sure I can't get you anything else, Mariah?' Connor teased him. 'White lilies, some frolicking puppies?'

He laughed, but defended himself. He doesn't drink much, so he makes it count when he does. He sloshes a couple of fingers into a tumbler. They're sitting at the kitchen table by silent mutual agreement. Far safer than that sofa. Someone's been in and turned on all the little lamps dotted around the vast room and lit the fire. It's exactly what he needs after the day he's had.

The woman sitting opposite him is the best part of the scene, by a country mile. She's taken off her shoes and her makeup is a little smudged under her eyes. She's pulled all her hair over one shoulder and it tumbles down over her chest, leaving the curve of her neck exposed. The lamplight makes her eyes look even more deep set and shows off her cheekbones. She gives him a tired smile and holds up her glass limply.

'To a successful day,' she says. 'Well done—you did brilliantly.'

He shrugs off the compliment. 'I'm far more interested in toasting us. Half a lifetime, and you're here, next to me. Of all the undeserved strokes of good fortune I've had, this takes the cake. To old friendships and new beginnings.'

He clinks his glass to hers and takes a sip, watching her face as he swallows and the smoky, silky burn hits his throat.

'To new beginnings.'

'So. How wanky was I today, on a scale of one to ten?'

He can't help asking. It kept hitting him today, how accustomed he is these days to spouting wellness chat and holistic advice and psycho-fucking-babble; he can turn it on like a tap, but this isn't the Alex she knew and loved.

'You were amazing. I was so impressed. But'—she takes a healthy slug of her wine—'I suspect old Alex would have wanted to beat you up, if you weren't so ripped. I thought about it a few times and had a giggle to myself.'

'Did you, now. Fuck load of good you are as a cheerleader. Must be weird for you, though. I've had twenty years to acclimatise to New Alex. I agree, old Alex would have been disgusted.'

She snorts, and he remembers that she always had a filthy, unladylike laugh. How could he have possibly allowed himself to forget that gorgeous detail about her?

'He wouldn't approve of you meditating or being gluten free, that's for sure. No pizza? He'd be horrified.'

'If he saw my bathroom shelf, he'd definitely deck me. I have serum. *Serum!* And eye cream, and a scrub. They're all freebies, but still.'

'Doesn't make it ok,' she agrees.

'You've hardly changed at all.' He runs his fingertip around the rim of his tumbler. Her gaze falters slightly, and he adds: 'That's a good thing. I was so fucked up, I would've been dead in an alleyway by twenty-five, if I hadn't got my act together. You were perfect. You didn't need to change a thing.'

Her smile tells him he's says the right thing, but there's disbelief in her eyes.

'Really? I haven't changed? I find that hard to believe.'

It's not entirely true. She must be freaked out by how much he's changed, but he's a bit freaked out by how much she's stayed true to herself. He can't mention the biggest change he sees, though. She's lost some of her spark. She's still got that Italian flame under there somewhere: when he warms her up, her conversation's peppered with feisty comebacks. But she's more subdued, more... subservient? She's lost some of that incredible aura of self-confidence that surrounded her at school, and that everyone was aware of and drawn to. The question is who killed it off: him or that tosser she's married to? He's not sure he can bear the idea of either option being the truth.

'You seem to have been true to yourself,' he says now. 'You've got a family of your own—you were always such a close family. And you're doing something creative, like I always hoped you would.'

Her smile is tighter. 'How predictable.'

'What's up, babe? You can tell me.'

She sighs. 'It's not the right time to discuss it now. You're tired; you've got another big day tomorrow.'

'It's the perfect time. We've got all evening. And I can tell you need to get something off your chest. So spill it.'

He has a decent idea of what's bothering her, so it's not a huge surprise when she says:

'You cut me off. You gave me no choice at all. I wanted to be there for you, and wouldn't let me. It was so—*cruel*.'

'I know, but—'

'It was so selfish. I can't imagine what you went through, Alex—well, I can—but you didn't give me a chance. You made it so much worse for both of us, and it didn't have to be like that. I would have waited for you. You know I would. I would have visited you as often as I was allowed, but you gave me no say whatsoever. I didn't see you for *twenty-one years* and it didn't have to be that way at all, if you hadn't been such a stubborn prick.'

She's distraught. Her eyes are huge and wet, and she systematically shreds a paper napkin while she speaks. He can't have this conversation with her sitting across a table from her. He gets up and sits himself down at the end of the table and puts his hand over hers as he thinks about what to say to her in response.

'I know. I'm not surprised that's how you feel—you must hate me.'

'I don't hate you; I've never, ever hated you, but you hurt me so badly.'

She's stopped shredding the napkin; he runs his fingers over her knuckles and squeezes her hand.

'I understand why you think I was selfish, but I promise you, I did it for you. I had to cut you off. I couldn't let you live in limbo while I was in there. I was in such a panic, babe! I was so full of self-loathing, and horror, and I knew I didn't deserve you, and I didn't deserve to let you waste one more day of your life on a worthless fucker like me.

'I didn't do it for selfish reasons; it nearly killed me. I tortured myself over you, every fucking day I was in there. I would have done anything to see you. But I had to keep you at arm's length because I had to let you move on. And when

Fr Pat told me you'd failed Lower Sixth, Jesus, I thought I would die from the pain. It was so fucking ironic, you telling me to fulfil my potential and then me hearing about you losing the plot at school.'

Some nights, the guilt over what he'd done to Clara nearly overwhelmed the guilt he had to live with over killing Lindsay Smith. He'd had this perfect, beautiful girl who was top of her class when he met her, and she'd *failed* the first year of her A Levels because of him! Everything he touched turned to shit. Everyone he touched got harmed.

'That was the turning point,' she admits. 'When Fr Pat passed on your message, I knew I owed it to my parents to pull my finger out.'

'Well, that's something. I promise you, angel, I was trying to set you free, and not pollute you any more with my worthless shit. I told you that in my letter, didn't I?'

'You did, but it wasn't your decision to make. We should have made it together. I didn't share your view of yourself. I knew you, Alex. I knew had so much to give. So did Fr Pat. And Mr Evans. You should have let us help you. I mean, I'm glad you let them help you, but I wish you'd let me be there for you too. Whatever you say, you did deserve that.'

He wasn't in a good state when they banged him up, especially after he was sentenced. They put him on suicide watch for the first few weeks, but he has no intention of telling her that. The burden he had to carry was too huge; he had no way of dealing with it. Thank fuck for Tom and Fr Pat. They were in there every week. Listening to Clara speak, for the first time ever he allows himself to wonder if he made the right decision, cutting her off. He allows himself to imagine an alternate past where he let her carry some of the burden with him and let her love him. But the fact that she's here in front of him now, looking well and happy, with two kids, is enough reassurance for him. Letting her drag herself down with him and keep a vigil for the whole of his sentence would have been way too big a gamble. He did the right thing for her, even if she can't appreciate it.

He attempts to explain. 'From where I was sitting, it was the only decent thing I could do. I couldn't bring Lindsay back. I couldn't get out of there and look after Mum the way I should have. The only tiny piece of power I had was to let you go off and live your life.'

She twists her hand over and lets it lie, palm up, under his. He traces her lifeline with his fingertip.

'When you put it like that, I can see that you were doing it for noble reasons. It's just—sometimes nobility is overrated.' She twists her mouth and hesitates. 'I still have your letter, you know. The one you wrote me from that place.'

A shiver goes down his spine. The idea that something that originated in that building still physically exists is almost a violation. If he held it now, the waves of pain it embodies would probably travel through him.

'Jesus. Burn the damn thing.'

'I hadn't read it for a few years, but I've read it every day this week.'

'That's fucked up.'

She looks embarrassed. 'It sounds cheesy, but I needed to know that what we felt was real. And I know I've had a go at you just now, but when I read it, I understand why you dumped me.'

'I didn't dump you, for fuck's sake.' He keeps his eyes fixed on the milky skin of her inner forearm, glides his fingers over it, up to the crook of her arm and back.

'You said in the letter that you'd love me forever, but you didn't even look up me up when you got out.'

Her breath has gone shuddery, and he jerks his head up. She's clenching her jaw and a tear runs down her cheek.

'That was the worst bit, I think: even worse than when you told me not to contact you. I thought you'd at least come and find me when you got out. And then one day I asked Fr Pat how you were doing, and he said they'd let you out the month before! And you were just gone! He wouldn't tell me anything except he said you'd moved to London and Mr Evans was helping you get a job. That was it. I mean, seriously, Alex! You were free, and you just buggered off! Of all the selfish—'

The spark is back. She's fucking furious. She pulls her arm away and wipes her nose with the back of her hand before jabbing her finger at him.

'That was when I said, *enough*. I took off your ring and put it away with your letter at the top of my wardrobe and I decided to get on with my life. But how could you just disappear like that, on everyone who loved you?'

The words are harder to say than he could ever have imagined. 'I didn't disappear on everyone. I just disappeared on you.'

Her eyes are wide. 'You came back?'

'From time to time, yeah. I wasn't going to leave Mum alone with Connor after everything I'd put her through. And you know I kept in touch with Tom and Fr Pat.'

'And did you ever think to look me up?' Her voice trembles with indignation. He can only imagine how hurtful this must sound to her.

'Only every minute of every day. You have to believe me; it took every fucking ounce of self-discipline I had to stay away from you. But just because I was out, I wasn't free in my own head. I still wasn't any more worthy of you than I was when I was inside. You'd just started Upper Sixth, and

Fr Pat said you were back on form at school; there was no way I was derailing that. I owed it to you to stay away.'

What he'll never tell her is that he saw her a few times in those first few months after he was released, before she went off to uni. He wasn't strong enough to stay away from her completely. The week after he got out, once he'd got settled in his bedsit in Lewisham, he came down to see Mum and found himself standing across the road from the school gates. It helped that it was just before Christmas, and the visibility by four o'clock was already bad, but he had his coat zipped up as far as it would go over his mouth and his hood pulled right down, for good measure. He watched the stream of kids coming out of the gates like a hawk, his heart racing.

When he saw her, he honestly thought he would collapse right there on the pavement. She had her same, ancient rucksack on both shoulders and a beanie pulled low, but that hair streamed out behind her. She was a vision. An absolute vision. He watched as she strode purposefully down the street, hands in her coat pockets, her breath visible. She held herself tall, and he thought, *she's not broken. I didn't break her. Thank fuck.* Since the day three years before when he'd pulled his smartest ever stunt and asked her if he could walk her home, he'd never, ever had to stand and watch her and know that he couldn't go to her, and the pain was almost more than the pain of not seeing her had been. She walked on her own, and the thought that she hadn't found a walking mate, male or female, to replace him, tore his heart apart. He followed her home that evening, mainly from the other side of the road, keeping a careful distance, just to make sure she got there safely.

The next time was in early February. She would have finished her mocks by then. It was a Saturday night and he was spending the weekend with Mum and Connor. He went for a walk and found himself standing across the main road from Casa Valentina, just on the off-chance. It was a filthy night and the restaurant was a beacon opposite him, golden light streaming from its windows. The din of voices and laughter from within was faint. He stood and watched for about ten minutes, feeling like a Dickensian orphan. He knew exactly what it must smell like in there. He'd imagined devouring a Casa Valentina pizza like a caveman so many times when he was inside.

She rewarded his patience by coming into view. She was in a stretchy black dress, her hair tied up in a bun, a huge pizza platter balanced on each hand. He was too far away to see much, but he could make out the size of her smile as she put the pizzas down in front of a lucky couple sitting in the window. Everything in that room represented love, happiness and wellbeing for Clara. As long as she was there, she was part of an extended family who loved her and would see her through life. And he could rest easy.

She's crying softly now, her arms wrapped protectively around herself, and it feels like stalemate. All the sacrifices he made, he made them for her, and they nearly fucking killed him, and she resents him for them. Despite what she says, it sounds like a part of her really does hate him for pushing her away. Or if she doesn't hate him, it'll take her a long time to forgive him.

'I'm so sorry for how much I hurt you,' he tells her. 'I will never, ever forgive myself for putting you through what I put you through. But you've got to know, babe, everything I did back then was because I loved you. I only thought about you, it wasn't about me.'

'I know.' Her voice is small. 'I know you did your best, in unimaginable circumstances. It's just—the utter agony of not being able to get to you at all, to reach you, to talk to you —it was like you were dead, but worse, almost, because I knew you were suffering.'

He has to accept something that he hoped for a long time was not the case: that despite his best efforts, she served that sentence with him, and she probably hasn't had the benefits of years of expensive therapists and trips to Tibet and holotropic breathing and meditation and all the other bollocks he's tried, to make peace with it all. She's probably just as fucked up over it all as he is.

She's still huddled in her chair, and even though her words are generous, he can tell she's wary. He has a brainwave. He picks up his phone.

'This is exhausting, rehashing this stuff. Can we take a break, just for a minute? Do you trust me?'

She nods tiredly, and he gets to his feet and holds out his free hand to her. She frowns a little but she humours him, taking his hand and standing up. He smiles to himself. Please let this not backfire. He presses play on Spotify and the iconic opening chords of Robbie Williams' *Angels* start up. She reels, and her mouth drops open in an O of disbelief. She takes a step backwards.

'Oh God, no way. I've avoided that song like the plague for years.'

'I know. Me too. But come here.'

He puts down the phone and drapes her arms around his neck, before putting his arm as tightly around her back as he can and pulling her right in towards him. Her head collapses on his chest, and he strokes her glossy hair from its crown to the tendrils falling over his arm as they begin to move together. It's a gentle little shuffle, but she lets out a huge, shuddery sigh into his chest, and he pulls her closer.

'I listened to this on repeat after they arrested you. Over and over and over. I wore the CD out, in the end.'

'They had some lame social event just after I'd been sentenced, and towards the end of the night they put this on. I legged it back to my cell and I nearly punched the fucking wall in, that night. The nurse had to bandage up my knuckles.'

Her hands clench behind his neck, twisting the collar of his sweater, and he attempts levity. 'But forget that. I put this on to cheer us up, not make us want to top ourselves. Remember the night of the GCSE party?'

Robbie Williams had released *Angels* right around the time they got together, and, probably because he always referred to her as his angel and the term of endearment caught on, it quickly became their song. They played it on a loop when they were in bed together. They requested it at the end-of-GCSEs party the school had thrown for the Fifth Form, and slow-danced in a manner that may have been too heated for a school event.

'I remember you snogged me on the dance floor in front of the entire year.' Her voice is shaky.

'It wasn't my fault. That backless red dress you were wearing—Jesus Christ, you looked so fucking gorgeous.'

'I can't believe my boobs stayed put in that thing.'

'Despite my best efforts. I have never been so proud in my life as I was, walking into that hall with you.'

They've found an easy rhythm now, swaying together as Williams' gravelly voice ushers in a tidal wave of memories. He's pressed repeat, so the song starts up again as soon as it's over. He wishes he could just press repeat on this moment and stay here with her forever. With her heels off, her head fits easily under his chin. Everything fits perfectly. His palm slides over her hair as he inhales it. Her face nestles between his pecs. His hand rests on the small of her back. He's come home after a twenty-one-year nightmare. He's sure of it. Connor's words of warning are a distant memory as he whispers into the crown of her head.

'I meant what I said in that letter. I've never, ever stopped loving you. I still love you. No one else has ever mattered to me, and no one ever will.'

18

2019

Since she sat down at the table in this beautiful room with this beautiful man who has informed the direction of her whole life, she's been spinning into a vortex of grief that feels as real and raw as it did twenty-one years ago. The utter waste of those years apart, and the irretrievability of those lost decades weigh heavily, so heavily she doesn't know how to process these feelings. Hearing from Alex himself that his grief matched or outweighed hers makes the pain worse, but it's also a strange relief to hear, after so long, that she left as big a hole in his world as he did in hers.

And now she's in his arms, swaying to a song that's overwhelming in its evocative power. She's back there with him, in that assembly hall at St Winnie's: young, and madly in love, and wallowing in the warm certainty of his feelings for her, and blissfully ignorant of the tragedy that will befall them all less than six months later and of the relentless ticking of an invisible clock, counting down the minutes until their worlds are shattered.

That they've come full circle and are back in each other's

arms, having opened their hearts, spurs elation and relief like nothing she's ever known. Abi was right; she needed to talk things through with Alex. She's needed this for years and years. The agony they've both suffered has been such a potent binding agent that she feels as close to him as if they'd never been parted. She lets her hands roam over his neck and shoulders and she revels in the sensation of his fingers stroking her hair. His other arm is a vice around her and she buries her face in his chest, inhaling him like an addict. Time and space are the oddest concepts. She's built a whole life away from him and, in this moment, it's as though nothing else exists outside of this room where they're dancing in a circle of lamplight. She's shrugged off her entire reality like a cloak and slipped into an alternate existence where it's just her and him, as if they've never been apart.

So when he tells her that he has always loved her, still loves her, and always will, she jolts while all the while knowing, deep down, that it couldn't be any other way. They've both kept their inner fires burning far too bright for them to have been extinguished by mere time apart. They've worked *so* hard at it; it's been so exhausting, surviving without him. The relief that's been settling around her blooms into happiness at the certain knowledge that the man in whose arms she's wrapped still loves her.

She pulls her head away and tilts it up to his face. The way he's looking at her makes her catch her breath; his eyes are shining with such adoration. There's relief there, also—he too must have found their conversation just now cathartic, even in the pain it surfaced. He's a sight for sore eyes: clean-shaven for today's event, the soft lamp-light playing on his beautiful bone structure. His eyes are the most incredible feline shape, and they're almost all pupil right now, with a circle of hypnotic green. She puts her hand up and strokes his eyebrows, cheekbones, jaw, lips with her fingertip, so she can learn him by heart all over again.

'I love you, too.' She stares at him as she says the words, to bore them into his brain. 'I've never stopped loving you, either. I've been broken ever since you went away. Just being here, with you—I finally feel like myself again.'

'I know you're married, and this is not a straightforward situation for you.' He's whispering; his hands come up to cup her face. 'I'm not trying to make your life more complicated. I fucked you up once; I have no intention of doing it again. I only want you to be happy, angel.'

It's impossible, trying to hold the thought of Jeremy and Violet and Charlie, all together in Dorset without her right now, oblivious to her betrayal of them. It's impossible because just acclimatising once again to the burden she and Alex have shared for so long over the course of this evening's conversation is exhausting enough. Her brain is full of anguish and trauma and grief. She can't possibly hold the burden of her responsibility to her family in her heart tonight. She cannot. Tonight she needs to find relief, not add to her load.

'Can we—not talk about the fact that I'm married right now?' she asks. 'I just can't. This is between you and me. We've got so much ground to cover, so much unfinished business between us. I'm so overwhelmed right now that I can hardly stand up.'

Before he can protest, she stands on her tiptoes and pulls his face towards her and kisses him. Their kiss last week was a knee-jerk reaction; this evening it's a considered choice. They've bled themselves dry; this is the only next step she can conceive of. Her lips meet the pillowy softness of his and she knows the following to be true: she has never felt this way about anyone else. Not Jeremy, not anyone. And no one else has ever kissed her like Alex. His kisses have always been movies: sensory paradises where the outside world ceases to exist and she experiences life only through the nerve-endings of her mouth and her skin.

And now she's back where she belongs, as this unhurried kiss unfolds and releases a butterfly-net of memories and emotions that float around her and add substance and meaning to what they're doing. His fingers skim her temples, smoothing back her hair as their lips slip and slide and their tongues find each other. His hands move down over her hair and clasp it into a ponytail; one coils its way around her waves and pulls in that way she loves, and the other pushes into the small of her back and presses her against him.

When his hand moves to her bum and slides the slippery fabric of her wrap dress over her skin, something darker ignites inside her and she kisses him with a new intensity. She clings onto his upper arms and revels shamelessly in the sensation of his triceps flexing under her hands. She goes on a little journey, down the S of his spine and onto his bum, which is *ridiculous*: rock hard and so perfectly curved. Meanwhile, his fingers dig into the underside of her buttocks and she starts to groan into his mouth.

He mumbles into her mouth, their lips still gliding against each other.

'How do you feel about going upstairs?'

She pulls away to meet his eyes and giggles. Suddenly she feels shy, again. What in the world is that all about? This man has been inside her a hundred times, but it's been a long time and while he's spent the interim working on every muscle group in his body, she's carried twins and eaten way too many bowls of carbonara and shot her pelvic floor to hell. That said, this lovely room would have to be on fire for her to leave right now. He's still, as always, the most beautiful thing she's ever seen, and he's now a bona fide pin-up for every housewife in the country, and many more overseas. This is ridiculous. She's about to get let loose on Alex Molloy. She thought she would never see him again, and he's standing in front of her, asking her to go to bed with him. It's *insane*. She licks her lips. She's salivating.

'Are you okay?' He strokes her cheek with the back of his knuckles. 'If it's not what you want, that's totally fine.'

'Alex.' Her voice sounds husky, even to her. 'All I have ever, *ever* wanted is to be with you. I just can't believe it's happening. I feel like I'm losing the plot. But *yes.* Please take me upstairs. Please.'

She does a little shimmy against his groin. He's gratifyingly hard. They're still nose to nose, and he touches her tongue with his.

'Minx. Come on, I have something to show you.'

Her nervous giggle is back. 'I hope it's what I think it is.'

'Not quite. Come on.'

She takes his hand and follows him upstairs.

'Wow, Alex!'

The room is vast, under the eaves of the stables. Once again, someone has turned on all the occasional lamps and drawn the curtains. There's a huge bed with a wooden frame and a crisp white duvet turned back. At the sight of it, her stomach flips. A roll-top bath stands under the window. She points to it.

'I want a go in that, at some point.'

'You'll get a bath. With me.'

'Is that what you wanted to show me?'

'Nope. It's under here.'

He's still holding her hand. He guides her over to the

bed and lets go, turning his back on her and pulling his sweater off in one easy movement. She gasps. The whole of his back, from one perfect shoulder to the other and down to the waistband of his trousers, is a veritable work of art: a tattoo that looks more like a delicate pencil sketch. Gossamer-fine wings, impossibly intricate, span his shoulders. The woman's head is downcast, a slender trumpet in her hands. Long, Pre-Raphaelite curls tumble over beautifully shadowed, twisted robes.

Alex has an angel on his back.

19

2019

The combination of Alex's flawless bare skin, glowing in the lamplight and this spectacular artistry is too much—she absolutely *has* to touch him. She edges forward and traces the outline of a wing with her fingertips. It blows her mind that it was etched with a needle and not shaded with a pencil. And his skin is still soft, so soft it breaks her heart.

'It's so beautiful,' she whispers.

'She's my guardian angel. She's you, basically.'

She can't speak for a moment. She drops the lightest of kisses on the little bumps at the very top of his spine and feels him shiver under her mouth. She trails her lips and nose across to one shoulder, inhaling his skin as she goes. The smell of it is the one she's always known, and that butterfly net is at work again, releasing hundreds of beautiful, fluttering memories from their slumber.

'When did you get this done?'

'About fifteen years ago. You haven't come across it before?'

'No—how could I have?' She's still busy exploring his skin and his art. Her hands glide from his shoulders down his arms as her mouth moves across to the other side of his back.

'Well, there are a few pictures of my back out there in cyberspace. Some photographers like to photograph her.'

'I bet they do.'

She sidles around him and stands in front of him and her arms drape languorously around his neck as she stands far enough back to get a good eyeful of him topless. He's good enough to eat; velvety skin glowing in the lamplight, his pecs curving softly above a perfectly toned, tapered torso. He doesn't have that over-muscled beefcake thing going, thank goodness; he's just a perfect, beautifully crafted specimen of manhood. Da Vinci would approve. That angel is not the only work of art around here. She's practically drooling.

He pulls her in closer and she asks him the question she needs to ask.

'So, fifteen years ago?'

'Yep. I'd been wanting to do it since I got out, but I needed to wait until I was making some decent money. You've seen how budget tattoos turn out.'

He rotates his arm to show off the blotchy *FULFIL YOUR FUCKING POTENTIAL* tattoo and she laughs.

'I take your point.'

'There's an artist who does these beautiful tattoos, and I saved up and went to her and she designed it for me and then she inked me, too. I knew I wanted to have something to remember you by, something beautiful enough to be worthy of you.'

Fifteen years ago, she had graduated from Bristol and

was making her way in London. She had given up on the hope that Alex Molloy would ever come back into her life, and all her memories of him were locked up in her heart and in a little box at the top of her wardrobe. And somewhere in London, likely fewer than ten miles away from her first flat in Battersea, Alex was sitting in a tattoo parlour and handing over probably thousands of pounds in a bid to immortalise her. She's struck once again by the stupid waste of them both suffering needlessly when they could have been together. She should have tried harder. She should have begged his mum to give her his details. She shouldn't have given up.

'I've made you sad again.' He kisses her eyelids with so much tenderness that they fill up against his lips. 'I'm sorry. I just wanted to show you, you've always been in my thoughts. You've been everywhere with me.'

Something in her snaps.

'We've both been such martyrs. I should have hunted you down and not taken no for an answer. I'm not wasting another minute.'

She pulls his head down and kisses him, her mouth already open, and slides her hands down firmly over his heavenly chest. He moans a little and gets to work untying her dress at the waist. It swings open like a coat. She's wearing embarrassingly sensible underwear—plain black bra and pants that don't show too much under the slinky dress—but it can't be helped, and she's too far gone to care.

He tugs the dress off down over her arms and chucks it on the floor before putting his forehead to hers. He's grinning, his eyes dancing between her face and body.

'I remember this.'

'No you don't. I'm unrecognisable. One of us turned our body into a brand, and one of us grew twins.'

'You're beautiful. You're so fucking beautiful.'

He kisses her, and his hand moves around to snap open her bra. He slides it down and cups her breasts reverently in his hands, his thumbs moving over her nipples.

'Hello girls.'

Her laughter is accompanied by a sharp inhale as her nipples stand to attention, almost painfully tight.

'I've missed these. Shit, you had the best tits in the whole school.'

'I always suspected that was the only reason you went out with me.' She doesn't deny the compliment. She was an early developer, and she had a lot of unwanted attention as a result. When she was younger, she was mortified by her boobs, but once she got together with Alex she thanked heaven for her assets. He made no secret of his absolute obsession with them. They're more gravitationally challenged than they were, but they've survived her breastfeeding days in decent shape. At least her nipples still point (very, very fractionally) upwards.

'They were two of the million excellent reasons I went out with you.' He punctuates his words with kisses as she wrestles with his belt buckle, and he releases her breasts so he can help her tug off his trousers. They're both in just their pants now, and he crushes her to him, one hand clawing at her hair and the other on her bum. His erection is surely going to rip his boxers in a moment, and bruise her thigh into the bargain. It's heavenly, as is the light friction of his skin against her nipples and the intensity of his tongue filling her mouth. She arches her back and pushes into him. This body of his is *incredible*. Her hands glide over knotted muscles in his back and slip under the waistband of his boxers to grope his bum. He's positively peachy. He tenses his buttocks dramatically a couple of times and she laughs and does the same. He slaps her bum lightly.

'Off.'

Then they're blissfully, fully, naked. *Finally*.

'*Finally*,' Alex says. 'Jesus Christ. Twenty-one fucking years. I'm never letting you go.'

His tone is light, and he's smiling at her with a boyish smile and they could be back in her bedroom, except that they're in a space that's a million times more luxurious than her poor old single room in Otford. But his words make her shiver. How the hell is she supposed to let him go after this? How is she supposed to even function?

He lays her down on the bed, and time slows down. He crouches over her, stroking her face.

'Don't look at me like that, angel. My heart can't take it.'

'My heart can't take *this*. How are we supposed to handle this?'

'I don't know. But we're going to enjoy ourselves, ok? Fuck knows, we deserve this. I'd like to try to take it slow, but honestly, I'm not sure I can.'

He bends his head to her nipple and sucks lazily, slowly, his tongue rolling it around like a bead in his mouth while his hand traces the same pattern on her other breast, and she finds herself utterly paralysed with desire. She inhales sharply, thoughts of emotional overwhelm blessedly erased by the heavenly force of this physical overwhelm. She stares at the top of his head, at his lips moving on her breast, and she stretches her legs wider. He releases her nipple and brings his face up to hers and stares into her eyes as he trails his fingers down over her stomach and slips a couple inside her. She whimpers at the hot stab of desire she feels, and he smiles against her mouth.

'You are so heavenly. So fucking heavenly. I've missed this so much.'

His fingers are still moving inside her as his thumb begins to stroke her. She can hear her own moaning, but it's as if she's been drugged and the moaning is coming from far away. His strokes stay slow, but he increases his pressure. It was always like this with him; he seemed to be able to read her mind, as if his body was an extension of hers. His tongue moves in her mouth with the same rhythm as his thumb. She reaches down to try to take hold of him, but he grabs her hand.

'Nope.'

'I need you inside me. I want you inside me all night.' She has been apart from this man for too fucking long and she cannot last another minute without being joined to him in the best, most perfect way she knows how.

'I want that too.' The emotion in his beautiful eyes is threatening to send her over the edge. He's still stroking her, his fingers still dipping in and out. She's running out of self-control and time.

He pulls his hand away. 'I'll grab a condom.'

'No. I have a coil in. I'm not letting anything else come between us, not even some latex.' She has no idea how much Alex Molloy gets around these days, but she'll take her chances.

'You sure, angel?'

She nods.

'Another first. You and me, skin on skin.' He lowers himself down onto one forearm and runs his tongue lazily over her bottom lip and she lifts her face up closer to him, and she feels him guide himself to her entrance, stroking her wetness with his tip, and just as she's adjusting to the heavenly, tortuous feeling, he pushes inside her and they both clutch each other and laugh-groan as if this is a feeling they've never, ever experienced before. And it isn't. After years and years of hell and pain and love and waste, Alex Molloy is inside her and on top of her and surrounding her and filling her up, and his eyes are blazing with so much emotion as he moves within her that she knows one thing for certain: she's never, ever letting anyone take him away from her again.

20

2019

The sight of her face on the pillow beneath him is like every fantasy he's ever had come true. Her beautiful eyes are half closed; her lips are parted and he puts his mouth to hers as he moves, not kissing, exactly—just touching.

'Is this ok?' he mutters against her lips, and they tug into a smile.

'Mmm. It's—amazing.' She's struggling to speak, and he adjusts his position so he can thrust deeper. He pulls his head up a little.

'How do you like it, these days?'

Something flickers across her face at his acknowledgement of the fact that their sex lives haven't included each other for a very long time.

'Anything—I'll take whatever you're—oh, *God*, that's good.'

'I'll give you a full sex buffet. We're just getting started.' He's struggling to speak now, too. He trails his fingers across her jaw, down her throat, and around her nipples, which are bigger now, and darker, possibly. They're fucking beautiful, like pink-brown cherries. They belong in his mouth. He makes do with drawing lazy figure-of-eights between them while he keeps up his rhythm inside her. She's breathtaking, lying here with her dark curls spilling around her on the pillow. She's different—more womanly, obviously—but he has the strangest impression of having gone back in time, to her bedroom in Otford.

If his memory's correct, she can't come like this, underneath him. He arches away from her, as far as he can, and slips his hand into this new space between them and she ignites, gasping and writhing under him, her beautiful, dark eyes flickering as she gets closer and closer. Her hands come up to grasp his shoulders and she bucks as she gives him everything, her nails digging into his flesh, her mouth a soft O, her cries the *exact* same as he remembers, and her muscles clenching around him in a way that's so perfect that he follows her over the edge, shuddering as he empties himself into her, his senses exploding as he bends his head to hers for ravenous, desperate kisses and waves of heat rippling outwards from his dick to every inch of his body. He buries his face in the crook of her neck and snorts in the scent of her hair, as she winds her legs more tightly around him and squeezes, sending an aftershock shuddering through him.

'I love you. So fucking much.' It's like someone's clubbed him over the head. He's spent. Her hair is like a drug; *she's* a drug he's been craving for all these years. He rubs his nose along her neck and half kisses, half licks it.

'I love you, too.' Her hands are wrapped around the back of his neck; she's clinging on for dear life, as if she, too, realises that being conjoined like this is the only way to get through life.

~

THEY DO it again as soon as they've recovered. He tells her he's going to take his time, this time, now that he's got that first release out of his system. She lies back and luxuriates in the unique pleasure of having Alex Molloy kiss every inch of her skin, as if he's never encountered something he wants to worship quite so much as her body. It seems he's still obsessed with her hair. And her boobs. But he works his way down her arms, and over the crepey skin of her stomach, which he doesn't seem to mind at all, and down her legs before he flips her over and works his way all the way back up again, with featherlight kisses on her calfs and thighs and bum and spine.

'Lie on me,' she tells him, and he does. He lies right on top of her, his head turned to the right, just like hers, so they're cheek to cheek, and his arms at exactly the same angle as hers so he can place his hands on top of hers and interlace their fingers. It's a feeling beyond words, having this astonishing mass of muscle on top of her, consuming her, while his heart beats against her upper back. The fact that he exists and lives seems such a beautiful, fragile truth that a tear rolls down over the bridge of her nose and onto the pillow. He's hardening again, and she opens her legs slightly to accommodate him between her thighs before squeezing them together.

He sighs and rubs his face against hers before letting go of her hands. She's about to complain as he moves upwards, away from her, before his hand comes under her stomach and pulls her bum up with him and she eases herself onto all fours. His hand massages her stomach as he presses against her bum, and she can feel the heat of his body hovering against her. She puts her hands on the headboard.

Within seconds he's inside her, his hand moving back to hold her hip in place, and they find a rhythm immediately. Their bodies definitely remember *this*. This was their speciality. The sensation of him filling her up so fully is creating a wall of pressure in her chest, and when he reaches forward and cups her breast, weighing it in his hand, her mouth starts watering. Every part of her that loves his touch the most is on fire. He releases her breast and slides his hand between her legs, and she pushes as far back against him as she physically can, and he picks up his pace. And the whole ridiculous, stupifying, melting, unravelling process begins again.

Afterwards, he reaches across the bed for a wad of tissues, and eases out of her, and they flop on the bed, curled into Cs, facing each other.

'Fuck me.' Alex rubs his face with his palm. 'I am crucified.'

'Me too.' She heard somewhere once that you should feel like you've lost a few IQ points after a good orgasm. Right now, she'd be hard pressed to spell her own name.

'You've still got it, Fiori.'

'You too, Molloy. Good stamina, for an old man.'

'I'm only a month older than you.' He kisses her nose.

'I'd just turned sixteen when you first pounced on me. I was barely legal.'

'Me too. And you were legal, that's all that matters. Not that I gave a shit about that at the time.'

'I have to say.' She pushes herself up onto one elbow and traces a line down his forehead, his nose, his lips. 'You were a very competent lover, for a sixteen-year-old.'

He throws his head back, and his laugh lights up the room, his white teeth gleaming as he grins at her in delight. 'Shagger's probably a better word. And I really had no clue. I just about knew how it all worked. Sam Carter gave me a few tips to get going—that girl knew what she wanted.'

She guffaws with laughter. 'I must remember to thank her if I ever bump into her.'

'I fucking love your dirty laugh. It turns me on so much. But most of my moves I learnt with you.' He pauses dramatically. 'You were my *muse*.'

'What an honour. But I'm glad I inspired you. It worked out very well for me.' She leans closer to him and drops a slow, sweet kiss on his lips. She's not sure she should ask the next question. 'Did you not go crazy in prison—not being able to have sex, I mean?'

He stiffens. 'Of course I did. We all did. That's why there were so many punch-ups: it was like a permanent bull fight, in there.'

'How did you manage?' She watches his face. His smile is soft and sad.

'I wanked myself stupid over you.'

'Oh.' It's the answer she expected, but the sadness is so palpable, and the image it conjures so vivid, it hurts her chest. 'Did you have a roommate?'

'A cellmate—no: we had our own cells, thank fuck. Do you want to know what I thought about, in particular?'

'Um—ok. If it's not too painful to talk about.' She pulls her arm out and lays her head on the pillow, wriggling forward so her face is as close to him as possible.

He smiles. 'Well, I was a seventeen-year-old boy, so my fantasies were pretty basic: you, bouncing on my cock, and you, sucking my cock, mainly.'

Her face breaks out into a smile, too.

'How original.'

'As I said—basic. But there were other fantasies, too.' His

face grows serious, and he puts a hand out to stroke her hair and shakes his head slightly, as if he can't believe she's real.

'I thought about everything. I replayed every way we did it. Every minute I'd spent with you. You in that red dress at the dance, with your tits pressed against me, and the feel of your arse through that satiny fabric. You in your netball kit —holy fuck. Kissing you, up against the science books in the library. Every time I kissed you, in fact. The back of your neck. The feel of your hair, wound around my hand. The *smell* of your hair. You, looking up at me in the dining hall every single day when I came to sit with you for lunch. It never got old, seeing you. I don't think it would ever have got old.

'Everything. Every single fucking moment. You were with me the whole time I was there. I went to sleep curled up around you, inside you, and I woke up with you, every morning. You were the only thing that kept me sane in there, angel. You really were my guardian angel.'

As he recites what's essentially a love poem to her, tears stream over the bridge of her nose and soak the pillow. This is the thing about the two of them. Most people have hazy memories of their first loves: recollections that are more like blurry snapshots. But because their relationship was so intense, and so brutally taken away from them, they've enshrined every memory. Alex isn't the only one who's immortalised their time together; her own memories play like a technicolour movie: picture-perfect. They both went over them so painstakingly and so repeatedly that they've preserved them flawlessly. They dated for just shy of a year, but their importance in each other's lives far, far outlasted their physical time together.

'I'm so sorry,' she tells him now, between sobs. 'But I'm

so happy if it made life even the slightest bit easier for you, in there.'

'It was everything.' He presses his forehead to hers. 'You were more real to me than anything that actually went on in there, thank fuck. I'll never be able to tell you how grateful I am.'

They're quiet for a moment. There's nothing to say that can make his past pain better.

He wipes away the tears from her nose with unbearable gentleness. 'I have a favour to ask you.'

'Anything.'

'Stay the night with me. We never got to spend the night together; it was the one thing I always wanted—to wake up with you—and I had to imagine it every morning. Stay.'

His hand loops around her waist and moves over her back in big, lazy laps. She thinks.

'Will you let me escape in time for me to get home and make myself look respectable for the conference?'

'Maybe. As long as I get you in that bathtub first. It's a ten o'clock kick-off. You'll have loads of time.'

He's not the only one who's mourned the fact that they never got to spend the night together. It was impossible, given her parents had absolutely no idea they were sleeping together. He was always gone before they got home from the restaurant. Waking up with him will be more intimate than practically anything else they've done, but she can't conceive of getting out of this bed and leaving him here after the evening they've spent. Normal life can wait for a few more hours: normal life, and all the hideous, complex dilemmas that await her when she surfaces from this fairytale.

'Then yes, please,' she says, and wraps her leg around him.

21

1999

He woke up before the bell. He was hard, as usual. He'd been dreaming about Clara, as usual. He turned stiffly onto his side—this fucking pathetic excuse for a mattress—and closed his eyes again. Imagined he was in her bedroom, that this smelly blanket was her soft white duvet, and that he was under it with her.

He imagined waking up with her, curled right up against her, his nose buried in that thick, silky, fragrant hair, his arm wrapped around her, her gorgeous tits weighing heavily on his hand. The smell of her hair and of her skin, warmed by sleep and by him. His cock pressed against her arse, rather than in his hand. He came quickly as he imagined turning her sleepily onto her back and how she would look, and feel, and taste.

He had photos of her in here, but he kept them well hidden. Didn't want anyone getting into his cell and nicking them, tossing themselves off over her. Mum had brought them in for him as soon as he was arrested. There was one of them at the GCSE party, her glowing and fucking gorgeous in that red dress that would always haunt him, him with his arm around her, grinning like he'd won the fucking lottery. Another of her on the pedalo on the Serpentine, head thrown back, laughing at him. They'd bought a disposable camera that day, but they'd taken too many shots of London and not enough of themselves. If he'd known what was in store for them, he'd have used up the whole roll on her.

It was Tuesday. Mum and Connor were coming to visit today. He had mixed feelings, as usual. He missed them so much, but it was enough of a burden to deal with his own pain in here. Coming face to face with Mum's pain in particular always broke him. But he would never ask her not to visit. He couldn't do that to her; he knew she needed to see him.

SHE LOOKED BROKEN, too. Since he'd been arrested, her permanent air of tiredness had given way to a deeper exhaustion. He'd aged his mum overnight. She was getting littler, more hunched in the shoulders. She only came up to Alex's chest now. Connor had his mouth set in a grim line. He kept looking behind him, even when they were sitting down. Alex didn't blame him. This place would give anyone the creeps. Mum, on the other hand, kept her eyes firmly on Alex and seemed intent on pretending that they weren't surrounded by other blokes here at her Majesty's pleasure.

They covered off whether Alex was eating (not really, but he said yes), and exercising (a fuck-load, Mr Evans had been in last week to discuss bodyweight exercise tips with him) and sleeping (yes, thank fuck). Then Connor spat out:

They burnt out Mum's car, y'know.

Alex sat bolt upright. *What? Who did?*

Lindsay Smith's boyfriend's cousins.

Connor! Mum said. *I told you not to say anything. Alex doesn't need to know about this.*

Fuuuuck. He put his head in his hands. Would there be no end to the pain and grief he could cause his mum? He could feel the horrifying sting of tears. He would not cry in here, not in public. *Those fucking wankers. Did they get caught?*

I knew Alex would want to know. Connor did look embarrassed, though. *No, but one of them came up to me at the bus stop a few days later and admitted it. Little fucker ran off before I could deck 'im.*

Language. Mum's tone was resigned. Her youngest son was a killer. Swearing was the least of her worries.

What you going to do without your car, Mum? You need it to get to work.

She waved her hand wearily. *I'll just take shifts closer to home. Don't worry about it, love. Connor and I are fine. We just need you to keep your strength up and stay positive.*

Fat fucking chance of that. He'd been worrying about retribution. At least a burnt-out car was better than a brick through Mum's window, but that could still happen. The frustration of being able to do fuck all to protect Mum from in here hit him sharply in the chest.

Mum put her hand on his and squeezed it briefly.

Clara came to see me again, she said quietly.

His head jerked up. God, he was jealous of his own mother. She'd seen her, hugged her, probably.

She reached into her bag. *She asked me to give you a letter.*

The nearest screw pegged it over to their table and held out his hand for the letter. He ripped open the envelope and searched through it before handing it back to Mum and begrudgingly nodding. Prick.

Mum held it out to him. He shook his head.

I don't want it. I want it I want it I want it.

She put it on the table. He could see Clara's neat, elegant handwriting on the front. *Alex.* As upright as her posture. He imagined her writing it painstakingly. Licking the envelope with her perfect little pink tongue. He stared at it as if it would explode. That was danger, right there, on the table. Pandora's box. A scent hit him so powerfully he thought he might pass out. She must have sprayed her body spray on the letter. The little beauty! Right there, in that second, she was there with him.

She was devastated, love. Mum took his hand again. *She was in an awful state—she'd got the letter you sent her. She really wants you to allow her to be part of this awful experience with you. She loves you so much—you're a lucky boy.*

He could not have felt less lucky in that moment. Mum's grief. Connor's grief. Clara's grief. Lindsay's whole family's grief. It was too much to bear. His own grief was already too huge, and at the same time he felt he should push it to the bottom of the pile. Everyone else was a good person who he'd pulled under the bus with him. He'd brought his own grief on himself.

I love her too. His voice was a mumble. *That's why I need her to stay the fuck away. I was clear in my letter. I don't deserve her. She needs to get on with her life.*

Mum gave him a sigh that told him she was disappointed in him, which was rich, considering everything he'd put her through over the past few weeks.

Just take the letter, love. I promised her I'd give it to you. The poor girl was desperate. You can do what you like with it, but just take it.

~

He took the letter back to his cell and inhaled the paper so hard that he snorted.

My darling Alex,

Your letter killed me. Please don't push me away. Please don't try to do this on your own.

What happened was a terrible accident, and I can't imagine how you're feeling in there, but I know this: you need the people who love you around you to get through it.

I can never, ever forget you exist. I will live every day with you, whether you let me or not. You're in my thoughts every second. Wondering how you're doing is making me crazy.

Please write. Please let me visit you. I can't live without you. I need to see you. I want to do this with you.

You say I'm your angel, but you're my angel too. You've changed my life, and I will never be the same again.

I will love you forever too.

Stay safe in there

Your Clara xxxxxxx

He ran his fingers, then his lips, then his nose, over the paper. He loved her so much; she was the purest and truest person he'd ever met. He would never let her come near this fucking place, never let her see him like this, never let her waste a minute more on him.

If the letter hadn't smelt of her, he would have torn it up and flushed it down the toilet, to get the temptation of her words and her love away from him. As it was, he folded it up and hid it behind his mirror during the day, and slept with it at night. The scent of her lasted for weeks. It was the best gift she could have given him.

22

2019

The conference today was a blur of exhaustion and love-drunkenness. She'd swear she saw a difference in Alex up there on stage, too. He was more at peace than he'd been on Saturday—possibly because their sensual pre-conference bath morphed into energetic, uninhibited love-making, their wet bodies sliding slickly against each other as bathwater sloshed over the sides of the roll-top tub.

She's both horrified and fascinated by the ease with which she assimilates back into her normal life. It's as though she's screwed off the top half of her skull when she came back through her front door, plopped it on the hall table and screwed her 'wife and mum' skull-cap back on. She gets home before Jeremy, Violet and Charlie, who are having a slow journey back from Dorset, and has the benefit of time to shower, throw on some leggings and a jumper, and defrost some chilli before tuning out from her own problems with her millionth re-read of her all-time favourite, Edith Wharton's *The Age of Innocence*.

While the twins chatter on about their adventures with

Granny and Grandpa, she watches Jeremy with an absent-minded curiosity, as if he's a dissected frog under her microscope. He corrects the twins' grammar, he corrects their table manners, he comments that the chilli could have done with more cumin, and she counts the number of questions he asks her about the conference. Answer: two, both closed-ended. *Did it go well, darling?* And *Are you tired?* At least there's no chance of him ever noticing anything is up with her. A pie-chart of Jeremy's brain function would show his capacity as being divvied up between work, their personal investment portfolio, the upcoming tournament at the golf club next weekend, his client lunch at Simpsons tomorrow, and possibly a slice of self-congratulation that he has (very loosely) looked after the kids all weekend. Not the smallest sliver of pie would be devoted to pondering whether his wife ever regretted her life choices.

No, it's much easier to deflect. She asks him how his parents are, whether they've decided to go to France or Italy this summer, how the M3 was, and whether Violet and Charlie have finished their homework. If a wife is cheating on her husband, and said husband's impression of their marriage is not in the tiniest, remotest way changed, does that really constitute cheating? Philosophers can go ponder that one.

As Jeremy fields a one-man debate about whether his parents should consider down-sizing before they get too frail, she stares at him dispassionately. He is very attractive, there's no doubt about that. Laughably different from Alex, with his fair hair (about which he is ridiculously vain) swept back off his face in a style that hasn't changed since she's known him, and a full, sulky mouth. That he and Alex exist in the same world—in her orbit—is actually so bizarre, it makes her head spin. Jeremy is flippantly saying that his parents would be fools not to take advantage of the current property boom. He is flippant about everything. It annoys her, and yet she it's one of the things she finds most attractive about him, although she despises herself for being so predictable.

He has that languid, slightly bored air that must be part of the core curriculum at top all-male public schools (Jeremy went to Harrow: shock horror), and that results in his being dismissive of everyone and everything. But again, those same character traits can be a turn-on. He's vaguely kinky, in a hot, posh, non-controversial way, so when he murmurs to her in that languid, flippant manner that she shouldn't wear knickers out to dinner that evening, or she should pop into his dressing room and find herself one of his ties because she's been a naughty girl, her body always responds.

So the sex has never been a problem, but as she watches him speak, she has the most peculiar feeling of complete disassociation. She's attracted to him, yes. She's grateful for the life he's given her. He's accomplished and successful and charming and much-admired by their social circle. She loves him, really. They have a nice life together, although they kind of co-exist, moving through their experiences in parallel rather than necessarily living every moment through each other's eyes or each feeling as though the other's presence is the single, magical thing that turns their experiences to technicolour.

But if he died tomorrow, she'd be—fine. Charlie and Violet's grief would, of course, be shocking and awful and something she'd never, ever wish on them, but she could walk out that door and really not miss him, or if she missed him, not in that visceral, primal way that felt as though her body was being torn in two. Not in the way she's always missed Alex. Not in the way she's missed Alex all morning, since she left that bedroom. And when she's with Jeremy, it's perfectly pleasant and nice and normal. When she's with Alex, even just in the same room as him, even just in the same massive conference space, it's like there's no air in her lungs and no ground under her feet and no conceivable reason for her to exist on this earth except to be with him.

A memory floats up from *The Age of Innocence.* Her love of it has always stemmed from the grievous torment the two protagonists, Newland and Ellen, suffer due to their love of each other. Newland is engaged to Ellen's virtuous cousin, May, when Ellen appears on the scene. This is late nineteenth century New York high society, where appearances are everything, and so Newland and Ellen have no option but to continue the paths that are so clearly laid out for them: his as May Welland's husband, and Ellen's as a disgraced and unorthodox divorcee. Their circumstances couldn't be more different from those of her and Alex, but the intensity of their love and grief has always resonated, as has the sickening waste of their lives lived separately.

There's a quote in the book that's always struck her because of Wharton's ability to conjure up the bizarre and inhuman disassociations that we humans are capable of: it's Newland's sudden, exhilarating realisation that his young wife, May, might die young and leave him free to be with Ellen (spoiler: she doesn't). Later, sitting up in bed while Jeremy reads next to her, she looks the quote up. It's towards the end of the book; she hasn't got there yet on this read but she's read it so many times that the words are burnt onto her heart.

"What if it were she *who was dead! If she were going to die —to die soon—and leave him free! The sensation of standing there, in that warm familiar room, and looking at her, and*

wishing her dead, was so strange, so fascinating and overmastering, that its enormity did not immediately strike him. He simply felt that chance had given him a new possibility to which his sick soul might cling."

She's not wishing her husband dead. Obviously. And unlike Wharton's hapless characters, she walked into marriage to Jeremy with all the freedom of a twenty-first century woman. But this alienation from a marriage that two weeks ago was a given, part of the fabric of her reality, is freaking her out, and it's comforting to know that it's a sentiment commonplace enough to warrant inclusion in great literary works. Not that that should elevate her current situation to any grandiose literary scale. It's tawdry. She's cheating on her husband. She's pathetic. She should be ashamed of herself. She should be—she just isn't. Not enough.

~

AFTER DROPPING the twins on Monday, she goes back to Abi's house for a snatched coffee. She sent Abi an SOS text when she woke up. Alex is recording some morning workout class at the farm first thing, but he's kept his schedule clear for the rest of the day—the benefit of having done a big event all weekend—and he's made it clear he wants to spend as much time with her as possible before she has to get the kids.

Abi wolf-whistles when she opens the door. 'Bloody hell. You look ravishing. Working today? With *Mr Molloy*?'

Clara's blow-dried her hair to perfection, laid the mascara on with a trowel, and opted for a black wool polo-necked dress that clings just the right amount. She's even put on her favourite high-heeled boots that Jeremy got her last Christmas. She tries not to think about that part. She walks past Abi into the kitchen and slumps onto a bar stool at the island.

'Oh Jesus, Abs. I need serious advice.'

Abi fetches the cafetiere and two mugs. She puts them down on the island.

'Tell me you shagged him.'

Clara scrunches up her face. 'I did.'

'*Fuuuuck.*' Abi does a little drum roll on the marble counter. 'Jesus, that is *so* exciting. I'm sorry, I know your life is not a soap opera, but it kind of is. Mine is so fucking boring and this is incredible! You are sleeping with a huge celebrity sex-god and you also have this unbelievably romantic history—it's too much! I've been thinking about you all weekend, wondering how it was going.'

She comes around to where Clara's sitting and gives her a huge hug.

'Wow, C,' she continues. 'I would just like to say, I'm your friend and I'm here to support you, but I also need salacious details, okay? This has to work both ways. There has to be something in it for me.' She winks at Clara and goes back to the coffee.

Clara puts her head in her hands. Abi's reaction is sweet and kind of amusing, but she's right. This is not a soap opera. This is Clara's life, and Jeremy's life, and the kids' lives, and Alex's life. Too many lives. Too much potential for messing everything up.

'Come *on*,' Abi puts a mug down in front of her. 'Shoot. When, how many times, where, what was it like?'

'Right.' She's embarrassed now; she sweeps her hand across her forehead before remembering that she's trying to preserve her makeup for when she sees Alex. She hasn't talked about her sex life for a long time. 'Um—we went back to The Stables after the conference ended on Saturday—that's where he's staying on the farm. We had a *huge* heart-to-heart, where I bawled my eyes out over the fact that he'd never looked me up after he got out of prison. He told me he'd stayed away for my sake, because he didn't feel worthy of me, and that he has always loved me, and that he still loves me, and then he took off his sweater and showed me this massive, beautiful angel tattoo on his back that he had done *fifteen years* ago to remember me by, because he always called me his angel.'

'Sweet Jesus.' Abi's fists clench, and she crosses her legs. 'This guy is too much. Holy shit, C. What then? Please tell me you shagged him senseless.'

Clara puts her head back in her hands. 'Basically, yes. Three times, so far. But I'm going to see him after this, so I suspect that number will go up again.'

'My plans today consist of booking the Algarve for July, and you're off to shag your sex god. Jesus, life is unfair. And?'

'And, it was amazing. Twenty years of, you know, so much sorrow and heartbreak, and regret all came out. I can't tell you, Abs; the connection was incredible. I haven't felt like that since—since I was seventeen.'

'Did you tell him you loved him too?' Abi's voice is soft.

'Yep. And it's true. I do. But we haven't talked about the future at all—I mean, I can't just ignore the fact that I have a life and a husband and two children! We've got to have that chat at some point.'

'Do you know what you want?'

'No. Not in practical terms, anyway. I just know I can't live without him. I cannot let him go again; we've been through way too much, and wasted so many bloody years apart. But the idea of tearing up this life is so horrifying; I'm not ready to think about that yet.'

'Do you think Jeremy suspects anything?' Abi asks, taking a sip of her coffee.

'Absolutely bugger all. That man can get so far up his own arse that I could have a sex change and he wouldn't notice.'

Abi puts her hand to her mouth to avoid spitting out her coffee.

'Sorry. That was mean. He's done nothing; I'm the one who's messing around with someone else.'

'It doesn't sound like you're messing about, from where I'm standing, C. It sounds deadly fucking serious.'

23

2019

Colourful, dishevelled shop fronts pan slowly behind the blackened windows of the chauffeur-driven Discovery Alex has sent to take her into Shoreditch. She's shooting still footage for another of his classes today; this one's a special session he's offering to members of Shoreditch House. East London is not her comfort zone. Not in the slightest. But when she gets to Shoreditch House, she can see that this corner of London has artisanal style and even some hipster gloss. It's been this way for years and years; she knows that; she's just never had a reason to come here.

She makes her way up to the fourth floor gym as instructed by Alex. Hmm. This is all a little industrial for her liking. She takes in the walls—a combination of bare brick and painted breeze-block. Whoever's designed it has stayed true to the industrial roots of the building, but it leaves her cold. That said, it's edgy and she can see it working well for Alex's brand and his website. The photos she creates for him will be moody and atmospheric.

Alex is there with a little huddle of people. She doesn't

recognise any of them. He dominates the room, and not just because of his height and build. As soon as he spots her, he waves the others off and heads over to her. He's in his workout gear: shorts and a sleeveless v-necked t-shirt that exposes the breadth of his shoulders and positively sings to her to be removed.

'Hi, gorgeous.' His voice is low; his double kiss would seem perfectly polite to any onlooker. He glances around and takes her bag off her, leads her by the hand around the corner to an empty space. Puts the bag down. She backs up against the breeze block wall. His hands brace the wall on either side of her head. He leans his forehead to hers. He sighs, then kisses her so softly and sweetly on the lips that her eyes prick.

Her palms go to the sides of his face, and she pulls him far enough away from her that she can see him. They roam over his skull and neck. Newland Archer's words from *The Age of Innocence* come to mind:

'Each time, you happen to me all over again.'

The delicious romance of that interchange between Newland and Ellen has always given her thrills, but this morning it seems to perfectly encapsulate how she feels when she sees Alex. No matter how much she's thought about him and obsessed over photos of him online, that moment where she sees and touches and tastes him for the first time is always the sweetest, headiest rush of understanding there is. Every time is a revelation. *Every time, he happens to her all over again,* and every time, the euphoria she feels is brand new.

Her hands stay on his head as he kisses her face as if he hasn't seen her for twenty-one years, as if he didn't spend hours lying next to her yesterday. She leans back against the wall and closes her eyes. Her fingers roam over his scalp.

There's always been something about his shaven head that she's found intensely vulnerable, as if the absence of a protective mop of hair allows her fuller access to the miracles of life and brain function that thrive mere millimetres under his shapely skull. And boy, can he carry off the bald look. This bone structure is insane. His cheekbones, so high and so prominent, the hollows below them that cry out to be kissed; the tight ridges of his jaw that curve downwards to his chin, the graceful, sweeping arches of his brow bones.

Her fingertips trace the planes of his face as he kisses her. She knows this face by heart. She opens her mouth and touches her tongue to his, and he pushes his miraculous body closer, presses himself along the length of her, her back to the wall. She slides her hands languidly down to his bare shoulders and squeezes. All she can think is, they'd better have rooms here.

~

THE CLASS IS HIDEOUS, from where she's standing. It's Tabata: twenty seconds of HIIT to thumping house music, followed by ten seconds of rest. And repeat. Even Alex is drenched by the end of it. The mood today is far more intense than that of the studio at Sorrel Farm when she shot his last class. Everyone here is seriously fit, and the gruelling two-to-one on-off ratio of Tabata leaves no time for joking around. Even Alex keeps his instructions short and terse.

Afterwards, he high-fives and bro-hugs and back-slaps the attendees before sauntering towards Clara. He has a towel strung around his neck and he wipes at his face with one end of it. The skin of his arms glistens with sweat, the sheen adding definition his muscles don't need.

'I'm going to grab a quick shower, all right?'

She licks her lips. 'Need some help?'

'I'd love some.' His grin is wolfish. 'But I don't fancy sharing you with the other blokes in the showers. I need some food after that. Wanna grab a table on Six and I'll see you up there?'

'Okay.' She's hungry, but she'd rather grab a room and eat her lunch off his stomach. It's as flat and hard as a table. He must hear the petulance in her voice, for he leans in.

'I'll see if I can get a room for after lunch.'

They're on the same page. Again.

The sixth floor is beautiful—far more her scene than the prison-chic of the gym. She passes along a glass corridor, on the other side of which is a rooftop pool bordered with cheery red and white striped sun loungers. The pool is empty, steam rising off it. It must be a great scene here in summer. And the dining area itself is delightful—wall-to-wall picture windows all around, and greenery hanging from wooden beams. A raised open fireplace stands in the middle, bar stools around it and a huge feature chimney hanging overhead.

By the time Alex finds her, she's drooling over the lunch menu. It's bang on twelve, and she's ready to pile in. He leans over to kiss her. He smells utterly wonderful. She shouldn't really be kissing gorgeous celebrities on the mouth in the middle of a busy restaurant, but the idea that any of these cool people with their tattoos and edgy haircuts and black-rimmed glasses would know Jeremy is laughable.

'I've got us a room.'

She has an instant stab of guilt. 'Alex, that's way too extravagant.'

'It's only extravagant if you're not planning on making it a worthwhile investment for me.' He's still holding her other hand. 'Relax. They know me well here. They gave me a good rate.'

'Okay. Well—thank you. It's very generous.'

'I can't think of anyone I'd rather spend my money on than you. Speaking of rates, did you agree a day rate with Connor for today and the stuff you did for our website?'

She squirms. 'Not yet. Honestly, I don't want you to pay me. I'm happy to do it for free.'

'Babe.' His mouth is in a thin line. 'You are not a charity. Your photography is beautiful, and it'll get millions of hits on our site. You need to be properly compensated. What the fuck is Connor thinking?'

He pulls his hand away and picks up his phone. '*Sort. Out. A. Day. Rate. For. Clara. And. Get. Her. Paid. Today.* Right. Is Evelyn paying you properly?'

She hates talking about money—it's uncomfortable. Besides, whatever she makes from her photographic work won't scratch the surface compared to what Jeremy brings in as a partner in a law firm. He's made that clear before, multiple times. He's the breadwinner. She's the homemaker, and whatever nice little creative hobbies she undertakes remain just those in his eyes.

'Of course she is,' she says now.

'How is she paying you?'

For God's sake. 'I'm on a day rate for stuff like the conference. And I have a contract for the cookbook; I get a flat fee for every image they use.'

'Okay, then.' He nods. 'I'm not trying to give you a hard time, angel. But it fucks me off if I think people are taking the piss with you. You have no idea how talented you are. You—'

She interrupts him with a smiling shake of her head. A hand on his, across the table.

'How did I get so lucky? To have this fierce cheerleader?'

'I've always been your cheerleader. I've always been dazzled by how amazing you are. And if I have to shout it from the rooftops, I will.'

'I know. But now you have this'—she gestures, arms open wide—'presence. No one ever gave you enough of a break at school to let it out. And now you're unleashed. You have a global platform, and now everyone knows how amazing *you* are. And nothing, *nothing* makes me happier.'

'I'm still me.' He takes a sip of his water. 'You were the only person who ever saw anything in me, before all the fucking sheep jumped on the bandwagon.'

Their mood is taking a melancholy turn. She smiles at him. 'Do you ever think what we'd be doing right now, if you hadn't gone to prison?'

His face is still serious. 'Every fucking day.'

'Really? Do you think we'd have stayed together, this whole time?'

'I do, yeah. I've thought about this so much.' He sits back in his chair, and his face clears. 'We would have got married young, maybe when you'd finished uni.'

'Would you have gone to uni?'

'I don't think so, no. I would have stuck out my A-levels and probably passed a couple, thanks to pressure from my swotty girlfriend.' He makes a face and she sticks her tongue out at him.

'But I would have started working, to help Mum out. Doing what, I don't know. I'd like to think I'd have found my way into fitness. But probably not at this level.'

'Maybe Mr Evans would still have helped you. Maybe you would still have been rich and famous.'

'Doubt it.'

'How disappointing.'

'Just as I thought—you're a star fucker. You only came out of the woodwork because I got famous.'

She throws her hands up. 'You've got me. Would we have kids, in this other life?'

'Yeah. Two. Maybe not twins. But they'd have Italian names. Valentina and maybe Luca. I always thought your mum's name was so pretty. And I always wanted to be a part of your big Italian family. You were the happiest family I'd ever seen.'

He says it so matter-of-factly that her eyes well up. He *was* a part of their family until he cut himself off from everyone who loved him and wanted to support him. But it's overwhelming to know that he still wants to subsume himself into the identity of her broader family.

'Valentina and Luca. I like it.' Her voice is soft. Imagine if Violet was Valentina, and Charlie was Luca. Those names would suit them.

He cuts into her reverie. 'And you'd be running the V&A, obviously. Or the National. I'd fit the kids in around my small but thriving PT business. And you'd come home on the train every night and I'd have dinner ready.'

She laughs. 'Come on. That's taking it a bit too far, don't you think? Can you even cook?'

'I can cook! I'm being offered a book contract at the moment, for a kind of nutritious family eating guide.'

Their laughter is interrupted when a girl approaches their table. Long, long dark hair, almost to her bum. Beautiful. Zero makeup—she doesn't need it. She's wearing beige yoga pants and a beige crop top under a floor-length cream cardigan, open to reveal a milky, flawless expanse of stomach. She can't be more than twenty-two or twenty-three. She apologetically asks Alex to sign the back of her pale pink phone case and explains that she's a huge fan and works out via his app several times a week. He's polite and sweet as he thanks her for her support and shoots her a dazzling grin.

Clara watches the interaction with mixed emotions. Her first reaction is a stab of insecurity: she doesn't need a reminder that *her* Alex is in fact a public figure with millions of fans who love his work and presumably love his face and body, too. There's only one Alex Molloy, and there are legions of women out there who'd happily take her place—some of whom are almost half her age.

But it's also a turn on. She's loved him, *him*, for over half a lifetime, but this public side of him, this confident guy who's comfortable with his celebrity and whose presence turns heads, is hot. Alex 2.0 is a bit of a bonus, really. Her reward for her loyalty. She fell in love with the boy version of him, and two decades later the universe has served her up a man who can silence a room when he enters it but who only seems to have eyes for her.

Her eyes travel over him. He's in some kind of zip-up navy knitted tracksuit that looks expensive and Italian and soft. There are still some tiny spots of damp on the white t-shirt below from where he didn't dry himself properly. She drinks in his 'on' status, the smile he gives the girl while he trots out some safe, easy banter. As soon as this lunch is done, she gets to take him to a room, away from all these people who want a piece of him, and get him *all to herself*. She squirms in her seat and crosses her legs.

When the girl has smilingly and reluctantly left them to it, he swivels back to her, his smile bashful, and she can tell he's on the verge of apologising or brushing off the incident. But she stops him. She leans forward and brushes her leg against his under the table.

'I need you in that bedroom as soon as we've eaten.'

ONCE THEY'VE CLOSED the bedroom door, she pushes him against the desk and kisses him. She unzips his hoodie and gets to her knees, pulling open the drawstring on his jogging bottoms. Tugging them and his boxers down past his knees. Her other hand pushes his t-shirt up, her palm gliding over his stomach, down his happy trail. She's drooling. She rubs her nose over the hair too.

'Who *are* you?'

His voice, filled with awe. His eyes, when she looks up at him, hopeful and disbelieving and amused.

'I want pudding.'

His burst of laughter at her answer turns to a sharp intake of breath through his teeth as her lips close around him. His hands move through her hair, winding it.

'Fuck, babe. Fuck.'

She's in her happy place: her mouth full of Alex, hearing and feeling and tasting his reaction to her. Her hands grip his perfect, perfect bum. Before she can make him come, he shifts and stops her, pulling her up, kissing her, tongue moving roughly in her mouth, hands in her hair.

'I want to come in you.'

Off comes her sweater. Her bra. His t-shirt. He pulls down her trousers and squats to help her get them off. Kicks off his own. Then he's up, standing in front of her, a vision of skin and sinew, the tip of his erection brushing her thighs. He slaps the desk behind her and raises his eyebrows and she clambers up, opens her legs. She's beaming at him, at this beautiful man who still carries around the shadow of the beautiful boy he used to be, but who is now grinning at her in a way that's ridiculous but infectious. And she's smitten. She's powerless.

'Oh, really?' is about all she can manage.

'Oh, really. I want to fuck you on this thing.'

'We didn't need a room, then. Maybe they could have lent us an office.' The words come out as a slur because he's stroking her with the tip of his erection and then he's inside her, and the combined delights of his thrusts and the slaps of her boobs against his gorgeous pecs and the way her scalp tingles when he pulls her hair and the fact that their mouths fit together perfectly here is all too much for this body of hers to handle. He's too much.

The bed does come in handy, it turns out, because after they've come and caught their breath, his head heavy and heavenly on her shoulder, his exhales warm on her neck, he helps her over to the bed. And he pulls back the covers and curls up behind her and they're suspended together, in this anonymous East London hotel room, where no one from their real lives can get to them.

24

2019

The following week, Alex is on the huge bed in The Stables, lying on his stomach in a patch of sunlight. They've just had sex, and she sits astride him, perched on his bum, admiring the delicious view in front of her. They've hardly spoken at all. He pulled her in through the door frame and up the stairs and told her *I missed you so much*, and *you look so beautiful*, before undressing her and laying her down on the bed. She could tell he felt the same as her: why talk when the far greater priority was to have as many square inches of skin touching skin as humanly possible?

She strokes his angel, traces the curves of her wings and the line of her robes and the locks of her hair.

'Has anyone ever asked you who she is?'

'You mean press, or women I sleep with?'

Her throat tightens. 'Both.'

'I've talked about you in the press. Not by name, but I've mentioned that I had the tattoo done to remind me of my ex-girlfriend, who I was so undeserving of and who showed me that goodness and purity existed in the world. I've told them you were my guardian angel.'

'And the women?' She slips off his bum and comes to lie down beside him, curled into him. He rolls onto his side and they're nose to nose.

'They don't ask. I imagine they don't want to know, or they don't expect it to be based on an actual person. It's not like I had *I LOVE CLARA 4 EVER* inked across my back. That would have cramped my style.'

'I imagine so. You'd have to have made sure they never saw your back.' She hesitates. 'Have there been lots of women, since me?'

'I've slept with plenty of women, angel. It won't come as a surprise to you that I like sex.'

She strokes his chest, his biceps. It's horrifying to think how easy he must find it to get laid, how often he gets propositioned. Women must fall over themselves every day. She noticed it at the conference, and at that workout she shot.

'I've seen some pictures in the *Daily Mail*,' she admits. 'Lots of celebrities, too.'

'Don't read too much into that. Often we just walk the red carpet together for publicity. I do like dating women in the public eye, though. It makes it easier; they know the gig, and they're usually super busy themselves so they don't want too much from me.'

Once again it hits her how far-fetched this is—it's ludicrous. He's hers right now; they're in a bubble born out of years of history, but he exists in a reality of celebrity and wealth that she can't even fathom.

'Do you actually date many people?'

'Not really. I'd rather just have no-strings-attached sex.'

'Like this?'

'Exactly.' He slides his hand down to her bum and gives it a squeeze. 'Off you go, now.'

'You're as charming as ever.'

His grin is dazzling, and his eyes are—warm. Soft. Infinitely loving. 'I'll tell you something for free. I have never felt like this about anyone else. Not even close. I've never got serious about anyone I've dated. Never had a relationship longer than a couple of months. You're the only girl who's ever won my heart.'

She's a soup of useless, conflicting emotions: overwhelmed that she has pride of place in his heart, and devastated that he hasn't found happiness. 'That sounds so lonely, Alex. You don't have to do it alone, you know. I want you to be happy.'

'I am happy, right here, right now. Happier than I've been in years. But what about you? Did I set you on a lifelong path of debauchery?'

Her relationship with Alex gave her the gift of a love of sex, but it wasn't until she fully accepted that he was gone for good, and she herself went off to Bristol, that she allowed herself to even contemplate scratching that particular itch with anyone else but him. By the time she went to uni, she was desperate to get way from Kent and all the terrible memories it embodied, and Bristol was a breath of fresh air: stunning surroundings, inspiring architecture, a humming Arts faculty, a crazy student union, and thousands of young people who were hungry and studious and stimulating. She found, to her pleasant surprise, that she was the object of plenty of attention from guys who were polished and smart and gorgeous and athletic, and she finally allowed herself to act on it.

She gives Alex a carefully edited version of this gap in her history.

'It's weird for me, though, thinking of you with other people,' she says afterwards.

'Not as weird as you having a fucking husband. Think about it, angel. There's a man in your life who's not me, and he gets to lie next to you every fucking night, and watch you grow his babies, and wake up next to you every morning. Do you have any idea how that feels? I think he must be the luckiest guy in the world.'

'No.' Her voice is small.

'Don't get me wrong; I've always wanted you to be happy. I'd be gutted if you were lonely and miserable, but of course you were never going to be. You were always going to get snapped up. You're so amazing—you're luminous. And I bet you're the most fantastic mother. I'm really, really happy you have kids. But I'm very conscious that I'm only a small part of your life. I have to be, because you have a family.'

'No, Alex.' She wriggles up against him as fully as she can. 'You're wrong. You're everything. You're my whole universe. I don't want to lose you again.'

'Then you've got a hell of a lot of shit to work out,' he whispers. His eyes shut, and tears bead on his long eyelashes.

She lies there. He's putting this all on her, and it's so unfair, but it's also understandable, because he's free to do whatever he likes and she's not. She kisses his wet eyes, and hugs and hugs him, and tries to communicate via skin-on-skin telepathy exactly how much he means to her, but she can see he's shutting down right in front of her.

She kisses his cheek. 'I'm going to get a glass of water.'

She pads downstairs, naked. On the breakfast bar, his laptop is open and glowing. She glances at the screensaver and freezes in horror. Dominating the screen is a grainy, low-res version of a photo she'd know anywhere, a face that has haunted her for twenty-one years. It's one of those photos where the ordinary happiness on the subject's face is eerily overshadowed by the tragic fate that is later to befall them. Like missing girls. Murdered schoolchildren.

She grabs the laptop and runs upstairs, throwing it down on the bed.

'Why the *hell* is your screensaver Lindsay Smith?'

~

SHE STANDS there in front of him, naked and livid. Fuck. He runs his hand over his face.

'Penance.' What else can he say?

'I *beg* your pardon?'

'It's so I remember her. Every time I look at it. Every day.'

She stares at him like he's a total fucking lunatic and pulls his shirt off the floor, pulling it on and buttoning it once across the chest. She looks so beautiful, with her hair falling over his shirt in long, lustrous tendrils, that the miraculous nature of her being here in the flesh hits him anew. She sits down on the bed next to him and takes his hand. Her voice is softer.

'I thought you'd worked through all that, sweetie.'

He squeezes her hand before releasing it and pulling himself up to seated. He leans back against a wad of pillows and covers himself with the sheet. She's speaking to him and looking at him as if he's an unstable child who may lose the plot at any point.

'Babe, I could go and sit in a fucking cave in Tibet till the end of my days and it won't change the fact that I took a person's life. There is no 'working through' that. I ruined her baby's life, and her boyfriend's, and her parents', and I deprived her of the opportunity to be a mother and have more kids. And I'm here today, rolling in dough, up to my fucking neck in privilege'—he gestures around the enormous room—'and I don't really feel like I paid the price. Not enough.'

'But you did pay the price. It was an *accident*, Alex! A horrible, cruel twist of fate! You went down for two years—everyone says that sentence was too harsh. Look at what you've suffered—and me, and your mum.'

'It was my fault, angel. I have to take responsibility for that. If I hadn't got behind that wheel and behaved like a total twat, Lindsay Smith would still be alive and her little boy would have grown up with a mum. Yeah, I had a shitty few years, but I bounced back like a fucking rubber duck, and she's still dead, and she always will be.'

'I had no idea you felt like this! What about all that... radical forgiveness, or whatever you call it?'

He shrugs. Radical forgiveness doesn't change anything, not really.

'It's helped a bit. Look, I'm functioning, aren't I? Before I met Je, I was still on a pretty self-destructive path, underneath all the fitness stuff. Now I can just about look at myself in the mirror. But nothing I ever, ever do will atone for killing her.'

They're both silent. She gets up onto her knees and crawls over and straddles him, her face collapsing onto his shoulder and her hair falling over his nose and mouth. He inhales and wraps his arms around her.

'This is Catholic guilt gone crazy, Alex. As you say, nothing can ever, ever make up for it so you've got to give yourself a break and find a way to live with it. What does Fr Pat say about all this?'

He gathers up her hair, away from his face, and twists it softly into a rope. 'It's all we've talked about for years. He knows I struggle. He's always told me I need to find a way to love myself, because I'm worthy of love as a child of Christ—blah, blah, blah. You can imagine.'

She lifts her head. Her eyes are huge with tears. Her voice is barely a whisper. 'And do you love yourself?'

He gives her a tight smile. 'Not a fucking chance.'

'And it's never let up, not even after twenty years?'

He tries to explain. 'The more successful I get, the more undeserving I feel. So I do what I can to give back. A few years ago, I set up a trust for her kid. He turned twenty-one last year, so he'll have access to it now. I make donations to youth charities. I spend as much time as I can visiting young offenders' institutes, talking to the kids about our mistakes and working with lobbying firms who are pushing for more rehabilitation in the prison system. It helps—it makes me feel like some good has come out of this shit-show. But I can never let myself forget her, because if I do, what does that say about me?'

She lets out a huge, exhausted sigh.

'You're doing amazing things, sweetie. You're right—good has come out of all this. And remember what Je says at the conference: we're all better than the worst things we've done. You did it; it's done; don't let it define your entire life. You're allowed to be happy, you know. Otherwise it's two lives wasted, and you know Fr Pat wouldn't approve of that.'

He smiles at her smile and her well-meaning words, but he has to level with her.

'I'll never really be happy. The best I can hope for is oblivion. I get it when I'm exercising, and when I'm working, and when I'm doing something useful for others. To be honest, that's the main reason I didn't top myself years ago. As long as I can do something that gives back, I'm not just a stain on this planet, and I can justify my existence.'

'Oh my God, Alex!' She puts her hands on his cheeks. 'I can't bear it! I cannot let you talk about yourself like this. You are *amazing*. You've changed so many people's lives already, and made them fitter and healthier and happier. You are a very, very special human being and I love you. It breaks my heart that you can't see yourself the way the world sees you.'

She puts her mouth to his and parts his lips with her tongue, and he drinks her in and gratefully takes the temporary oblivion she's offering him.

25

2019

This time, it's slower, and deeper, and more transcendent than it's been yet. This time, she knows instinctively that it's about using her body to reach his soul, to touch the wounded part of him so hideously scarred that he's allowed access to nobody. This time, it's about using her physical display of love where words are useless. She kisses adoration into his mouth and stares into his eyes, so close to hers that their eyelashes are practically brushing. He fumbles for the single fastened button of his shirt and opens it, sliding it off her shoulders so it hangs around her elbows. She tugs it off impatiently and returns her hands to cupping the face of this man who moves her so much.

He places his palms on her breasts as if giving her a benediction, before moving them slowly, agonisingly slowly, in tiny circles. Her nipples tighten and harden and ache so much for him that she pushes her breasts into his palms and feels his smile. That's better. She reaches down and finds that he's already hard, and she pulls herself up so she can take him in. As she lowers herself down, he moans, and she rewards him with a sweep of her tongue along his lower lip. She begins to move slowly, greedily, rolling her hips in circles and pulling back so she can see the ecstasy flit across his beautiful face. He's smiling now. That's all she wants: to make him smile, to make him forget his torments.

As they move, she has the sense that he's trying to tell her something, beg her for something, show her what he needs. She glues herself to every inch of him, as firmly as she can. His hands are around her waist now, and in her hair, and she digs into his shoulders as she grinds down onto him as fully as she can. They are both slick with sweat. Every single nerve-ending in her body sings at his proximity. Every drop of her consciousness is consumed by the force of the connection she feels to this man. She prays this connection has the power to heal. It has to. It's the only tool she has to reach him with.

He falls over the edge with a low roar into her mouth as he holds her to him, and they stay in that position as his shudders subside, and his breathing slows, and his kisses go from feverish to dreamy. She has him trapped against the pillows, against the headboard, pinned between her legs, his head in her hands. He's safe here, cocooned within her body.

~

When they've recovered sufficiently, they order room service, and they perch at the breakfast bar downstairs in the robes and pick at an assortment of goodies from the Oast House—padron peppers, and creamy humous, and crispy-skinned chicken breast, and some delicious-looking, vibrant winter salad with roasted beetroots and squash and lentils. Alex spoons big mounds onto both their plates. The sex, and the emotional exhaustion of their conversation, have left her knackered and ravenous. She attacks the salad, which is still warm, with gusto, before using her knife and fork to pull the skin away from the chicken. It's incredibly crisp and fragrant; she lays it reluctantly on the side of her plate.

Alex points. 'What are you doing? You've got to eat that. It's delicious!'

'I'm trying to be good. I want to shift a few pounds.' It's all very well for him; Mr Lean Muscle Machine works off God knows how many calories a day, working out.

'Babe, fat doesn't make you fat. Sugar does. And you're not fat, so you have nothing to worry about. This is Sorrel Farm chicken. It's the best, and the fat is part of the deal. I really believe in eating the whole animal—the fat as well as the protein.'

She doesn't need to be told twice. 'If you say so. You're the expert.' She stuffs a piece of her chicken skin into her mouth. Jesus. It's orgasmic. She closes her eyes and moans with her mouth full. When she opens them, Alex is smiling at her. He covers her hand with his and squeezes.

'Better than sex, eh?'

'Almost. It's setting a high bar, I've got to say.'

'I'll consider myself warned. Life's too short not to eat chicken skin.'

'I like that motto. Sex *and* chicken skin. It's been a good morning.' She sucks the fat off her finger.

He's still grinning at her. He strokes her hand with his thumb.

'Thanks for looking after me. I'm sorry I'm such a fucking headcase.'

'You're not a headcase. You're a wonderful person who has a heavy cross to bear. It would mess anyone up.'

They fall silent and enjoy the food. She looks at the clock behind Alex's head. Two o'clock. She has an hour before she has to go pick up the twins. She feels sick at the thought of being without him, and uneasy about leaving him alone with his thoughts, despite her efforts to distract him after their chat.

'Will you be ok, when I go?'

He nods. 'Yep. You've cheered me up. Thank you.'

'Do you think seeing me again has brought all these feelings about Lindsay to the surface?'

'Maybe a little. But they're never too far from the surface, babe. Don't worry about me. I've learnt to live with them. I'll be fine.'

She can't believe he's only been back in her life a few weeks. How the hell did she last two decades without him? Who was that person who went through life with no Alex in it and felt contented and fulfilled? Life without him is inconceivable: drab and flat and hopeless. They've been back together for the blink of an eye, but they've come too far and bared too much of their souls to shy away from talking about the direction of their relationship from here. She swallows. It's the scariest thing to ask someone, but this is *Alex*, and she can't let a fear of vulnerability get in the way of what's important.

'If I was with you properly, do you think it would fix things—make you happy?'

He stares at her. 'How do you mean?'

'I mean if'—oh, God. She feels nauseous—'I left Jeremy, and you and I were a couple. I could get a divorce.'

The ripple-effects of heartbreak and betrayal and disappointment, not to mention the miles of red-tape and organisational and bureaucratic nightmares that stand between her current situation and the solution she's painted so easily, in a few short words, taunt her. They are *horrifying*. But she stands firm.

He bows his head and squeezes his eyes shut as if he's in great pain, and he presses the creased skin at the bridge of his nose with his fingertips before looking up at her and taking her hand again. He exhales.

'That is the most... generous, and beautiful, and unselfish thing anyone has ever, ever asked me. But I will never break up your marriage. I can't.'

'It's not unselfish.' Her words come out in a tumble. 'I'm not trying to make you feel like a charity case. I love you; I want to be with you. There's no way I can go back to Jeremy now and pretend everything's fine.'

'Babe. What we have'—he looks up at the ceiling for inspiration—'is more than most people get to experience in their lifetime. I'm not sure what we've been doing, these past few weeks, except acting on what is an enormous fucking well of passion and emotion and history. Am I right? But what I told you earlier is true. I'm still here because I want to make amends; I want to try to do some good in the world. That does not include breaking up people's families. Even yours. Even though I think your husband sounds like a twat who doesn't appreciate you.'

'No. No.' She grabs at his shoulders. 'You wouldn't be doing a bad thing; I want to be with you—I need to be.'

'Clara. My dad pissed off and left my mum because he thought with his dick and he didn't give a shit about anyone else but himself. I will not do that—not to your husband, not to your kids, not to their grandparents or to any of the other people who have invested in you as a family. I will not be my father. The price is too high. I told you anyway, I'm broken. I'm past saving, babe. I will not break up a family and take your kids away from their father, just because I can. That's not who I am. Do not ask me to be that person.'

The finality of his words is a sickening thud to her stomach. She realises that the whole time she's been in this weird… bubble with him, she's been held aloft by a small, flickering flame of hope. It was faint, but it was there—hope that they'd find a way to be together; hope that they couldn't possibly, *surely*, throw away this second chance they'd been given? It's impossible for her to accept that they haven't come back into each other's lives for a reason, but apparently he finds it entirely possible.

She shouldn't be surprised. She's *so stupid* to be surprised. He's done this before, of course: cut her off for no reason that makes sense beyond his own twisted logic and moral framework. At least this time, he has the decency to do it to her face. Not like last time, when all she had to go on was a shitty letter. But in every other respect, it's the same. He's making a unilateral decision about her entire future happiness, and it makes her so. Fucking. Angry.

'So what are you telling me?' The blood is rising to her brain and making her light-headed. 'That after all that, you really do see this as just no-strings-attached sex?'

'Babe. Of course not.' He puts his hand on hers and she jerks it off. 'I *love* you. You are everything to me.'

'But you won't let me in, will you? You'll sleep with me, but you won't let our lives overlap, not really. You won't even entertain the idea of trying to find a way to make this work; you won't fight for any kind of future for us. *Again*. Jesus Christ, I am so stupid.'

'Please, angel. I can't tell you how much I wish things were different. But I'm not ready to let you go.' His face is almost too much for her. Almost. Those beautiful eyes are luminous with tears. She's never doubted for a second that he loves her. But it's not enough for him. It's fear, even if he can't see it himself.

He's so bloody broken and weighed down with the guilt and trauma and responsibility of what he did all those years ago that he's built the most enormous bloody barricade around himself, and he won't even let her through. Not in the way that she wants him to. He's terrified that if he starts to dismantle the barricade, he'll collapse. She wants nothing more than to be with him and help him face that seething mass of darkness together, but he won't let her in, and his shit is way beyond her pay-grade.

She slides off the stool. 'That's inconvenient for you then, isn't it? Because I have to protect myself too, and I'm not willing to just be on standby for whatever sex you need to obliterate your pain, Alex. There are lots of other women you can go to for that. You ruined my life once, and I'm damned if I'm going to let you do it again. I'm going *home* now.'

26

2006

Last night's rehearsal dinner at The Wolseley had been a little more raucous than it should have been. She'd eaten carbs, which she'd sworn not to do. And she'd had four glasses of wine, which she'd sworn not to do. But it had been great fun. Jeremy had held court, charming both his mum and Clara's mum. He'd been on fire. He was *hot* when he was on form like that: cavalier and handsome and witty and irreverent.

When she'd left him last night, he'd kissed her in a deeply inappropriate manner in front of the cab and laughed when he saw the desire on her face as he pulled away.

You need to wait another twenty-four hours for that, until you're Mrs Winters. He slapped her on the bum. *Go on, off with you. I'll see you at the church. Maria, take her back to the hotel.*

She'd been seriously turned on when she walked away from her fiancé last night. She couldn't wait to get him to herself for their wedding night, which would take place in a suite at the Savoy after their reception in the hotel. She could imagine how good he'd look in his morning suit today, how much fun she'd have undoing it later on in their suite.

So she couldn't explain why, this morning, standing in a smaller room at the Savoy with her sister Maria, the sight of her reflection made her want to run to the loo and throw up her breakfast. Her dress fitted perfectly, despite last night's carbs. The hairdresser had done an incredible job with her hair. She loved her fiancé—and she definitely fancied him. So what was the problem?

Maria. I think I'm having a freak-out.

Maria spun around. *Really? A big freak-out, or a standard 'I'm getting married today' freak-out?*

I don't know. She sat carefully down on the bed, not wanting to crease this stunning fishtail gown any more than she had to.

You guys looked pretty fucking loved-up last night, from where I was standing? Maria came and sat next to her, held her hand.

Yeah, we are. I mean, he's great, and I love him. It's just—till death do us part. You know?

Scarier words were never spoken. Seriously. Everyone feels like this on their wedding day. Maria spoke with the wisdom of a woman who'd been married for a year.

I know. She looked down at their hands and said the words that had been threatening to burst out of her for days now, for weeks. *It's just—it doesn't feel like I thought it would. Love. It doesn't feel like it did with Alex. I love Jeremy, very much, but Alex was my whole world. I thought that's what I'd feel when I got married.*

Oh, sweetie. Maria laid her head on Clara's shoulder. Carefully, because she'd had her hair done too.

No one else has ever come close to him; I've never felt that way about anyone else. Even Jeremy. What if he was my one true love, and it was all over before I even turned eighteen?

My darling. We've been through this so many times. You were both so young! Things can be so intense at that age, because of all the hormones, and because it's all so fresh and new. And the problem is, you and Alex never got the chance to fizzle out, or grow apart, or... anything. So it's not fair to compare Jeremy to Alex. You have Alex on a pedestal, and no one else will ever come close, even poor Jeremy, even though he worships you and he hasn't put a foot wrong.

She let out a shuddery sigh. *I know you're right. It's not a fair comparison.*

It's really not. You and Alex were seriously intense. And the pain he caused you... I'd never wish that on anyone. But you know Jeremy will never do that to you, right? You guys have a healthy, functional, grown-up relationship from where I'm standing. That said, if you don't love him, you shouldn't marry him. You don't have to do anything you don't want to do.

Clara squeezed her sister's hand as if, by doing so, she could somehow absorb Maria's sanity and maturity and perspective. She would not think about Alex now. He left her. He left her twice—when he refused to let her visit him in prison, and when he got out and fucked off to London of his own accord. Jeremy would never, ever do that to her. She would not insult her fiancé on their wedding day by allowing herself for even a second to imagine how she'd be feeling, right now, if she knew that Alex would be waiting for her at the end of the aisle in an hour's time.

I want to do it, she said. *I want to be Jeremy's wife.*

Later, as she straddled her smoking hot husband on an enormous bed in the same hotel, and got to work unbuttoning his shirt as he grinned up at her with undisguised delight and lust, she knew she was exactly where she was supposed to be. Or that's what she told herself, anyway.

27

2019

Her devastation is total. Alex still wouldn't let her in, not properly, not after everything they went through. They fused their bodies together, and bared their souls to each other, and still, after all that, he kept himself locked away. She can't understand how he could do it to himself and to her. Once again, he called the bloody shots and she was utterly powerless to change his mind.

She had no idea how damaged he still was. She bought into all the crap he gave her (and everyone at the conference) about radical self-forgiveness. That first time she had coffee with him, he told her how well he was doing and what healing powers exercise had. Bullshit. Beneath the incredibly slick, self-assured public persona he's built for himself, he's still the same insecure, unworthy boy she knew, but he's worse now because he's measuring every step he takes in his own life against a yardstick of having taken away someone else's life, and if that's the barometer he insists on using then he's never, ever going to be able to find peace in himself. He's broken.

She hasn't heard from him for almost two weeks; no surprise after the way she left. She didn't exactly leave the door open for him to seek her out. It's clear he thinks he's being selfless, making the ultimate sacrifice—his own chance for future happiness—because it's the noble thing to do, but really, she sees it as selfish. Or self-indulgent. She's not sure which. He's making it all about him. The burden he has to carry is undeniably horrific, but he doesn't have to shoulder it alone. That's what she's been trying to tell him. It sounds like that's what Fr Pat's been trying to tell him for two decades.

He's so bloody black and white. Surely, after everything he's seen and suffered, he of all people should understand that life is grey? It's ironic, for someone who's never embraced Catholicism, that he's so unflinchingly judgemental about things.

Thou shalt not kill. He killed, and he committed a mortal sin, and he's seemingly beyond redemption, even in this life.

Thou shalt not covet thy neighbour's wife. His dad, who sounds like he was a total waste of space, walked out on his wife and kids and Alex is so quick to put his actions in the same bucket as his dad's. He won't let himself be *that person.* She's not asking him to be any kind of person; she's asking him to let her love him, for God's sake. And she bloody well covets him, that's for sure. She's damned and she couldn't give a shit.

He slept with her. He asked her to spend the night with him, and she did. He told her it was the one thing he'd always wanted, and she obliged. It was the one thing she'd always wanted, too. And when they were asleep together, he did the same thing he told her he'd imagined doing in prison, every night, every morning. He curled himself around her, as if he was her protective shell, as if *he* were *her* guardian angel.

The feeling of surfacing briefly in the darkest depths of the night, cocooned within Alex, was incomparable. The scent of his skin warmed within the sheets. The heavenly solidity of his muscles and the improbable, ridiculous softness of his skin, in parallel. The steady rhythm of his breath. Her knowledge that right then, in that moment, he had everything he'd told her he wanted so badly, and he could sleep in peace. She's offering him a lifetime of that, and he cannot get out of his own way and out of his own head sufficiently to give her the only answer she wants: *yes*.

She's following him on Instagram now, and she despises herself, but she tells herself it's so she can keep track of his movements and avoid him at the farm. Whatever. But his Stories tell her he's up in London this week, shooting at some swanky gym in the East End. It means she can go to the farm without the constant, sickening buzz of dread and hope assaulting her, and actually get on with her job.

There's a hairy moment where Charlie turns on the TV in the kitchen one morning before school. He's ready to go; Violet's upstairs revising for a maths test, and Jeremy has already left to get the train into Cannon Street. Before he has a chance to flick over to Netflix, Good Morning Britain comes on, and there's Alex, sitting with Piers Morgan and Susanna Reid, looking heart stoppingly gorgeous in his workout gear. He's Nike-d up from head to toe.

'It's Alex!' Charlie says. 'Can we watch it, Mum?'

'Um, sure.' She goes to switch the coffee machine on. It's already on. She stays at the island, strumming her fingers on the marble, watching it over Charlie's head so he can't see her reaction to Alex. Her heart is beating wildly. She feels simultaneously sick that he won't be at the farm today, and positively voyeuristic that she gets to watch him live from the privacy of her kitchen.

He's saying something about the importance of physical exercise for young people, and how critical it is for them to move their bodies—even if they don't like team sports, they should find a form of exercise that works for them and brings them joy and relief. Susanna smiles dreamily at him. She's only human. Then she says:

'Alex is going to do a five-minute workout for us right now, in the studio. What are you going to have us do, Alex?'

He grins and turns to the camera. He's looking at her. She can't breathe for a moment. His face. His skin. How much makeup have they put on him? She can't tell he's wearing any, but he's radiant and it's bloody February, for God's sake. He's a vision. His eyes are luminous green and his smile is brilliant.

'It's just five minutes. Anyone can do it! This is a low-impact routine, so it's suitable for all ages and fitness levels. It's just a warm-up, really. If you've got school today, this will wake your body up. If you're a grown-up, and you're feeling stiff this morning, this will get your joints working nicely. You'll feel better afterwards, I promise!'

'Thanks, Alex.' Piers gestures towards the other end of the studio. 'Go for it.'

'I'm going to do it, Mum!' Charlie jumps up. And so she stands there in her spacious kitchen with the dawn barely breaking beyond, and watches her son twist and bend and squat in time with her lover, with the love of her life. And on screen, Alex grins and moves and stares into her eyes, and once again it hits her: the enormity of the journey this man has been on. There are millions of people watching this—watching him—right now. He's not hers anymore. He hasn't been hers for years. He's public property, a national treasure, even. But he's made it clear that no one owns him, that no matter how much each member of the public feels like they own a bit of him, he's a closed door, really. And there's nothing she can do about any of it, except hug her bewildered son very, very tightly when it's over and breathe her devastation into the top of his silky head.

~

SHE GOES straight to the farm after school run. She'll have an hour or two to herself before Zoe finishes breakfast service. She gets her wellies out of the car boot and takes herself and her camera straight out to the fields. It's a stunning morning with a hazily bright sky, and the wonderfully acrid smell of firewood hits her nostrils as she crunches over the still-icy grass.

She should do this more often. She averts her eyes as she passes The Stables, giving them a wide berth. That charming building has been the setting for what she hoped would be a miraculous Act Three in her life, and now she can't bear to look at it. The memories are too vivid, too raw. They stripped everything away in there, figuratively and literally, and it still wasn't enough to quash his demons.

As she trudges around the farm, her mood shifts ever so slightly. It's hard not to find resilience among such beauty; when faced with it, it's hard to forget that the world keeps on turning amid sorrow and heartbreak and injustice. The watery sun, so low in the sky, is slow to thaw the light frost this morning.

She walks all the way over to the lavender fields. They were a wondrous haze of chalky grey-purple over the summer and now they're uniform rows of endless pale sage mounds, but still beautiful, their frost-tipped ends subtly lustrous. At the far end of the largest field, she turns and stops. In the distance, the Oast House's sculptural funnels rise above the rest of the farm buildings, and a spire of smoke from its chimney winds its way up into the sky. It's a perfect vista and a perfect shot for the Winter section of the book. She stands there and stomps her feet and curls her toes up inside her thick welly socks to keep the blood flowing. And she wonders what her life will look like without him, having rediscovered just how it can feel with him at its centre.

Abi asked her the other day how she knew she and Alex were soulmates.

'The physical side I get,' she said. 'He's so fuckable, it's ridiculous. But you guys aren't the most obvious fit, if you don't mind my saying so. The reformed bad boy and the impeccably behaved Clara Winters? What's that all about—is it just a case of opposites attracting?'

'We're less opposite than you think. We really are soulmates. I know it doesn't look like it from the outside, but it's true.'

She's thought about this—or over-analysed it—for years. That she and Alex came together at school was improbable, given that the crowds they both hung out with could not have been more different. But it was the very fact of their differences that allowed them to see each other properly. Each of them was a breath of fresh air to the other, a being so different and so new that they were able to fully appreciate every tiny thing that made the other precisely who they were.

They saw each other. That was the crux of it. Clara felt seen, and accepted, and celebrated by Alex in a way that she'd never experienced. Sure, her friends and her family accepted everything about her, but to Alex, she seemed miraculous. And it was exactly the same for her, with him. His Alex-ness was so wonderfully different from her own construction that she worshipped every facet of it. They were mirrors for each other. That they existed well beyond each other's usual circle meant they could be completely themselves and know that the other would rejoice in that.

Alex told her a million times that her intelligence, her talents, ambition, her self-assurance were awe-inspiring, and the things he loved most about her. Over those precious, heady months together, he began to internalise those facets, too. It was as if she unlocked parts of him that were dormant, waiting for a partner who wouldn't laugh at him if he worked hard. He was super smart, and she'd like to think she gave him the safe space to explore that side of him. He certainly did fulfil his *fucking potential* when he was with her. Yikes.

He was really, really good for her, too. She knew her parents were suspicious when they first got together—everyone was suspicious of the Jubilee kids—but she blossomed with him. She already had the confidence that came with being top of her year group and surrounded by supportive, loving family and friends, but her self-confidence was very much based on her achievements. Her persona was that of the good girl, and sometimes she felt as though there was only downside.

Everyone—friends, parents, teachers—expected her to get straight As, all the time. She worked her arse off, and she kept on getting them, but they weren't celebrated so much as expected. But if she'd got a B, there would have been raised eyebrows. Alex's love cut through all that; he was so focused on the essence of *her* that he showed her her worthiness without the trappings of achievement and the validation of academic success. With him by her side, she gradually became less of a people-pleaser.

Together, they were so perfectly whole and deliriously self-sufficient in their bubble. That was why, when they took him away, it was like asking her to breathe with only one lung.

She also asked herself a million times, during those precious few weeks, whether their intrinsic bond was still intact. There would have been nothing more catastrophic for either of them than forging ahead based on an ancient dynamic that didn't exist anymore, or mistaking two decades' worth of lack of closure for eternal love.

The truth, as far as she can see it, is that their bond was different this time around, but still undeniable. It morphed with his fame and success and also his trauma and heartbreak. It evolved by virtue of her having experienced marriage and parenthood and the rejigging of what success in life meant to her. But they still saw each other in a way that no one else could. He certainly saw her far more fully in those few weeks than Jeremy has ever done. Jeremy has always had a clear vision of the wife and marriage he intended to have, and she fell into line and assimilated perfectly into that vision. She's never showed him the fullest expression of herself, and he's never shown the slightest interest in finding it.

The physical side was still perfect with Alex, but to call sex with him physical would be to miss the point completely. Of course, he's stunning; she wouldn't be a fully functioning woman if she didn't react to his bodily beauty. But when they were wrapped around each other and he was moving inside her, the alchemy was far, far more than the scratching of a physical itch. It was transcendent, just as it always had been. She knows how lucky she is to have found this magic with another human being, but she had eleven months with him and then a few meagre weeks, and she's never had anything like this with the man she gave her future to. And it's not fair. It's not in the least bit bloody fair.

She fell down a rabbit hole of his old press interviews yesterday. She wasn't due at the farm, and it gave her far too much time to think. She scoured Google and found vast amounts of long-form interviews. The Sunday supplements seem to love him, and he's even had a *GQ* cover feature. They interviewed him last year and went with a shot of his back, his head turned to one side, his face in perfect profile. How in the name of all that was holy had she missed this? It was just as well; she couldn't imagine what kind of meltdown she'd have had if she'd spotted that cover while browsing the magazine aisle in the Sevenoaks branch of Waitrose.

She kissed her fingertip before stroking it down the line of his spine on her laptop. Beautiful, beautiful man. She closed her eyes, imagined for a moment that he was lying next to her as she traced her fingers over his back and feasted on the artistry above and below the surface. Envisaged bending her head to brush his skin with her lips.

The interview was even more heart-rending than the additional stunning, moody photography that accompanied it.

When I was at school, I had a girlfriend.

It's her on my back.

She was so beautiful, I can't even tell you.

She was also the purest, best person I've ever known.

The thought of her got me through every day in prison.

She was my guardian angel. She still is.

The interviewer asked: *Is she still in your life?*

No. I never saw her again after the night I got arrested. She's married now.

He told the world about her.

He had her immortalised, with ink and a needle, all over his back.

Fifteen years ago.

And then he found her again, and she handed herself to him on a bloody platter, and he couldn't do it. He couldn't say yes to a future with her.

It's so fucked up.

He's so fucked up.

28

2019

Once she's in the Oast House kitchen with Zoe, she's calmer. She's calmer because Zoe's like a human metronome, and the serenity she exudes is so infectious that all other beings who come into contact with her can't resist recalibrating to her level of zen. Even the other chefs are seriously chilled. Clara thinks back to the kitchen at Casa Valentina. The mood was always warm, but the air was usually thick with Italian cursing as too many Mediterraneans shared and worked in the small space. What a contrast.

Today they're photographing one of the seasonal recipes for the cookbook. Zoe is preparing a slow-cooked venison stew for tonight's menu. She explains that the venison has come from Angus' family's estate in Derbyshire, a by-product of the necessary culling process, and that the fantastic nutritional density of this meat makes it a wonderful choice for the depths of winter. She's going to add swedes, which normally Clara would hate but which will probably taste divine when Zoe cooks them, and port, and blackberries at the end.

This is the part of the job she loves most: being a fly on the wall in this beautiful kitchen, its endless gleaming copper pans hanging from the ceiling and its lustrous wooden surfaces. She loves watching the harmonious, often unspoken, choreography between the chefs, the reverence with which they treat the food, and the wondrous sights and smells of the cooking process itself. She's picked up quite a few tips, from sauteing methods to unexpected pairings.

She meanders around the kitchen, her camera never far from her eye: assessing, framing how the sights in front of her convert behind the lens. A long-distance tableau of the four chefs, taken from the other end of the oast house. The jewel-like lustre of the mounds of blackberries. Zoe's cleaver catching the light as she slices cleanly through the venison. She'll end the session capturing Zoe as she plates up and styles the dish on the mismatched blue-and-white china that reflects the traditional charm of the Oast House so well.

This is where she's happiest, these days. Hiding behind the lens. It's become her eye. She can rarely see things in real life anymore without wondering how they'll look when she's shot them and edited them to bring out the colours. It's perverse, she knows it, but she can control and edit and perfect her images in a way she learnt long ago she couldn't do with life.

'You're not at peace.' It's a statement, and Zoe doesn't look up from the venison as she utters it. It's an odd way of phrasing her observation, but she's hit the nail on the head.

'Not really, no.' She flicks through the last few photos she's taken on the camera's digital display to avoid having to make eye contact.

'I'm sorry. If you want to talk about it, I'm here.'

And talk she does. The kitchen feels monastic; Zoe's depths of compassion and lack of judgement make her the perfect confessor. She tells this kind, warm woman to whom she's grown close over the past few months about Alex, about their story twenty-one years ago, and their stalemate today, and the impossible cauldron of worry and conflict and desire and heartbreak that her brain has become. Zoe listens and chops and moves mounds of cubed meat into a huge casserole for browning. She tells Clara she's not really familiar with Alex or with his story. No surprise—she doesn't strike Clara as a tabloid reader. When she's finished her tale of woe, Zoe stills and looks at her.

'You poor darling.' She puts down her cleaver and wraps her arms around Clara and her camera and hugs her. 'That is such a terrible burden for you both to bear,' she whispers in Clara's ear.

Clara's eyes smart at the kindness in her tone. 'Thank you.'

Zoe releases her and goes back to browning the meat.

'Any advice?' Clara attempts levity, but she'll take any wisdom this woman can offer. Zoe has a perspective on life that has always seemed infinitely more measured than anyone else she knows, and a couple of weeks ago she belatedly discovered why. The *Sunday Times Magazine* published a cover feature on Zoe entitled *Heaven on Earth.* The title reflected not just the delights of Sorrel Farm or Zoe's philosophy for using sustainably sourced food to commune with nature, but Zoe's own jaw-dropping story. When she was much younger, she underwent an operation to remove a brain tumour and was pronounced clinically dead for six minutes before her heart rate and brain function restarted. Her tumour vanished a few weeks later.

When she read the article, Clara was stunned by this revelation. She hasn't openly discussed any of the content with Zoe, beyond congratulating her on the piece, but she's been observing this amazing woman with fresh eyes for the past fortnight. Zoe came back from the dead and Clara suspects the article merely touched the surface of how deeply her near-death experience has coloured her outlook on life.

Now, Zoe's still for a moment, spatula poised in mid-air above the casserole. She always does this: reflects before she speaks.

'You want to walk away from your home and your marriage for this guy.' Once again, it's a statement, not a question.

'Yes. I mean, I'm willing to. I can't live without him, not now I've felt what it's like to be with him again. He's the person I should always have been with.'

'He tells you he doesn't want to be like his father, but really, it sounds like it's this woman's death that's the problem. He cannot live with the guilt; he still hasn't found a way to make peace with it.'

'You're right. Despite everything he's done, it's still tearing him apart, and he doesn't seem to be able to allow himself to be happy because of that.'

Zoe pushes at the meat with the spatula and inhales the aroma from the depths of the casserole before answering. '*Rien n'arrive par hasard.*'

Clara frowns. 'Nothing—what?'

'Nothing happens by accident. You guys say "everything happens for a reason". Do you know if he's ever allowed himself to think it was meant to be—her death? That it was all part of a grand plan that he or you or I can't comprehend, and that he was just a pawn in this great universal chess game we're all playing?'

'I can tell you now,' Clara says. 'I know Alex, and he will never, ever have allowed himself to entertain that theory.

He's all about taking responsibility. That sounds far too convenient; it would absolve him, basically.'

'Look.' Zoe throws her hands up. 'I don't know. We all have the freedom to make choices, yes, and we create our own paths by doing so. Alex made choices that night that had disastrous consequences for so many people. *But.* I truly believe the length of our stay on this physical plane is determined for us. I was not meant to die on that operating table, that day. Maybe this woman was only meant to live for—how old was she?'

'Twenty-six,' Clara whispers.

'For twenty-six years. Maybe that was all she was ever supposed to get in her physical form. I understand—it's tragic, mainly because her baby lost its mother. But I've seen the other side, albeit super, super briefly. Her death was not the end of her. She's still here.' She waves her hand. 'She's not lost. She's an infinite being, and neither Alex nor anyone else can ever take that from her.

'All I'm saying is that perhaps, if he broadens his perspective to think of it like that, he will stop taking on one hundred percent of the responsibility and pain. There were so many factors at play that night, to throw them into each other's paths like that. He had to leave your house at the *exact* time he did. She had to leave wherever she was at an exact time too, and walk at an exact pace, in order for him to be the instrument of her death. If you think of it like that, it blows the mind, the complexity of the operation that was her dying at his hands. Does one human have the power to orchestrate something like that? I'm not sure.'

Clara's skin has broken out in goosebumps. She stares at Zoe, but her mind's eye is playing a scene from far above, as if she's some omniscient being watching tiny figures reenacting that fateful night in miniature.

Her fury. Her choice of words to Alex.

Alex, leaving her house.

Heading back to the estate.

Drinking and snorting whatever he did.

Taking his mum's car keys.

Putting his foot on the accelerator.

Lindsay Smith, saying goodbye to her friends.

Leaving the Queen's Head.

Walking, choosing her pace, passing the darkened Spar and the fluorescent lights of the twenty-four-hour chemist.

Stepping out onto the zebra crossing as Alex's headlights approached and didn't slow.

When you think of it like that, what are the chances of it happening? Infinitesimal, that's what they are.

Their whole lives, she and Alex have asked themselves until they've been blue in the face: *what if?* What if he'd left five minutes later? Five seconds later?

But now, she asks herself, what if he and she both learn to accept it? To move on, finally? Alex will never yield responsibility for what happened to Lindsay, and he shouldn't. But perhaps he can stop the endless asking *what if?* Perhaps he can accept *what is*.

If he can finally make peace with what's happened, and his role in it, and the fact that he has done his time, served his sentence, then perhaps he can learn to accept this second revolution in the wheel of his life, this opportunity that he and she have been given to pick up their love story again. Perhaps he can shift his perspective to see that this reunion is miraculous, and that it must be a sign from someone, somewhere, that he's deserving of happiness. Then was then, and now is now. Maybe it's time to drop the past and move forward.

29

2019

Work. It's what's kept him sane over the past two decades. It's the only thing that really takes his mind off the unbearable burden of having ended Lindsay's life and having ruined Clara's. And it's going to have to save him now, too, because he's never needed it more. It's so fucked up. He had Clara back in his life; his angel, whom he dreamed of for so many years, was here and she gave so much of herself to him and offered even more, and he couldn't take it.

His possible future shimmers before him. A future shot through with love and happiness and the chance of a family, and yet it feels as impossible as if he'd never found her again. He will not be that guy. He cannot be the guy who breaks up a family and deprives two kids of the chance to grow up with both their parents. His mum would be so ashamed of him. He's put her through so much already, but this would kill her.

And so he works. He knuckles down, much to Connor's relief, and he refocuses on the people who actually need him, the people he might help. Clara doesn't need him. She thinks she does, but all he's done since he showed up again is fuck her up, and mess up the life she's built for herself.

He spends a few days up in London, shooting Good Morning Britain and hosting a massive charity fitness event that HSBC has put on in Tower Hamlets. And he enjoys himself. He draws so much energy from the faces of the people around him as he shows them the power of movement. Kids; pensioners, people who could do with losing up to half their body weight. Their faces are beautiful. They show courage and pain and resilience and surprised joy and, best of all, that priceless look of pride and satisfaction when they complete a workout they didn't know they were capable of. Clara was right. The humanity he witnesses through exercise is everything. She should be here to photograph this. She would love this.

Evelyn showed him some photography Clara had done for Sorrel Farm's foundation, which runs school trips to the farm to educate kids on ecology and biodynamic farming. The photos are breathtaking. The children's faces, alive with glee as they get stuck into the soil, are priceless. One shot, of the quiet awe she captured on a little lad's pale face as he bottle-fed a lamb, choked him up especially. She has an undeniable talent for conveying the human experience through her lens.

'We should make the charitable section of the site much more prominent,' he tells Connor later. 'We should have had Clara there today.'

He's crashing at Connor's pad in Victoria Park, which has the added benefit to him of getting to spend time with Connor's partner Nikki and their three kids. Thankfully, Connor and Nikki have given Mum grandkids. God knows she deserves to know the intense happiness of grandparenting, and God knows, he's fucked up his personal life beyond all belief. They're sitting at the kitchen table, finishing off a bottle of red and browsing through his website. Nikki has taken herself off to watch Netflix in bed.

'If you hadn't fucked her, and fucked her up, then maybe you could have asked her.'

'Give me a break, man. It's all very well for you to say—you're with the love of your life; she's the mother of your kids. Clara and I couldn't help ourselves.' He takes an impatient swig of what is an excellent Zinfandel.

'I know, mate.' Connor's tone softens. 'You know you did the right thing, right? Walking away was the only option.'

'Was it, though?' He doesn't know anymore. Walking away from her feels, in fact, like total fucking lunacy. He got her back, against all odds, and he let her go again.

'Fuck knows, I want you to be happy. But let Fiori go, for the love of God. You cannot break up her kids' family. You of all people should know that. Every single shitty thing that's ever happened to us, we've blamed on Dad not being there.'

'I know.' He leans his head heavily into his hands. Fuck. It hurts so, so much. He's gone around and around this dilemma in his head a million times since he let her walk out of The Stables. He cannot do it. It's too binary. He cannot demand his own happiness by destroying that of anyone else, and in particular, her kids. He's here to try to make some kind of amends for what he did to Lindsay and her entire family; he cannot wreck another one.

He scrolls absently through the website. Connor has put Clara's images up as huge banners across the top of the key pages. The Transform page, which was previously just a load of Before and After pictures, now has a banner image showing a couple of members of the Sorrel Farm class. He remembers that girl, who said she had a toddler, and that bloke who was on leave from the City who, God love him, was soaked with sweat about three minutes in. Clara got a shot of their entire row jumping in the air after their final chest-to-floor burpees, but it's those two whose faces are in focus, and their expressions are fucking priceless. They're exhausted and *euphoric*. He grins despite himself. She was right. Of course she was. The Transform page needed that bit of humanity. Transformation is not just about inches off the waist.

He clicks into the About Me section and comes face to face with his own stupid mug, which Connor has plastered across the top, but the look on his face makes him pause. He's lit up. His eyes are glowing green—they look a bit spooky, actually—but his expression is one he's never seen on himself before. Rapturous. Like he can't believe what he's looking at. He's transfixed. His lips are slightly parted and turned up into a grin, and he's staring intently into the camera, like he can't get enough.

So that's how she sees him, through her own eyes, through her lens. And that's what she does to him. He's a different version of himself with her. That's total fucking transformation, right there.

~

He shifts in the hard plastic chair and leans his elbows on the table. Today he's wearing bottom-of-the-range Nike jogging bottoms and a zip-up top, and basic trainers that he bought especially for these visits. He doesn't want to look flash in here. He wants to look as much like them as possible. They need to know that he's the same as them, that they can be him.

He's only been doing these sessions for nine years or so, since he made a name for himself. He's wanted to do them for far longer, but he was so fucking scared. The first time he came back here, to Cookham, the fear that built in him was like nothing he'd known since getting out: a claustrophobic wave of panic and horror hit him as soon as he set foot inside and smelt that unforgettable fucking stench. Fresh BO, stale BO on unwashed clothes, fags, cabbage, shit, and the industrial cleaner that never quite masked the other smells. Instantly, he was once again the terrified kid they locked up.

He really struggled that day, and the next few times he went in. He had to draw on all his Tibetan training not to lose the fucking plot. Breathe slow. Deep. Even. Choose your reaction. That was then. This is now. You can walk out of here in an hour, mate. You can do this. Helping them is more important than being comfortable.

Now, he fucking loves it. He loves being confronted with how low he was, because it means he takes nothing about his cushty existence these days for granted. He loves hammering home to these kids that if he could salvage some sort of life for himself, then they can. Above all, he loves telling them they have a worth. That they are seen. That they are better than whatever they've done to bring them here.

He visits a Young Offenders' Institution twice a month, usually in the South East. Cookham Wood and Rochester are his most regular destinations, but he's been up to Reading and Aylesbury a few times, and even Brinsford in the Black Country. He has plans to go up to Deerbolt in Durham next month. He doesn't do workouts, though the conversation almost always leads to keeping fit, and how to get ripped in your cell. He's here to talk to these kids, to hear their worries and try, though it's so fucking hard, to give them some perspective that goes beyond their current experiences in lock-up.

Today, there's a skinny kid who's breaking his heart a little. He hasn't seen him before. He's got the unmistakable look of a former addict: gaunt, hollowed-out face, with skin that's far older and more ravaged than his biological age dictates. He's twitchy, too.

'What's your name?' he asks him.

'Kyle.'

'How long you been in here, Kyle?'

'Two months.' The kid wipes his nose on his sleeve.

'Are they treating you okay? Giving you what you need?'

He won't ask what he's in for, but it's clear he'll have needed rehab when they brought him in.

He shrugs. 'Spent a week in the infirmary when I got here, didn't I, while I came down. Now I'm just getting on with it.'

'When you out?'

Another shrug. 'It's a three-year sentence, so...'

Jesus. There's not much to say, except, 'Good man. Hang in there. Hopefully that means I'll get to see a bit more of you, yeah?'

It's fucking tough on addicts who come in. Even if they spend a week cleaning up in the infirmary, they get their hands on all sorts of stuff as soon as they're in the main wing. He'd put money on Kyle being on something; he's way too twitchy to be two months clean. When Alex was banged up, he saw all sorts of addicts drying out, their withdrawals adding a whole other element of pain to the horror of adjusting to life inside. He could empathise. He was an addict, too. Adjusting to life without Clara was so fucking painful, the agony felt physical. He climbed the fucking walls in there. He wanted to crawl out of his skin. The withdrawal symptoms never fully went away. He's never been fully clean. And he went back for another hit, and look what's happened. He's a fucking mess again; every cell in his body screams out for her, constantly.

The young blokes move the conversation back to Alex. This happens a lot. He's here to talk about them, but of course they're desperate for distraction, and he's an exotic entity: a bona fide celebrity who was once in their shoes. They tend to ask all sorts of inappropriate questions that he can't in good conscience answer: how often he gets laid; how much money he makes. The worst was a couple of years ago when he briefly dated a glamour model. Some of them had read the *Sun*, and they were far more interested in asking him about her than in hearing anything he had to say.

This group, thankfully, is more interested in what his experiences at Cookham were like, twenty years previously, and how he got his big breaks. He repeats his usual advice on coping mechanisms.

'Don't worry about what the others say is wanky. You can be sure that if people call it wanky, it's good for you. There's no point talking about nutrition in this place; I remember the state of the food.'

This earns a laugh.

'But any other tools you can master—breath work, exercise, yoga, meditation, will help you. No one here is short on time. These things will help you cope, they'll help you accept your circumstances, and they'll calm you down when things get out of control and you feel like you're going to explode, okay?'

'What about wanking?' some wise-arse shouts out, and Alex grins.

'That definitely helps, too. And see the people who love you as much as you can.'

'Fuck, I miss my missus,' says one guy, who's previously introduced himself as Gez.

'I know, mate. It's so tough. I had a serious girlfriend when I came in, but I didn't let her visit me. Ever, not in two years.'

'Why the fuck not?' Gez asks. 'You must have been mental not to see your missus.'

'It was too hard. I didn't want her to see me like this, and I definitely didn't want her coming to this place. And I was so ashamed of myself, man. I told myself I didn't deserve to see her. I just wanted her to forget me and get on with her life.'

'But you was in an accident, right?' Another kid pipes up. 'You killed someone accidentally.'

'I hit a woman, a young mother, with my mum's car when I was off my face. And I killed her. I didn't mean to, but it was all my fault, and I deserved to go down. I fucked up very, very badly.'

'Look who you're talking to, man.' It's Gez again. 'We've all fucked up. Kid arrived last week; killed his little sister. *On purpose*. They've put him in the Ding Wing, for now. You're not like him. You were a kid who fucked up. It happens.'

'Yeah, but I needed to take responsibility for what I did, then and now. I can't ever let myself forget what I did.'

'You did take responsibility, man.' It's Kyle, his voice quiet. 'You did your time. It's been twenty years, innit? You need to get over it. Fuck's sake. '

It's unhelpful of him to even hint at his current demons in front of these lads. Right now, they're so deep in the vortex of shame and frustration and pain that they can't see a way to the other side of these walls. They want to hear about his wonderful life of fame and fortune. They need to hold him up as a poster child for what's possible when they get out. It's not fair for him to even suggest that in two decades' time, they'll still be haunted by what they did. He needs to do a better job of bigging them up and keeping his fucking demons to himself.

He can't quite articulate why Kyle's unlikely absolution, from a scrawny kid with a whole host of problems of his own, makes him sob into his pillow like a baby when he's back at Sorrel Farm that night.

30

2019

The Oast House is transformed into a sensory paradise of red and pink for Sorrel Farm's Heart Ball: a white-tie event for the British Heart Foundation. Round tables dot the space, swathed in red or pink cloths, their centres bursting with silver candelabras, tapered candles, and bowl after silver bowl of peonies, roses, anemones and ranunculus. Huge, tumbling arrangements of the same flowers punctuate the sides of the room, and between them, the banks of glass doors reflect back the twinkling candlelight. Hundreds of red and pink and white helium balloons jostle up on the double-height ceiling, their strings suspended prettily below them. Guests gather in clusters, pink champagne in hand, and their laughter rises above the soft crooning of the band's saxophonist. Despite herself, despite her nerves, Clara is enchanted.

She and Jeremy have purchased a table with Rick and Abi and some other friends from school and the golf club. Abi organised it ages ago and cajoled them all into parting with hundreds of pounds and giving up an evening for a format Clara has long outgrown: the endless, silver-service dinner followed by charity auction and dancing. But there is something magical about getting ready to go out to a formal event, and at least at Sorrel Farm the food is guaranteed to be good: no plasticky chicken for them tonight. Jeremy looks particularly handsome, in a patrician sort of way, in his white tie. He's like a character from an Evelyn Waugh novel.

The main reason for her emotional turmoil, though, is that Alex will be here. Evelyn pulled her aside last week and told her apologetically that he was confirmed to come alongside some other celebrities. It would be a big pull for the charity, she explained. At least Clara's not on photography duty tonight; she plans to stay well clear of him and his famous, glamorous chums, whoever they are. It's been a couple of days since her talk with Zoe, and she wants to sit Alex down and speak to him properly, but tonight's not the night for a chat about predestination versus free will. She hasn't heard from him at all since she stormed out of The Stables. Neither of them have made any contact. Two weeks, five days and... about six hours. Not that she's counting. Not that she's been crawling out of her bloody skin since she left him. She's sat on her hands every day, desperate to hear from him but refusing to sell herself short by going back to him on his terms which, as far as she can tell, are just very, very good sex. That's all he seems capable of offering her, and it's not enough.

She adjusts the fabric of her dress. It's a few years old, but it stands the test of time: a red silk panelled Amanda Wakeley number, old-school glamour with the ultimate in corsetry which means she doesn't need to suck her stomach in all night and her boobs look like they've been served up on a platter. Jeremy has already expressed his surprise that she can still fit into it. She takes a large mouthful of champagne. She'd better not drink too much, but God knows, she needs some Dutch courage. Her plan is to stick close to Abi, whom she's charged with keeping her in check: no mooning over Alex, no approaching him, no embarrassing displays of emotion.

Jeremy, Rick and another friend, Jimmy, are arguing about who's had the most lessons with the golf club's new pro so far.

'You look amazing, C,' Abi murmurs as they zone out of the conversation and people-watch. 'It's really not fair, how gorgeous you are. Your tits are the star of the show tonight. Alex Molloy won't know what's hit him.'

'If it was just about my boobs, he'd have a ring on my finger already, believe me. But yours are looking fabulous too.'

Abi made Rick buy her a boob job and tummy tuck for Christmas a couple of years ago. Apparently, they both agree it's the best money they've ever spent. Hers are standing to attention, jaunty and unsupported, in a black, strappy Valentino dress that formed part of an enormous Net-à-Porter delivery last week after Abi declared she had nothing to wear for the ball.

There's a buzz of commotion, and Clara's head jerks back towards the entrance of the event, where Evelyn's had a step-and-repeat wall set up for photographs, covered in British Heart Foundation logos.

'The celebs are here!' Abi squeals excitedly, and puts her arm around Clara's waist. 'Ohmigod, it's *Jackson James*! Holy shit!'

Clara laughs. Abi's uncool enthusiasm is infectious. Jackson James is a British action film star who's made it huge in Hollywood, thanks to his *Adrenalin* movie franchise. He's all shaven head and cheekbones, not unlike Alex really, except that this guy really is built like a brick shit-house—he could make Alex look willowy.

'And there's Honor.' She gestures subtly with her champagne flute. Jackson's wife, Honor Chapman, is a former morning television presenter whom Jackson met and, legend has it, charmed, on her studio sofa. She now runs a successful cosmetic line. She must be a similar age to Clara, but she's like a creature from another planet: coltish and delicate in a white dress that offsets her glossy auburn hair perfectly as she poses with Jackson for the photographers. She must get a better, closer look at her later.

Abi reads her mind. 'We'll have to stalk her later. Maybe we can follow her to the ladies' room.'

'Totally agree.' They laugh. Then—shit. It's Alex.

He's so handsome, it makes her head spin. His clothes these days are a big upgrade from the Umbro crap he used to wear when he was sixteen, but seeing him in white-tie is another level. Unlike Jackson James, who looks like he may go all Incredible Hulk at any minute and burst out of his dinner jacket, Alex is a true bloody clothes horse. He's *breathtaking*. She's too far away to see his beautiful eyes, but she can tell he's 'on'—this is the version of Alex's persona the public gets access to. He grins at the photographers, teeth gleaming, bantering with them, looking like he does this every day of his life.

And the absolute worst bit is that his arm is draped around a breathtakingly beautiful woman, gazelle-like in a sheath dress of palest pink, with the most lustrous mahogany skin Clara's ever seen. Her collarbones positively gleam above the dress. She's almost as tall as Alex, but she's so slim and delicate, she looks like she could snap. She's absolutely stunning. Her hair is pulled tightly back to showcase her flawless bone structure, and shoulder-length earrings sparkle against her skin. She can't be more than thirty, and she's Clara's complete physical opposite, and she's on Alex's arm. She must be a model—she's got to be.

'Oh, crap.' Abi's arm tightens around her waist. 'Shit. You ok, C? That guy is so hot, it should be illegal. I can't imagine how you're feeling right now, hon.'

There's a jostle among the photographers as Alex's date moves away from the wall and Jackson James comes back and throws his arm around Alex's shoulder. He goes in for a theatrical kiss on Alex's cheek, before releasing him; they both then stand shoulder to shoulder, arms crossed, grins blinding. The kiss is likely the shot that will make the papers tomorrow morning. They're both so handsome in their white tie—creatures from another planet. Clara had no idea Alex knew Jackson James; he never even mentioned it. She stares blindly as Alex and Jackson move on and Seb Macleod takes their place with a handsome guy who must be Gino, his boyfriend. Alex disappears into the crowd and she blinks and turns to Abi.

'I feel like I want to die. I shouldn't have come.'

'I know. But I'm going to look after you, and we're going to make sure you have a good time. We haven't danced for ages! I just can't believe he brought Ronnie Stewart.'

'Who?'

'That girl Alex is with. That's Ronnie Stewart. She's a yoga teacher. She has, like, four million YouTube subscribers.'

'Oh, for fuck's sake.' Of course she's a yoga teacher. It makes sense—she looks all lithe and limber. She can probably contort herself into a pretzel for Alex. She remembers his comments about liking dating people in the public eye. She hopes to God this is just a publicity stunt, a date of convenience.

Dinner is miserable for her, despite the delicious food and excellent wine: miserable and interminable. It's saved only by Abi, who proceeds to get very drunk. With each drink her indiscretion grows, and soon they're all howling over her revelations about various parents from school. The other people at the table are fine; they're all close in the way that having had kids at the same school for eight years has made them, but they're not what Clara would call kindred spirits. Her conversations with them tend to revolve around school logistics and parental struggles: common ground for all of them. She could never imagine herself having ecstatic conversations about why she prefers Sargent to Gainsborough, or why the Frick is the best museum in New York, or why the classics beat contemporary literature every time for a cracking read. They don't feed that part of her that's been hungry ever since she left the National Gallery: the part of her soul that needs to feast on the output of the most creative minds in history.

After dinner, she's forced to watch the live auction, which is held by an auctioneer from Christie's. Jeremy bids on, and wins, a round of golf for four down at Royal St George's in Sandwich. He's thrilled with himself. There's a lot of money in this room, but the highest-value lot of the night is lunch with Jackson James and Honor Chapman at Scott's in Mayfair, which fetches eleven thousand pounds. A gym-honed forty-something woman at the next table wins a one-on-one personal training session with Alex, for the princely sum of six thousand pounds. She smiles like the cat who got the cream, and Clara wants to slap her.

There's a brief lull when the auction finishes, and they reshuffle their positions at the table so the husbands can catch up on one side and the wives can gossip freely on the other.

'I wish I could have afforded a bid on Alex Molloy,' says Karen, a slim brunette with a predatory manner who's actually harmless enough. 'Jesus Christ, that man is divine. Though I would have had to take a hundred TRX classes to get into shape for him.'

'Clara knows him, don't you, C?' Abi shoves her with her elbow.

'Shut up.' Clara shoots her a death stare.

'They've been *working together*.' Abi annunciates her words carefully. She returns the death stare with a cheerful wink. 'Clara's been doing some photography for him.'

'Oh. My. God.' Karen slams her hands on the table. 'I can't believe this! Tell me *everything*, you lucky bitch.'

'Well, speak of the devil,' Abi drawls. 'Look who it is.'

Clara follows her gaze, and the bottom falls out of her stomach as Alex approaches their table. He's taken off his jacket and undone the top two buttons of his dress shirt. His white tie hangs around his neck, exposing a deep V of skin that she just wants to run her mouth down. He has never, ever looked so beautiful, and the look he's giving her right now is up there with the best, most charged, most intoxicating looks he's ever given her. Her red dress is a rag, and she experiences a sharp jolt of shameful satisfaction that her outfit choice is having the desired effect on this particular bull.

He comes right around to between where she and Abi are seated, and she puts her napkin on the table in a hurried, flustered move and pushes her chair back so she can stand up. His hands go to her bare shoulders and he kisses her: first cheek, second cheek. So slowly. So deliberately. And as his face moves next to hers, she closes her eyes briefly and drinks in his scent, including that heady cologne that has now formed part of her experience of him. He pulls away and there's a moment where a million unspoken sentiments flash between them, before he puts his 'on' face back on and shoots her a blinding smile.

'I didn't see you bidding for the PT session with me.'

'You'd have to *pay* me six grand to work out with you. Or more. You're a maniac.'

Abi is tugging at her dress, and so she begrudgingly drags her eyes from Alex's and introduces him to Abi and Karen and the other women at the table, and he completely dazzles them: she can see it on their faces and in the raised pitch of their voices and in the arc of their bodies; they're like sunflowers to his rays, moths to the heat of his flame. Who can blame them? He's peerless.

And then he turns back to her. 'I'd love to meet your husband.' His tone is even, but there's menace in his eyes.

She narrows hers at him before smiling sweetly. 'Of course.'

As she watches Alex shake hands with Jeremy, and then with the other guys at the table, she can't help but compare them. Jeremy is always completely at home in these social situations, but Alex has something else: a gravitas and a self-sufficiency that sets him apart from everyone else in the room. She recalls Jeremy referring to him as a thug. It's laughable. He looks a million dollars, and he's gone through shit that none of the entitled pricks at this table—her husband included—could even imagine, and got himself *here*. Jeremy has miraculously warmed to Alex as he, Rick and Jimmy indulge in alpha-male banter with him in front of their social acquaintances on the surrounding tables. Funny, that.

31

2019

Alex slaps Jeremy on the shoulder in a manly fashion. 'D'you mind if I borrow your wife, mate? There's someone I want to introduce her to.'

'Be my guest.' Jeremy is all smiles.

'Excuse us.' Alex puts his hand lightly on her waist and steers her away. As they weave between the tables, he murmurs a stream of angst in her ear. 'I've missed you so much. So fucking much, I can't tell you, angel. You look stunning. You're the most beautiful woman in this room by a million miles.'

She's not, obviously, but she doesn't doubt that he believes it. And she's still furious with him for being so utterly pig-headed.

'I missed you too,' is all she will give him.

His hand tightens on her waist.

'Who do you want to introduce me to, or was that a ploy?'

'No ploy. Jackson.'

'Jackson? You want *me* to meet Jackson James?'

'Nope, I want him to meet you.'

'Why? How do you guys even know each other?'

'I'm his trainer. I've trained him for years.'

'You built those muscles?' she asks, and he laughs.

'Yep. But he did the work himself. That guy has discipline like no one else I know—when it comes to his body, anyway; he's far less disciplined where women are concerned. But we're very tight. He's always known about you; I've always talked to him about you, and I've been basically crying on his shoulder all the way through dinner. He can't believe we found each other again. He says he's not leaving until he meets the woman who's had my heart for over half my lifetime.'

She's charmed, flattered and pissed off simultaneously. She may be the one with the wedding ring, but it's he who has the insurmountable issues. He presumably thinks he's being noble by staying away, that depriving himself of her is one more penance on this endless bloody road of self-flagellation he seems to be on.

She thinks of the perverted nobility of Ellen Olenska's words to Newland Archer in *The Age of Innocence*:

I can't love you unless I give you up.

This is the crux of their own problem; Alex is presumably operating within a similarly fucked-up moral framework. He seems to think that if he were to go against all of these self-inflicted rules (killers aren't ever allowed to be happy; our happiness can't come at a cost to anyone else) then he would be paying too high a price for his happiness. It's impossible to swallow, but his words now are like a heavenly balm. For some unfathomable reason, knowing he's been suffering just as much as her helps.

They arrive at Alex's table. Evelyn's there, looking ravishing as always, with her fiancé Angus. She wouldn't have Angus pegged as someone who'd particularly enjoy hobnobbing with celebrities. But then again, he's so delightful that he probably gets on with everybody. Sure enough, he has his trademark charming grin on his face and an arm draped around Evelyn. They jump up to greet her, as does Seb. His partner, Gino, is absolutely gorgeous in the flesh. The white-tie dress code loves his Mediterranean colouring, and his gleaming black hair is slicked back from his face. He could be a film star, with those looks. She can see him standing at the helm of a wood-panelled Italian motorboat, the Med foaming behind him as he jets around Capri with A Summer Place by Percy Faith playing in the background.

'Clara's Italian too,' Alex says, as Gino kisses her. He too smells heavenly. Do all these guys patronise some secret apothecary somewhere, that rustles up otherworldly herbal scents for them?

'Only second generation. My parents run an Italian restaurant nearby, in Otford.'

'Best pizza I've tasted beyond the Amalfi Coast,' Alex adds smoothly, and she jolts with the reminder that this guy has seen so much of the world since she knew him before. His younger self had never left the UK.

Next up, he steers her over to Ronnie, muttering *She's just a mate, I promise,* in Clara's ear before making the introduction. She's even more beautiful up close, with skin that looks as though every inch of it's been painted with Touche Eclat. She's skeletally thin, though, and although very sweet, seems to be on another planet. Clara can't quite work out if she's on something or just very zen from all that yoga.

Finally, she's in front of Jackson James and Honor Chapman, and they both stand as Alex makes the introductions. Honor is mesmerising—Abi would kill for this moment. Clara finds herself doing a mental analysis of Honor's makeup, not that she could ever recreate such gorgeousness herself at home. She has neither Honor's face nor makeup skills. Her huge eyes are green flecked with hazel, and they're defined by creamy gold eyeshadow and some kind of liner that looks green gold.

Her skin must have a biological age of twenty-five: it's radiant and dewy. She's the sort of person on whom pale skin looks creamy and aristocratic, rather than gaunt and pallid. Who even has skin like that at this point in the winter? Sargent would have killed to paint this woman. Her auburn hair is pinned in an artfully loose chignon. She's just magic; everything about her is refined and luxurious. Her smile when she shakes Clara's hand seems genuinely sweet. Clara's possibly more chuffed at getting to meet Honor than Jackson.

That is until she puts out her hand to Jackson and he gives her the full benefit of his multi-million-dollar grin and pulls her in for a kiss.

'So this is the angel, eh? Fuckin' 'ell, who knew you actually existed?'

Alex punches him in the arm and shoots Clara an apologetic smile, but it's okay. It seems highly improbable that Jackson will end up shooting the breeze with any of her social circle tonight and spilling her secret.

'Well,' Jackson continues, 'it's wonderful to *finally* meet you, Clara. I've heard a lot about you, these past few years. Molloy said you were a knockout, and he wasn't wrong.' He winks at her and her insides do a little dance. It's impossible not to be charmed by this guy. It's no wonder he fronts one of the biggest movie franchises on the planet. Charisma pours off him in waves, and that *smile*!

'So.' He waits until Honor has made her excuses and sat back down next to Ronnie, with whom she's probably discussing extreme diets. 'You two have a serious history. I mean, I don't know of any other couple with history like yours. It's amazing. You could write a book about it.'

'We're not a couple,' Alex points out. 'But yeah, it's a pretty crazy story. I just wish it had a happy ending.' The look he shoots Clara is that of a lost puppy, and she reminds herself that they're in a room full of people and she cannot take this man in her arms, no matter how much she wants to.

'It does—it can. You found each other again, man. You're both adults. Your ending can be whatever you want it to be.'

'Spoken like a true child of Hollywood.'

'Hollywood would adore this guy and his story.' Jackson jerks his thumb towards Alex. 'They love an underdog. But you need your Happy Ever After with your beautiful leading lady, otherwise they wouldn't be interested. Seriously'—he turns the full force of his piercing stare on Clara—'I hope you don't think I'm speaking out of turn, love, but think about it. That ring on your finger doesn't have to be the final act of your story. You're young and gorgeous. You both had a shitty time of it when you were younger, from what I hear. Maybe it's time you put yourselves and each other first.'

~

'He seemed to be under the impression that I was the one holding back on us,' Clara says. He's steered her over to the bar for an Old Fashioned before he has to deliver her back to her husband. The DJ has started up and pop music is blaring; it gives him a legitimate excuse to lean right in to speak to her. Her breath is warm on the side of his neck as she speaks, and it's all he can do not to pull her in against him. To be honest, it's all he can do not to bury his face in her cleavage. This is a million times worse than the end-of-GCSE party. It was bad enough then, having to watch her get into her dad's car at the end of the night, but at least he got to show the whole school she was his on that dance floor.

Tonight she's in another stunning red dress that makes her look like a siren, but that's the only constant. Then, he knew he was unworthy of her, but now, he knows he can only be bad news in her life. Tonight she's wearing another man's ring and she'll go home and get into bed with another man and possibly fuck him. He can practically taste the bile that thought conjures up in his mouth. And to make matters worse, tonight he's more in love with her than ever and he's also more conscious than he ever was, in the prime of his youth, that they can have no future together.

'I didn't tell him you were holding back.' He accepts the tumblers from the barman and taps his Amex. 'I just told him you weren't going to be leaving your husband.'

'You know I would. You know I would do anything for you; I'd walk away from my whole life to be with you. Not my kids, obviously, but everything else.'

There's no doubting the sincerity in her voice, or in her face. He can't believe this woman, who was willing to put her life on hold for him and wait for him while he was in prison twenty years ago, and is now willing to walk away on the entire life she's rebuilt—to throw everything away again, for him.

'It's not going to happen, babe. I've told you; I can't let you do that. This is not the place for this conversation.' He looks around and keeps his voice low. 'Too many busybodies. We can talk about it during the week, if you like? Go for a walk? I'm in London a fair bit at the moment, but I'll make it work.'

'Fine.' She reaches for her drink, her mouth set in a tight line. She's categorically not fine. 'Do what you normally do and push me away. It's the Alex Show, right? You're saving the world, all by yourself, and God forbid you should let anyone help you. All you need is a bit of arm candy for the press, someone you can have no-strings-attached sex with after this and send home again in the morning.' She necks almost half her drink and slams the glass down.

She's impossible, and it's impossible to speak to her in this setting, when he can't touch her or make her see.

'You have absolutely no fucking right to say that to me when you are one hundred percent guaranteed to go home and get into bed with your husband,' he hisses, and has the gratification of seeing her look embarrassed. Unfortunately, the gratification turns to shame pretty damn quickly.

'I have no intention of having sex with Ronnie. I told you, she's a friend. Besides, she's fucking neurotic. She talked about her chakras the whole way through dinner.'

A small smile appears on her face, and she raises her eyes to his. That's better. 'I'm not going to fuck her, ok? She's emaciated. The only thing she ate at dinner was the wilted greens.'

'No chicken skin?'

'No. I ate hers. I wasn't going to let that go to waste.' It's on the tip of his tongue to ask her to promise him she won't go home and fuck that twat, Jeremy, but it's not cool. She's married; he knew what he was taking on when he allowed her back into his life.

'Okay, then. I believe you. I'm glad you don't fancy her, because she's my physical opposite.'

'Oh, you want to play that game? Let's talk about your husband, shall we?' He counts on his fingers. 'White.

Blonde. Posh. Obviously a public schoolboy. Could you have found anyone more different from me?'

'No.' Her voice is small.

'Was that deliberate?'

'I suppose so.' She studies the contents of her tumbler intently. 'It didn't exactly work out brilliantly for me, being with you. Jeremy was the safe bet. I knew he'd never—'

'—crash a car and kill someone, and end up in prison?'

'You're putting words in my mouth, but kind of, I suppose. I knew he'd never hurt me, anyway. I knew he wouldn't push me away.'

He stares at her until she meets his eyes. What the fuck has he done to her? He let her down so badly, broke her so badly, that she ran off and married some posh sap to play it safe. When he met her, she was top of the year group, insanely creative and full of fire. Now she's living a small, safe life and colouring painstakingly within the lines, because of *him*.

There's nothing he can say to make her feel better. She's made it clear the only thing she wants to hear from him is that he'll make a future with her. And he can't say that, do that.

She leaves shortly afterwards. With her husband. He watches them from the bar. He puts her coat around her shoulders and his hand on the small of her back as he ushers her out the door.

32

2019

The bottle of Johnny Walker Blue is half-empty on the table next to Alex. His head is in his hands. He can't stop thinking about the path Clara's life has taken. Sure, on paper she's done great. They seem comfortable, financially—her clothes and car are expensive. And she dotes on her twins. Charlie's a great kid, and if Violet's as much like her mum as she sounds... his heart hurts just thinking about what Violet must be like.

But at school, she was so ambitious—she used to tell him she planned to run the V&A Museum one day. She had a deep appreciation of and passion for art and culture that very few kids at that school had. And now, despite her talents, photography is something she seems to treat as a hobby. Sure, she's a mum too, but she told him she gave up her National Gallery post when she got engaged to Jeremy. Something's not quite right there.

She's doing fine, but everything Alex has seen in his nearly four decades has told him that *fine* is not why we're on this earth, and the horror grows that he caused this erosion of her fire and ambition and her ability to trust that life would reward you for taking risks. He damaged her faith in the world so badly that she went for the safest, most *appropriate* fucking life partner she could find.

A hand slaps his stooped shoulder heartily and Seb's face appears next to him.

'What the hell does Alex Molloy have to look so down about? Mind if I join you?'

He sits down heavily next to Alex and drains a water glass so he can pour himself a decent measure of scotch.

'Hiya, mate.' Alex rubs his hand across his forehead. He's knackered; he needs to drag himself across the courtyard and get himself to bed. 'Where's Gino?'

'Ev and Angus have taken him home—he's trolleyed. Ev's given me a key so I can follow them back later.'

'You're staying with them? Jesus, you guys really have it sorted, don't you?'

'I'm very lucky. Christ, this stuff is good. I'm madly in love, and I have an ex-wife who's my best friend in the world and who will always be an amazing partner in crime. Did I tell you she's coming back to join our board? It's not the same without her; I'm the face, but I just don't have the vision that she does.'

'She's rejoining the board? Doesn't she have enough on her plate, down here?'

'You try telling her that. She's relentless. I'll be glad to have her back. It was so much fun, building the business together. And I can tell she's had FOMO since she left; this way, she gets to stay involved without a massive time commitment. Honestly, mate, I'm glad we're not married anymore, but the business partnership was—that was something else.'

Alex knows Evelyn well from his associations with her and Seb over the years, and he's always been captivated by her. Her energy levels are incredible, but she approaches everything softly and from a place of fun. She's almost childlike in her boundless enthusiasm for new projects. He has a sudden, painfully sharp image of what it would be like to work with Clara. She'd wipe the floor with him, like she always did at school. Her eye is just as good in front of the lens as behind it. She knew instantly what was missing from his website when he and Connor were oblivious. Her photography is live now, and it sings. Collaborating with her would be so creative, so joyful. Doing anything with her would be joyful.

'You've got the best of both worlds, mate.' Alex feels suddenly teary. It's something about seeing the softer side of Seb, whose public persona is flippant and jocular and very, very slick. 'But you know what, you deserve it. You did the bravest fucking thing I've ever seen: you put absolutely everything at risk—your marriage, Eddie, your business partnership—to tell the truth about who you were and what you wanted. Honestly, hats off. You're a braver man than I'll ever be.'

'It was all a load of bollocks.' Seb leans closer, his tone conspiratorial.

'What do you mean?'

'I got stitched up. By the *Post.* They got pap shots of me and Gino kissing outside a bar in Soho, and they gave me a choice: I came out to them exclusively or they'd publish the photos. There was nothing brave about it. I just went along with what Ev and our PR manager told me to do, and I came out on the other side smiling. I'm a jammy bastard; it all just fell into place for me.'

'Holy fuck.'

'Yep. But do you know what's crazy? I'm not sure I would ever have been brave enough to take the leap and upset

Evelyn like that, but now I would never, ever go back. I'm going to marry Gino—we're looking at Positano for this summer—and Evelyn's so delirious with Angus. He's a great guy, and he makes her so much happier than I ever did, because he's besotted with her. And Eddie's cool. More than cool; he's doing great. We all got what we wanted, but I couldn't see that any of that would be possible and I just couldn't see past the fear of coming out, to Ev, to the public. All I could think about was how fucking terrifying it would be to jump, rather than what might be waiting on the other side.'

'Wow, man.' Alex shakes his head and pours them each another few fingers of Johnny Walker.

'Now you know. I'm a total pussy. I've had so much goodwill for coming out, and I don't deserve any of it. Not really. I've had everything handed to me on a platter, and I've always taken the path of least resistance. Not like you. You're my hero: what you've been through, and what you've achieved. Look at you. I hope Eddie turns out like you.'

'Stint behind bars aside, you mean.'

'Ideally, yeah.'

'I'm no hero, mate.' He puts his head back in his hands. 'I've fucked everything up so badly, and I've totally ruined the life of the only person I've ever loved. Nothing I've done has come to any good, and I feel like I'm on the fucking brink.'

'Jesus.' Seb's arm goes around him. 'I hope that's the whiskey talking. Tell me: what have you done? And who is she?'

'It's Clara Winters,' he begins, and he proceeds to tell Seb the whole, godawful story.

'So,' Seb says when he's finished his pity-party for one, 'let's see if I've got this straight. She's the love of your life;

you're the love of her life. You messed up once—big time; no one's denying that—and now you've found each other again. She's offering to leave her husband for you, and you have a real, proper chance of a future together, and you've says no because you don't think you deserve happiness—or her—and you don't want to break up her marriage. Right?'

'Yeah.' Situations are always so easy, so black and white, when they belong to other people. Seb's looking at him like he's lost the plot.

'Mate. If jammy, pathetic bastards like me are allowed to be happy, guys like you who've had a really rough fucking ride of it are allowed to be happy. Seriously, dude. I just told you how well my life has turned out after I took my big leap—not just for me, but for everyone else in my life, too.'

'That's great, but this is a different situation. I'd be breaking up her family.'

'You would, or she would?'

'Same difference.'

'Listen to me, mate. Do you know what the biggest mistake I ever made was? Not being honest with Ev from the start about the fact that I was gay. It was so presumptuous of me that now, looking back, I can't believe I kept her in the dark. That was what she was most furious about: I treated her like a child and I didn't give her a chance to choose for herself. It was her life too, and she had a right to know the facts, and I made it all about me. You're making it all about you! No—let me finish.

'You've just sat here and told me how furious she still is about you cutting her off when you got locked up. She's *still* not over that, and you've gone and done the exact same thing to her again! You've made it all about you and what you think is right, and you're really not listening to her.

'She's not a fucking nineteenth century chattel, mate,

where the guys get to decide who owns her. *She gets to decide.* She gets to choose her own partner, and her future. So she made a decision on who to marry, based on her state of mind at the time, and now she's found you again. And she loves you. You might think you're not worthy, but guess what? You're not the only one whose opinion counts. You've got way too much baggage to be able to tell whether you're worthy of her. You make her *happy*. She wants *you*. You're a fucking idiot if you make the same mistake twice.'

He looks into Seb's tired face as he exasperatedly slicks a lock of hair back off his forehead, and it's like a lightbulb has gone off, but the clarity is tinged with horror as he realises Seb is right. He's made all the decisions, both times, and both times he's completely discounted what she has to say and what she wants. She's so much smarter than him, and he's been so fucking patronising, assuming that her viewpoint isn't valid. What if it's all pretty simple? Maybe it's not about whether he thinks he's worthy of her. Maybe it's not about him at all: it's about her, and what she wants. Maybe it's about finally, after twenty-plus years of making her utterly miserable, giving her everything single thing she wants, and making her happy for the rest of her life.

~

CLARA WRIGGLES OUT of her corsetry, and her entire abdomen breathes a sigh of relief. How Victorian women did it, she'll never know. No wonder they were always having fainting spells. She puts on her cosiest pyjamas and practically crawls into bed. She was quiet the whole way home, but Jeremy, Abi and Rick made enough noise for all of them. They were all hammered. She's had a fair amount to drink herself, but all it's done is make her more sad.

Her conversation with Alex was highly unsatisfactory. That man is so frustrating. He's always been mulish, but the barriers he's put up since they were kids are so bloody impenetrable that trying to get through to him is impossible. Being there with him tonight, in a crowded place, and not being able to collapse against him was utterly exhausting. And she could see in his eyes that he was struggling similarly. Why he cannot get out of his own way, she doesn't know. She curls herself into a ball and hugs her legs; she wishes she'd had the foresight to put a hot water bottle in the bed before they went out.

Jeremy gets into bed and sidles up behind her. His arm goes around her waist and slides under her pyjama top; his fingers stroke her stomach.

'How's my beautiful wife doing?'

'I'm okay,' she mumbles. 'Tired.'

'That dress you were wearing tonight was very, very sexy. In the old days, we would have found somewhere to go and have sex.'

'True.' It is true; their sex life was pretty good back in the day, and Jeremy was never one to turn down the opportunity for an adventure. Unfortunately, it seems that tonight, Alex isn't the only bull whose fire her red rag has stoked. She dreads these moments, but she's managed to avoid sex with Jeremy as much as possible since she started sleeping with Alex.

He kisses the side of her neck. It's now or never. She's torn between self-loathing that she can sleep with two men at once, and the knowledge that it's easier this way; that she owes her poor, oblivious husband this at the very least, and that she can buy herself more time to work out what the hell to do with her life if she goes along with this and pretends everything's okay.

She sighs and rolls onto her back, and her husband of thirteen years begins to kiss her. And it's not awful. It's totally fine; she can go along with this easily. He bunches the fabric of her pyjama top higher, while simultaneously nudging the waistband of her bottoms lower. She sits up and tugs off the top in one go, then lies back down and lifts her bum off the bed so he can get her bottoms off. Then his head moves lower, down her body, and she has to stop this immediately because she absolutely cannot bear if he goes down on her; having an orgasm tonight, with Jeremy, would be a physical impossibility. So she pulls him back up to her face, and kisses him, and eases him inside her, and wraps her legs around him.

'Don't you want to come first, darling?' His breath is coming in sharp huffs.

'It's fine. I'm too tired,' she says, and it's at least partly true. And as he moves inside her, she shuts her eyes and lies there and wonders what the fucking hell has brought her to this place, where she can go through the motions of sleeping with her husband while feeling like she's betraying another man whose claim on her body and her soul precedes Jeremy's by a decade and runs so much deeper than any claim a ring and a piece of paper can possess.

Sex with Jeremy is fine; it's absolutely fine, and it's such a well-trodden path that doing it is easy. And she does love her husband. She *does*. They have years of memories and shared experience, and he's undeniably attractive—he's gorgeous. But it's terrifying to think that the same act with Alex is nothing like this. When Alex is moving inside her, and his skin is slick against hers, and she's wrapped around him or pressing down on him or pushing back against him, every cell in her body is alive and she feels as though every atom in the universe has conspired to bring them together.

It hits her in an instant download as her husband shudders inside her, his face buried in her neck.

This isn't what she wants.

Alex has ruined her for good.

And even if he won't let her in, he's made a mockery of what she thought was a perfectly happy, decent life.

She doesn't want to do this anymore.

33

2019

The last thing she feels like is a coffee morning at Abi's where everyone is intent on gossiping about the ball, but somehow, here she is, hoping they'll all bugger off home or to the golf club or the gym, and leave her to vent on Abi. The conversation has inevitably turned to Alex and Jackson, and their relative hotness. She can't blame them. It's a far more interesting topic of conversation than the latest letter from the school informing them of a fee hike next term.

'They're both gorgeous.' Karen takes a thoughtful sip of her oat-milk latte. 'But I reckon Jackson is dirtier.'

'That's only because of the rumours in the press,' another mum, Sybil, points out. She was at the ball, at another table.

'No smoke without fire,' Karen says sagely.

Clara remembers Alex's words about Jackson. *He's far less disciplined where women are concerned*. The endless speculation in the press about his fidelity must be true.

'I'd go for Alex.' Sybil has a dreamy look in her eyes, and she exhales heavily before continuing. 'He's not as ripped as

Jackson, but he's far quieter. There's something in those green eyes of his—he's like a caged animal. I bet if you got him into bed, he'd be fucking unleashed.'

Abi turns quickly towards the sink, and her shoulders shake unmistakably. Clara can feel the colour rising up her neck. Sybil has no idea how right she is. Unleashed is an excellent, inspired word to describe Alex in bed. She grips her mug and thinks about the intensity in his eyes when he moves inside her, the slickness of his hips when he rolls them against her and the incomparable sensation of being totally immersed in him.

'He might be gay,' Karen offers. 'He doesn't seem to do long relationships. He was in prison, wasn't he? He probably got turned in there.'

Abi mercifully rescues Clara from this hell. 'I'd go with Jackson. I reckon he's a dirty bastard. You can tell from that grin.'

'Do you really think the rumours are true? That he cheats on Honor? What the hell hope do the rest of us have, if even she can't hold her man?'

'Maybe they have an open marriage,' Abi says. Maybe she's far too busy starving herself and working out to shag her husband every day, so she just turns a blind eye while he sorts himself out. That marriage is a very valuable brand.'

'I'm with Abi,' Sybil says. 'And it's not just guys. We all go nuts when we think about a guy cheating, but you mark my words, a lot of the marriages in Year Seven will be toast by the time the kids have done their GCSEs, and it won't just be the husbands doing the leaving. The forties are a dangerous decade. Look at us. We've been married for long enough to feel totally secure, and a bit bored. Am I right? Or, if not bored, then definitely complacent. We're at TRX and spin class four times a week; meanwhile our husbands are growing paunches. We know we're only going to go downhill physically from here. Is it any surprise we end up shagging our tennis coaches while the window is open?'

'That's kind of what happened to me,' Karen admits, and Clara stares. She forgot Karen was on her second marriage. Her kids only joined the school in Year Four, so she didn't know Karen's first husband, but she and her current husband, Todd, seem great together. Totally normal. It's hard to remember he's not the father of her kids.

'What happened, if you don't mind me asking?'

'I was bored.' Karen shrugs her shoulders. 'I'd left the City, and was stuck at home with young kids, and he worked all the time. It was shit. I think if I'd gone back to work, it would have been different, but he was insistent that Annie and Alfie have one parent at home full-time. And once they went to school, I just snapped out of it. I wasn't prepared to put up with a shit life. So I retrained as a coach and went back to work, and met Todd through my coaching. He saw me. Bill didn't. Not rocket science. So I left him.'

Just like that. She doesn't deny Karen must have had her reasons, but she makes it sound so easy. Like exchanging an item of clothing. Comfort and ease and lethargy are such enormous obstacles to change. That's why Clara has never even moved banks, although she hates her bank. She just can't be arsed with the faff of it. But Karen, whose kids must have been small at the time, rose above that, and took charge of her future, and presumably went off and found herself a divorce lawyer. And made it happen. And even found a lovely new husband. And *told her ex husband that she didn't want to be with him*, and that she was taking her children and setting up a new life without him. How does she even function after something like that? But she looks perfectly serene as she sips her coffee and examines her nails.

She can't help herself. 'Would you do it again?' she asks Karen. 'I mean, if you got bored with Todd.'

Karen's eyebrows rise. 'Probably. But I think Todd's a keeper. I really do love him.'

Clara persists. 'It must be hard to know, though, what the tipping point is. I mean, obviously if he's mean to you, or he's a dick, or one of you falls for someone else, they're all clear reasons to get out. But if it's just a case of wondering if the grass is really greener, or whether life would be better with someone else, or just alone, it must be super hard to just walk away and break up a life together.'

Karen shrugs. 'I suppose so. But my view is that we only get one life, and if I'm in a marriage that doesn't make me ecstatic, then I want out. I have far too much self-respect to settle.'

Brave words. She has to hand it to her for knowing what she wants and going for it.

'I agree with Karen,' Sybil says, '*but* I also think it's a long game, marriage. It won't be fun and games the whole way. It's a commitment you make to be there for each other when you're old and incontinent and sick. I think the tough times define the quality of a marriage far more than the good times do.'

'Amen to that.' Abi presses her palms together. 'But that is also fucking depressing. Why can't we have both?'

'I do want both,' Karen says. 'I agree, cutting and running for the sake of it is silly. None of us wants to grow old alone. But if you can't have both in your marriage, then you need to go and get your needs met elsewhere. Life is definitely too short not to have lots of great sex.'

LATER, in her quiet kitchen, Clara sips a cup of tea (unnecessary, given how much coffee she drank at Abi's, but comforting) and concludes that Karen's generalisations about marriage and affairs fall wide of the mark. That isn't how it is at all for her. She married Jeremy in good faith, and before Alex came along, she was in it for the long term. But the awful, unbearably painful thing about Alex and her is that they *could* have it all.

Their love has survived two decades and more trauma than most people ever experience, and if he gave himself up to her, their *death do us part* would be the real deal. And the sex… the sex would continue to be desperate and greedy and charged and transcendent. And the profound connection between them would make every single, tiny thing they did, from school runs to washing up, magical.

She doesn't want to be single. She doesn't want to end up alone. She doesn't want to essentially single-parent Charlie and Violet. She doesn't want to shatter their stability. She's bloody terrified. But if she can't have what she knows is possible with Alex, then she doesn't want what she has with Jeremy. She'd rather have nothing.

Everything is different with Alex. If anyone told her, five or six weeks ago, that she'd be ready to walk away from her marriage, she would have laughed at them. But the inescapable truth is that she is different with Alex. She is herself with him, but he reflects this authentic version of herself that she shows to him back at her in a way that's radiant. Their colours just *go* together. It's as if her unfettered soul is a glorious cerulean blue, but over the years Jeremy has dampened it down to a sad, sludgy imitation of itself. It's lost its brilliance. Alex's soul is pure gold, when he lets it shine through and doesn't let guilt and torment dial it down. Together, they shine brightly, and their souls' rays intermingle to a vibrant, vital green.

Good Lord. Jeremy would probably have her committed if he could read her mind. But Alex wouldn't. He'd get it. He's always celebrated her arty side, which Jeremy sees as a little boho and weird for his liking. Jeremy tolerates it. Alex applauds it. She's had enough of being apologetic and not showing off her talents or taking them seriously. She knows Jeremy's proud of her—in the early days, he dragged her out to every corporate event he had—but she's always suspected it's her looks and gloss, and ability to discuss the latest exhibition at the Royal Academy in an intelligent fashion, rather than the very essence of her, that he's proud of.

What she's not proud of is that she's always gone along with it. It's not Jeremy's fault. Not at all. She let him get away with moulding her into the nice, quiet, cultured corporate wife he wanted. She's never called him out on it, never forcibly inflicted the full extent of her personality on him. The truth is, by the time she met him, she had a pretty jaded view on the merits of true, life-changing love. Because loving Alex had done nothing but fuck her up for years afterwards.

In Jeremy she found a decent life partner, a good, if not massively engaged dad (though a lot of the dads in their social circle are equally disengaged), a generous provider and a husband who gave her no complaints in bed. It should have been enough, and for years it was, because she had no expectations that she'd ever feel for anyone again what she felt for Alex.

And now, she doesn't want to do it anymore. She doesn't like it anymore. She remembers Violet's tantrums as a toddler, when she would throw her dinner (a previous firm favourite) off the table and announce in a steely fashion: *I don't* like *it anymore*. That's how she feels. That's what she wants to say. I don't *like* this marriage anymore. I want to *go*.

Where she'll go is anyone's guess. She'll have to do this in a sensible fashion, she'll have to do her homework before she goes up against Jeremy who's a bloody lawyer. The enormity of the mountain that stands between her life today and the freedom she knows she wants is enough to make her want to run to the loo and throw up. Legal. Financial. Logistical. Not to mention the heartbreak she'll cause, to Jeremy, to their kids, to Jeremy's lovely parents, who have always treated her as a daughter. To her parents, even. Jeremy has never made a ton of effort with them, but when he does see them, he's always incredibly charming, and they've embraced him happily.

She's breaking up her kids' childhood and family for purely selfish reasons. There's nothing technically wrong with her marriage. It's not like he's cruel or abusive. It's just not enough anymore.

'You're ending a marriage that doesn't serve you,' Abi tells her on the phone when she calls in a tearful heap. 'Yes, it's always a shame when there are kids involved, but you changed your mind. You made a decision based on what you knew to be true at the time, and now everything's changed; you've changed, and *nobody can make you stay in a marriage if you're not happy*. Remember that, sweetie. Marriage should not feel like prison. Everything else is just details.'

Marriage shouldn't feel like a prison. And now it does. It used to feel... inevitable. But she has rights. And she has options. She needs to hold on to that.

Abi's right. She's changed. Alex has made her blue again. Or green. Whatever. At least she's not sludgy anymore. She takes out her favourite sunshine yellow Smythson diary and writes down the things that, amidst all the mental crap in her head, she knows to be true.

I don't want to be in this marriage anymore.

I want a divorce.

I will never love Jeremy like I love Alex.

I will be more myself when I am out of this marriage, and by being more myself, I will be a better mother.

I want to work again. Properly.

I want to follow my creativity.

I want to be me again.

When she writes it down, it's all so clear.

She knows what she needs to do.

Except that they're supposed to be going skiing in two weeks. Her, Jeremy, and the twins.

So she has two weeks to pull this off, and ruin her kids' Easter holiday, and ruin her husband's life. And all so she can start again. Alone.

34

2010

Her phone rang. She ignored it. She had both twins sitting at their tiny dedicated table on some plastic sheeting in the middle of the floor. They were eating porridge and jam on toast and the sheeting already looked like a murder scene. One false move and she'd have to go shower again. She watched them as they attempted to aim the plastic spoons at their mouths. There were few things less appetising than watching small children eat. The porridge was already congealing on their noses, cheeks, chins, down the bibs that fully covered their upper bodies, and all over the table. She should just feed them in the walk-in shower so she could hose them down afterwards. They were revolting. But so bloody cute.

Her phone rang again. She risked a glance at the display. Maria. She made a *grrr* sound to herself and swiped to answer, hitting speakerphone.

I'm feeding the twins!

Turn on the TV! BBC!

Maria had recently given birth to her second child and was in that phase of her life where she relentlessly watched breakfast TV because it made her feel less like she was the only person on the planet each morning after a sleepless night. Clara remembered those days. Well.

It's carnage here. I can't.

Maria sounded breathless. *It's Alex! He's on BBC Breakfast! Seriously, turn on the fucking TV!*

Clara felt her pulse in her ears immediately. What the hell?

Ok, she managed. She scrabbled on the island for the remote and pressed the power button. Come on, come on. She hit *one* for BBC. And there he was. Oh, God. Oh, God. Oh, sweet Jesus.

Are you watching?

She was. She was watching, and gazing, and staring, and drinking him in like a bloody addict.

Yeah. Her voice was deflated, defeated. Because who had she been kidding all these years? She'd moved on with her life and she had a husband she loved and the two sweetest babies on the planet. But there was Alex, and he looked *extraordinary*. She'd always thought he was the best sight she'd ever, ever seen, but this was another level. He wasn't an effusive person when she knew him—he was pretty introverted, actually, and he kept his best smiles just for her. And they really were the best. But today he was glowing.

He smiled at the presenters: a huge, confident smile. She could tell he was nervous from the way he sat forward and bolt upright, and kept his fingers splayed awkwardly on his thighs, but he put on a good show. Watching him smiling and chatting with them was one of the most surreal moments of her life. Who was this guy in Alex's skin, who bantered with the presenters like he'd always done it?

He was gorgeous. So gorgeous. Seeing him in the (digital) flesh reminded her that his combination of features was her favourite ever sight. He still had a totally shaven head, and his bone structure was dreamy. His skin was luminous to an extent that was just wrong for a guy. And his muscles... her greedy, knackered, housewife eyes followed the curves of his biceps under his snug workout top and the way his shorts pulled taut over his thighs as he leaned forward on the sofa. She wanted to climb into the fucking TV and lick his skin. And his muscles.

She was so exhausted from processing the kids all day that she hadn't had sex in weeks, but if Alex was in front of her for real right now, he wouldn't stand a chance. She'd have him down on the kitchen floor in no time. In front of the twins, if need be. Nutella on those thighs. Peanut butter along his jaw. She stared and stared and stared.

It was a short slot to discuss a fitness event in Regent's Park that Alex would headline during the school holidays. She and Maria watched the rest of it in silence.

You still there? Maria asked when they'd moved onto the news.

Yeah.

You okay? I probably shouldn't have called you... I'm so sorry. I just got overexcited when I spotted him. It must be so fucked-up for you, seeing him on TV.

No, she told her sister. *I'm glad you called me. It's good to see him doing well.*

She'd known Alex was a rising star in the fitness world; Mum had sent her a few early articles about him in the *Kent Chronicle*, and his so-called 'tragic backstory' was included in every feature she read about him. He was gorgeous, and he'd remade himself. He was a dream for the press. And she was genuinely relieved he'd found a passion for personal training and an outlet for his athletic talents.

It just made her sad. Really sad. He'd always said silly

things about how he would hold her back in life if they stayed together, but look at him now. He'd left her, he'd walked away, and he'd never come back to find her. And now he was on the way to becoming a bit of a national treasure, she could tell, and millions of other housewives would be ogling him alongside her right now. He was public property now, and even after all these years, the feeling that he wasn't hers anymore had never felt quite this bloody painful.

35

2019

Alex hasn't been able to get Seb's words out of his head.

If jammy, pathetic bastards like me are allowed to be happy, guys like you who've had a really rough fucking ride of it are allowed to be happy.

You've gone and done the exact same thing to her again!

She gets to decide.

She wants you. *You're a fucking idiot if you make the same mistake twice.*

Fuck's sake. He whips the skipping rope around even faster. It's barely visible in the mirrored wall in front of him; just a blur of neon orange as it flashes around him. Jump jump jump jump jump jump jump.

When he's done, he throws himself onto the mat with a groan and collapses into child's pose, his forehead to the mat. When he lifts his head, he marvels at the stillness of the view in the mirror's reflection. This place has been worth the wait. He moved back in last week, and it's a relief to be away from the farm and know there's no chance of him running into Clara, or more accurately, engineering a way of running into Clara.

The mirrored wall reflects the full wall of bi-fold doors behind him. The studio and the kitchen extension are the only parts of the house that have been built from scratch. Right now he's staring out at a barren nut orchard, but once spring kicks in properly, the trees will be a vision. Clara would love them. Stop that thought. He's completely alone, and right now that suits him perfectly. It's what he needs, to be in this beautiful place with space to heal. But he suspects that novelty will wear off very quickly. When he bought this place, he intended it as a refuge, but now he can't stop thinking about what it's missing. What he's missing.

He knows what he needs to do since he woke up on Sunday morning with the whiskey hangover from hell. He's known it for three days, thanks to Seb's words ringing in his ears. He needs to go see Mum.

~

She looks well, when he drops in on her at her flat. She's still only in her early sixties, and she's always been a beautiful woman. He doesn't remember Dad, only has a few old photos to go on, but he always thought Mum was the most beautiful woman he'd ever seen when he was a kid. Until Clara seeped into his consciousness, that was.

Over the past decade or so, that tight, worried look that defined her face for his entire youth has faded, and she seems to be ageing backwards now. She's been able to give up cleaning, and she's been able to stop worrying about her pesky sons. He gets his cheekbones from her; he knows that much, and her skin is radiant now. Some fifty-year-olds would kill for that skin. She could have been a model. She could still be a model.

'My baby,' she croons in her warm voice, and cups his face in her hands as she kisses it. He smiles at the term. He's always been her baby. She's always held herself responsible for all the shit that went down, for not being able to provide him with a stable enough home life to protect him from the gangs and the drugs. For fuck's sake. As if anyone was responsible for Lindsay's death apart from him. Mum had a useless husband and two useless sons. She was the one who was owed an apology from all of them.

He's still making amends for his failures, even though he's never had to earn her forgiveness. She's walked the red carpet with him, and he's taken her to Cannes and even LA with him, but nothing will ever make up for the heartache she endured: knowing her son took a human life, and then knowing that his sentence was widely considered to be far too severe, knowing that her baby was dying in there. It was she who begged Fr Pat and Tom Evans to visit him frequently; it was she who tried unsuccessfully to have his sentence overturned or lessened.

He doesn't know where she's drawn her strength from all these years. The men in her life have caused her such heartbreak and suffering. Her resilience is staggering. She's always been his hero.

Her airy living room is a shrine to childhood photos: him and Connor, and Connor and Nikki's kids. School photos. Action shots on the football pitch. None of them with Dad. He takes a sip of his tea and puts his hand on her knee. Takes a deep breath.

'Guess who I'm back in contact with, Mum? Clara.'

Her face is almost as expressive as Clara's. She presses

her free hand to her heart and smiles delightedly. Yep. Clara's name has that effect on him, too.

'Clara! How did you find Clara?'

'Coincidence, really. Or fate. She does photography now, and Sorrel Farm—that's the resort I've been staying at—hosted a wellness conference with me last month and they suggested her to photograph the event. I couldn't believe it.'

'This is wonderful!' She's positively beaming. 'Is she well?'

'Yeah, she's very well. She's got twins—Charlie and Violet. They're eleven.'

'So she's married?'

'Yep.' He hangs his head, rubs his hand over his face. 'But I'm still in love with her, Mum, and she says she is too.'

The smile is gone. 'Alex.'

'I know.'

'Baby, she's *married*.'

'I *know*, Mum. Believe me, I've been torturing myself with that fact. I told her I couldn't break up her family, not when we all went through so much after Dad…' He trails off. 'But her marriage isn't great. Her husband doesn't really value her, not properly. She gave up her career; he just sees her as some kind of trophy wife. She's not as fulfilled creatively as she could be, and you know how creative she's always been.'

'Marriage is marriage, baby. She made vows to this man. More importantly, she has children with him.'

'I know. And I told her I couldn't do it, couldn't break up her family. But as a mate pointed out to me pretty bluntly this week, I refused to consider her point of view first time around, when I got banged up. I wouldn't see her; I cut her off. And she was devastated; she's told me how much it fu—

messed her up. My mate said maybe it's time I listen to her for a change, y'know?'

He braves a look at her face. It's the first time in years he's seen proper angst on it, and he hates himself right now for shattering her calm.

'What does Clara want?' she asks quietly.

'Me. That's what she says, anyway, though it's a massive decision to make in such a short time. And for her kids to be happy. She's a great mum, honestly.'

'Does she not worry that leaving their father will make them unhappy?'

It's the elephant in the room, and it's the question she must ask herself every day, if she's still mourning him as much as he's mourning her. He shifts uncomfortably.

'We haven't even got that far, y'know? I've dug my heels in so much; I've refused to even have the discussion with her. I've been so adamant that I won't break up their family. I won't be like Dad.'

The other elephant in the room.

'Your dad was...' She stops, sighs. 'I know I've always blamed every bit of trouble we've had on the fact that your dad left us. And I know it's been a big burden for you and Connor to live with, not having him around. But the truth is, really—it wasn't him leaving that caused the problem. It was him, full stop. He wasn't cut out to be a husband or a father. He was far too selfish.

'If he'd stuck around, I'm not sure things would have been any better. I don't know... you were both so little. But he drank too much and he couldn't hold down a job, and in many ways my life was easier once he'd cleared off. I don't think I've told you that enough. I didn't want to completely ruin your view of him. But maybe that was a mistake, because I don't want you to think all our problems were because he left us. Sometimes life is just hard.'

It's a relief to hear her say it. Dad was a disappointment, but his leaving didn't define them. He feels a rush of love for Mum, for her stoicism, for the shitty fucking jobs she held down, for the fact that she got both of them through school (well, nearly, until he got himself banged up) and kept the flat immaculate and always had food for them.

'Your life's been too hard,' he tells her. 'No one deserves that less than you, and you know how sorry I am for the part I've played in that. I don't know how you did it, when we were younger. Day after day, year after year. I don't know how you just kept going.'

She shrugs.

'You keep going because there's no other option. I had two beautiful, intelligent sons, and I wanted you to have the world. That drove everything I did. And look at me now'—she gestures around her—'in the lap of luxury, spoilt rotten by my clever, beautiful baby.'

She smiles at him. 'I have everything I want, but what do you want, baby?'

'I don't really know,' he begins, and she tuts.

'Come on, now. You have never, ever given yourself a break from the guilt. You're more Catholic than any of us ever were! I'm not asking you what you think you deserve. I'm asking you what you *want*.'

That she can see this is still the case for him is incredibly moving. And so he looks at his mum and he does her the honour of being truthful, and he tells her exactly what he wants.

'A life with Clara. A proper future with her, the future we should always have had. And with her kids. And maybe more kids, if she's up for it.'

‘Have you met her babies?’

He knows she means the word as she means it when she calls him *baby*—she’s referring to Clara’s precious, precious children, who will always be the people she loves the most, no matter how tall they grow.

‘I’ve met Charlie. He’s a lovely kid, very funny. I haven’t met Violet, but Clara says she takes after her—very studious.’ He grins at the thought of Violet. ‘So I already know I’ll love her.’

Mum reflects his smile back at him. ‘So Clara doesn’t know what you want, really?’

‘Not really, no. She knows how much I love her. But she doesn’t know I’m even entertaining the idea of allowing myself to go for it.’

Mum leans forward. ‘The thing is, baby. I was so scared when your dad left, even though he was a useless twat.’

He’s never heard her swear, ever. A surprised honk of laughter escapes him.

She continues. ‘I just felt so alone. I had to be the grown-up every second of every day and keep you two safe. If you want to do this with Clara, you need to be very, very straight with her and with yourself about what you can offer her. Otherwise, you’re asking her to take her two babies by the hands and jump into the unknown with them. She may not have the happiest marriage, in your view, but at least they all have stability and a home.

‘You need to know, before you mess her around and mess up her marriage, that you are ready to catch all three of those very special people when they jump. And you need to tell her that. Very, very clearly.’

36

2019

Clara is in full-on research mode this week, but her research isn't organised. It's a panicked flurry of googling divorce procedure and custody law and rifling through her and Jeremy's savings and investments and pension plans and mortgage liabilities. She's so lax on the financial side of things, and it's coming back to bite her. She has no idea how much money they have, or whether they could both live comfortably and provide well for the kids if they had to split everything.

There are a million questions in her head. He wouldn't try for joint custody, surely? No, he couldn't even look after the kids on his own when she was at the conference (she quickly shuts down an unhelpful visual of her in bed with Alex that weekend). Who'd pay the school fees? Him, presumably, as the main breadwinner? How can she find a decent lawyer through word-of-mouth when she's not ready to tell anyone except Abi? And worst: how the hell will she broach the subject with Jeremy? And how the hell will they tell the kids?

Alex's number flashes up on her phone, and she's

surprised by the mix of joy and resentment it ignites. She momentarily considers not picking up, but who is she kidding? She picks up.

'Hi.'

'Hi.' He sounds funny, out of breath, perhaps.

There's a pause while she waits for him to explain why he's calling her. 'Is everything okay?'

'I need to talk to you, angel. Like, a proper talk. Are you free now?'

She wonders what his response would be if she said, *Sorry, I'm busy trying to research how I can divorce my husband, actually.* Instead, she tries to ignore the thrills deep in her stomach and clears her throat. He wants to have a talk with her. God knows what that means, but it's an excuse to see him. It's like the sun just came out.

'Okay. Shall I meet you at the farm?'

'I'm not there anymore. I've moved into my new place.'

'Oh.'

'Should I come to you? I feel a bit funny coming to his house. Would you be willing to come over here?'

She definitely doesn't want Alex here. It would be far too weird. And the idea of checking out his new pad, of seeing him in his natural habitat, is like very ill-advised catnip.

'I'll come to you,' she says. 'Text me the address, and give me forty-five minutes.'

~

HIS NEW PAD is near Hildenborough, a fifteen minute drive, but she needs the forty-five minutes for a quick shower, a quick run of her tongs over her hair, a quick dusting of makeup and a quick change of clothes, including some very optimistic underwear. She can dream. He's texted her the gate code, and she punches it into the keypad and watches as very smart wrought-iron gates swing smoothly open. She steers the car around a curved drive, noting the massive rhododendron bushes, which will be glorious in a couple of months. This place is seriously grown up. Her wheels crunch the gravel underfoot and he pulls to a stop.

Holy shit. Holy shit on all fronts. A beautiful, square Georgian house in the most immaculate condition. A bare, gnarly sculpture of wisteria over the porch. Huge windows, with low, low sills. They must be incredible from the inside. A lawn sweeping down to a copse, and a body of water over behind the house. And best of all, Alex. Alex, standing in front of his majestic new home, his hands in his pockets, looking at her and then hurrying around to open her door before she has a chance to get out of the car.

He takes her hand and helps her to her feet and she's about to tell him it's all glorious, but before she can, he hugs her so tightly and buries his head between her neck and her shoulder and she can feel him trembling, and dammit, she's a mess again. *Each time, you happen to me all over again.* Each time, she's reminded that nothing else on earth compares to this, to him.

He shifts, and cups a hand around the back of her head, and lets out a huge, shuddery sigh.

'Jesus, I've missed you,' he mutters into her neck and she laughs, because, ditto.

He pulls his head up and holds her by the shoulders and smiles. 'Welcome to my home'.

There's something about that smile that's hopeful and naughty and knowing—what *on earth* is he playing at?

'It's stunning,' she tells him. 'I want a tour.'

'Come on in, then.' He takes her hand and leads her inside, and she's in house-porn heaven. Huge, square hallway with a black and white tiled floor, and a sweeping staircase with what is clearly an original banister, and a very elegant round table supporting a bloody enormous arrangement of flowers and greenery. It's all *gorgeous*. Before she has time to react, he steers her through a wide square archway into a vast white kitchen, and now she really does gasp, because staring her in the face from the other end of the room is a huge white and pink and yellow painting that she would stake her life on being a Cy Twombly.

'Is that a Twombly?' She points like a kid, and Alex laughs bashfully and nods. 'It is. But I prefer the artist at the other end of the room, myself.'

And he takes her by the shoulders and turns her gently around until she comes face-to-face with a cluster of box-framed sketches and paintings that are hers. They're her GCSE project of fruit and vegetable cross-sections: pomegranates, and oranges, and cauliflowers.

She can't believe her eyes. 'Are you *kidding* me?' She looks at him in amazement.

'You gave them to me, remember? Mum kept them for me. We found them a few years ago, when she moved out of the Jubilee. I knew I wanted them in my kitchen, someday.'

She's shaking her head. 'I never thought I'd see the day I'd hang next to Twombly. That's the sweetest thing I've ever seen.'

He drops a kiss on her hair. 'I didn't do it for you. I did it for me. You've always had a beautiful talent. I wanted to be surrounded by your art but you didn't give me enough of it so'—he gestures down the far end of the room—'I had to give Gagosian a call.'

She laughs, and turns her head so she can look up at him, and she finds he's smiling down at her, his eyes shining.

'Can we have a chat before I give you the grand tour? Or I'll lose my nerve.'

'Of course.' Her own nerves instantly go on high alert. As he coaxes a couple of coffees out of the Nespresso machine, she wanders down to the Twombly. He's far from being her period of expertise, and she's not exactly a contemporary art fan, but the painting is undeniably beautiful, hypnotic, even. She sits down on the plump sofa opposite it to better enjoy it. This would be a glorious place to curl up with a good book. The kitchen has bifold doors along the length of one wall, and it's airy even on a dismal day like today.

A moment later, Alex follows with the coffees. He sets them down on an aquamarine coloured, heavily lacquered coffee table. Whoever helped him put this place together had impeccable taste.

'So.' He sits and twists his body towards her, and she does the same. He takes her hand.

'Thanks for coming, angel. I'm not sure where to start, but I know I should have said this weeks ago. I was really unclear about what I wanted, and I'm sorry.'

A humming starts up in her ears. He can't possibly have brought her here for *closure*, can he? She can feel her heart rate begin to mount.

'What I'm trying to say. Ugh.' He squeezes his eyes shut. 'I'm fucking useless at this. Okay.' He opens them again, and gazes at her. 'I'm trying to say I love you. And you were right. We belong together. And I should never, ever have tried to call all the shots *again*. I can't *fucking* believe I tried to pull that stunt twice, y'know?'

Her heart rate is mounting again, but for a very different reason, and the humming in her ears is surely being caused by the blood that's rushing to her head as she attempts to take in what he says. She wants to ask him what he's saying, really, but her instincts tell her to stay quiet. Let the man speak. After all, what he's saying sounds very, very good.

'I still struggle,' he says, 'to accept what I've done, and the pain I've caused so many people. But what Seb rammed into my thick skull at the ball is that it's not all about me. It's about *you*, angel. I cut you off once and I'll never forgive myself for that, not now I know how you felt. You're far smarter than me, and I didn't listen to you. Twice. So if you want to be with me, then I am so fucking in, I can't even tell you. All I want is for you to be happy. Nothing else matters.'

He's offering her everything she wants, everything she's ever wanted, really. But she needs to hear him say it.

'But you want to be with me?'

'Of course!' His smile tells her everything she needs to know. He leans his forehead to hers. 'Jesus, are you kidding me? I want to spend the rest of my life with you. I've just got very, very good at saying no to myself. But I can't say no to you. So save me from myself, and tell me you want this, and I'll be putty in your hands. I promise I won't listen to my own bullshit anymore. God knows, I'm sick of the sound of my own thoughts.'

'I want this,' she tells him, as intently as she can, and she puts her mouth to his to seal the deal. There's so much more to say, but this kiss will show him more than words can. He presses his hands on either side of her face and trembles as his tongue touches hers and they kiss, dreamily, for a few magic moments before he pulls away.

'I have some things I need to say, angel.' His voice is shaky; his eyes search her face. 'Tell me if I'm coming on too strong. Right. Here goes.'

He clears his throat and she laughs to herself. As if he could ever come on too strong with her.

'I want to spend the rest of my life with you.' He exhales. 'Whew. I want to do it the proper way. I want you to divorce him and marry me. If you want to. I want to be a part of your beautiful children's lives. And I'd love more kids with you, if that's an option.'

She's crying now, and she opens her mouth to speak, to tell him *yes* to every bloody thing he's asking her and could ever ask her, but he puts his finger on her lips.

'Give me a second. This is really important. I know you're the one taking all the risks here. You have a husband, and kids, and a home. It's all great for me, but I know this is fucking scary for you, no matter how I dress it up. If this is what you want, I will be with you every step of the way. I'll find you a lawyer. I'll be waiting for you and Charlie and Violet if and when you make the jump. I'll come with you when you tell him, if you like. I'll give up my career and be a house-husband if you want to go back to the National, or try your hand at running the fucking V&A. I'll sell this place, if you and the kids don't like it.

'I will do everything in my power to make this as painless as possible for you, and I will never underestimate how much I'm asking of you right now. But I'm here. For all of it. I told you I'm here on this earth to make things good, and I can just about live with myself for breaking up your marriage, if you let me spend every single day trying my best to make your and your children's lives as happy, and as full of love as possible. And I should probably pitch myself to Violet at some point. Fuck. I'm a mess.'

She reaches up and, with infinite love, wipes away the crocodile tears cascading down his beautiful face. She has never loved him as much as she does in this moment. She's in awe of how far he's come, and how far he's willing to go to make her happy. She's in awe of his generosity towards her and her children, one of whom he hasn't even met. He's sitting here, holding her and offering her every single thing he can think of, and things she hasn't even thought of, to make her happy.

Their future together has always been so filled with potential, but now Alex has allowed himself to feel worthy of it, it's transformed from potential into fact. This is going to happen. It's their destiny. She's always known they deserve this, and now he's accepted it too. And his courage gives her courage. He's finally found it in him to demand what he wants, and it's about time she demanded what she wants, too. She doesn't doubt for a second that her children will be happier in the long-term with Alex in their lives. He'll love them as much as he loves her, and she can't think of a better role model for them.

'There's nothing else I want, ever.' She strokes down his temple, along his damp cheekbone. 'I want everything you're offering me. All of it. Don't ever leave me again.'

'I will never, ever leave you again. Everything revolves around you, from now on. We decide everything together.' He kisses her, slowly, languorously. God, this man is a ridiculous kisser. He can turn her to jelly with those heavenly, pillowy lips and that tongue. His hands smooth back her hair, and her scalp tingles with heavenly tension as he twists it into a rope and begins to wind it around his fist. He turns her head to the side and whispers in her ear.

'I think we should take the tour upstairs.'

She leans her head in towards his touch. 'Definitely. Show me the rest of our home.'

37

2019

They stumble around the house in a kind of three-legged race, arms wrapped as tightly as possible around each other.

'I'll show you the outside first, otherwise you'll never see it,' he says. The extension he's had built for a studio is stunning. It's a starkly modern glass cube that doesn't try to compete with the Georgian architecture of the house. Just outside it is a beautiful flagstone terrace and a large pool that's currently covered.

Alex tells her it's slate-lined. 'Hopefully we can open it up in a few more weeks.'

They both glance at the dense, grey sky and the barren trees and laugh. Spring feels a long way away.

Then they finish the ground floor tour: a double drawing room with two huge limestone fireplaces. Sculptural chandeliers and more art, mainly contemporary and modern. Huge sofas that look good enough to sleep a whole night on. A utility room of dreams: it's possibly her favourite room in the house. And Alex's study, white and minimalist. None of the accolades she knows he's won hang there;

instead there's a grid of identically framed photos on the wall, all featuring him with his famous clients. One catches her eye, and she thumps him on the bicep and gasps.

'Robbie Williams! You *didn't*!'

He grins at her. 'I was too scared to tell you. I knew you'd be jealous. I've only trained him once, when I was out in LA. That's his house.'

She groans theatrically. 'You're killing me! What was he like?'

'Fucking awesome. We had a great laugh. And I told him our story. He loved it. He actually shed a tear for us.' He kisses her hair. 'I'll find a way to invite myself back, one day, and I'll bring you. I promise.'

It's a ridiculous promise, and what makes it even more ridiculous is that he may well be able to keep it. Nothing about the rest of her life with Alex will be ordinary.

'I'll save the master bedroom for last,' he tells her smilingly as they head up the shallow sweep of the staircase. Instead, he shows her a couple of chic guest rooms, both ensuite, with marble wet rooms. And as they mount a narrower staircase to the top floor, he pauses.

'This can all be changed—the designers kept things very neutral up here, cos I wasn't sure what to use it for. But I thought it might be a fun spot for the twins.'

This is a huge attic space, airy thanks to numerous dormer windows, which features a low, white L-shaped sofa that looks suspiciously like Roche Bobois. Oh no. One hot dog, and it'll be ruined forever. There's a kitchenette with an island and bar stools, and a pool table. It's every teenager's dream, and it's incredibly indulgent for two little tweenies. Whatever difficult conversations and confusion and heartbreak lie ahead for her kids, this space will undoubtedly help to sweeten the deal.

At each end of the attic is a door, and behind each door is a large room with a king-sized bed and swanky ensuite. As Alex mentioned, they're neutrally but beautifully decorated. She turns to him.

'Who did you have in mind when you went for this layout?'

He shrugs. 'Just—you know—guests. I wanted to keep it flexible. But I thought it might work out well for the twins.'

His tone is casual, but the uncertainty and hope on his face hurts her heart.

'It's amazing.' She tells him. 'They'll go crazy for it.'

'There's one more room to show you,' he tells her, as they traipse back down to the first floor. It's a stunning square room with French doors and its own little terrace. It's unfurnished, but painted the most charming dove grey. The floors are stripped and the boards varnished to a high shine under an exquisite rug in muted blues and whites.

'I thought maybe you could build your empire from here. Paint, edit your photography, plan your world domination... you know.'

'I love it.' She sighs out the words. She cannot believe this man, and his generosity, and his thoughtfulness, and his love. 'There's a bit in *The Age of Innocence*—'

He pretends to roll his eyes. 'Here she goes again. Quoting Edith Wharton at me.'

'Oi. It's after Ellen and Newland share some precious moments in a little cottage on the grounds of his relatives' estate. Ellen says afterwards that it's the only house in America she can imagine being perfectly happy in.' She drops her voice. 'I feel the same about this house already.'

Her future shimmers before her eyes. *Their* future. In this house. With Violet and Charlie. Days and nights in all the seasons; swims and alfresco lunches in summer, and scrabble by the fire in winter. She can see it already, clear as anything.

~

THE MASTER BEDROOM IS *BEYOND*. She has to show Abi this. She would die. How has a guy managed this, even with professional help? It's incredible. The same lacquered floorboards as in her heavenly little Clara Room. A huge, ornate Louis Quinze fireplace. A massive bay window with a deep, cushioned window seat, and two more windows with floor-length curtains. A gorgeous, copper, roll-top bathtub in front of the fire. *In* the bedroom. Someone was paying attention at The Stables! The walls are papered with a fabulously bold blue-and-white print that must be Schumacher, and the chimney breast boasts a divine rococo mirror. And the bed! The bed is massive. Four posters in some dark wood, but no canopy. Classic, but clean.

'There's a bathroom through there.' Alex gestures. 'And a massive dressing room, which I can't even begin to fill on my own.'

He walks over to her and folds his arms around her, rests his chin on the top of her head. 'Do you like it?'

'I love it. I love every single detail. I can't believe we get to live here with you.'

'Good.' He kisses the top of her head, and she hears him inhale her hair. 'You can change anything you want. I want you to have some good art, too—my stuff might be a bit modern for you. We can go shopping for art together; you can educate me.'

'Shopping for *art*?' she murmurs into his neck. 'Seriously? You're turning me on.'

'Even better. Want to christen our bed?'

Our bed. Oh, God.

'I love you.' He tilts her head back and rains kisses down on her face. She closes her eyes. She's in Alex heaven, standing here with him in this beautiful home he wants to share with her, awash with emotion at everything he's just told her and shown her, and at the incomparable sensation of finally being alone with him after weeks of thinking her future didn't include him.

'I love you.' A deep kiss on the lips, tongue touching hers, before he moves to her neck and runs his tongue down it. She shivers in delight.

'I love you.' He peels up her sweater and she raises her arms floppily. Off it comes, over her head. Off comes her extremely gorgeous pink satin and lace bra.

'Jesus. I *love* this bra. And I love you.' He caresses her nipples before getting to his knees and laying his head against her stomach. She cradles his beautiful skull, marvelling at the feel of his scalp under her fingertips, at the sensation of his breath against her skin. He pulls off her socks and unbuttons her trousers and slides them down her legs, helps her step out of them.

'I love you. So. Fucking. Much.' His hands stroke her thighs, up to her bum, and she shivers again. God, this man. These hands. This mouth, kissing a line across the skin just above her pants. He slides his hand across her bum and stops abruptly.

'What the hell are these?'

She giggles, and turns around to show him her most decadent, naughty pants. They match the bra, but there's a hole cut out in the back and a satin bow holds them up. She *loves* these pants.

'Fuck. You are—' His voice sounds strangled, and his breath is warm on her arse. He licks down between the section of her cheeks exposed by the pants, and his hand moves up her inner thigh. He trails his fingers up, up, lightly enough that they leave a trail of fiery nerve endings in their wake. *Oh*. The anticipation is divine. She moans a little and widens her stance, and she hears him groan behind her, too.

'You're so beautiful,' he whispers. 'I can't believe these pants. They make me want to do seriously bad things to you.' His words are like kindling, and his fingers reach the satin between her legs and stroke it. Oh, God.

'Do, them, please,' she begs, and he rewards her with a lazy circle of his tongue around her exposed arse.

The pressure of his fingers is far too light, too teasing. He dips one finger inside the elastic and encounters her skin, and they both inhale sharply. He pulls it back out.

'Jesus, you're wet.'

'Alex, *please*.'

He kisses up her spine as he gets to his feet behind her. Gathers her hair up in his hands and twists it, laying it over one shoulder. The kisses continue over her shoulders, and she can't help it; she turns and grabs the back of his neck and kisses him. She's naked aside from these ridiculous pants, but he has all his clothes on. She pushes against him. There is no denying he's as aroused as she is. They keep their eyes open as they kiss, their tongues twisting desperately in each other's mouths, their breathing ragged. She breaks off the kiss to tug off his sweater and his t-shirt, smiling at the perfection that is Alex Molloy topless. She smooths her palms across his pecs and over the perfect curves of his shoulders.

'Beautiful, beautiful man.' She kisses his collarbones, one by one. When she looks up, he's watching her with a heartbreaking mix of love and desire in those green, green eyes.

'I love you.' She returns his words to him as she makes quick work of his belt buckle and jeans. She pulls down his boxers and takes his magnificent erection in her hand. 'Now, can we please make each other come? It's been three weeks and I'm going crazy.'

He rewards her with a guffaw of laughter and a jerk of his head.

'Minx. I want you on the bed. On your stomach.'

He chucks the throw pillows on the floor and she settles on the downy softness of the duvet on her front, her face to one side and resting on her hands as if she's sunbathing. She shuffles her legs wider and revels in anticipation as her naked, beautiful Alex climbs onto the bed and crouches on top of her. She can see him if he cranes her neck, and he drops a kiss on her lips before kissing his way back down her spine.

'Now, back to these pants.'

One hand strokes the satin gusset again, and she tenses and grits her teeth. *Control, Clara. You can do this. Enjoy it and don't wish for it to be over already.* The fingers of the other hand find the hole in her pants again and trail down the line of her arse. He manages to wiggle them further down inside her pants and finally they hit the place where she wants them, skin on skin, and she gasps and pushes into his hand as far as she can.

'This hole is just not big enough,' he drawls. 'Shame.'

He begins to untie the blessed bow, thank God, and he slides the pants down a little over her arse. His mouth moves over her cheeks, before thankfully, eventually, pulling them the whole way down her legs and flipping her over onto her back. She sighs in relief and drinks in the sight of him, crouching over her, naked.

Then, thank God, his tongue is everywhere, his fingers

are inside her, his other hand comes up to pinch and roll and press down on her nipple, and she comes so quickly and so hard that Alex has to hold her pelvis down while he finishes the job, and she sees sunspots where her vision should be when she opens her eyes.

'Get inside me, quick,' she whimpers and he's up like a shot, his mouth on hers and his arms wrapped around her like a vice. She tastes herself on him while she drowns in him, and lifts her legs so he can push inside her. And they're off, moving together as she wraps her legs around him. She grabs his utterly gorgeous arse and pulls him deeper into herself, and tells him *more, harder, harder*, because the dam has burst and from now on she's not afraid to demand what she wants.

There is nothing quite like this on this earth. There is no one else like him, no one who can make her feel this way, like sex is a sacred, magical, elemental act. And this is how it's going to be with him, day after day, year after year, for the rest of their lives.

38

2019

Afterwards, they lie side by side, face to face, the duvet wrapped tightly around them, like a two-person burrito. This is her safe space. This is her new home.

'You doing okay?' Alex kisses her on the nose. 'I've sprung a lot on you today.'

'Best day of my life,' she tells him. 'But you should know what I've been doing, the past couple of weeks.'

'What?'

'Preparing to ask Jeremy for a divorce.'

'*What?*' He pulls his head back. 'Seriously?'

'I didn't expect you to come around to the idea of us. But I knew, after I saw you at the ball, that I couldn't stay married to him. It just felt like a pathetic joke, after what I'd experienced with you. So I've been doing some research—trying to understand what my options are.'

'Angel.' He groans the word, presses his lips to her forehead. 'You poor sweetheart. So you've been doing exactly what I wanted to avoid? Planning to jump ship, all by yourself? Fucking hell, I am so sorry. I should have come to my senses sooner.'

'It's okay. I haven't actually done the scary bit yet—told Jeremy. And I haven't really got very far. But hopefully it will make you feel a bit less guilty, knowing I was going to leave him anyway.'

'Jesus. I am such a dick. You are so brave, taking that step as a mum with two kids. I'm just really sorry I haven't been by your side for the whole thing.'

She wraps her top leg around him, basking in a fresh flood of relief that she won't have to go through any of it by herself now. Alex will be there; he has his hands held out to her already and he'll hold hers tightly as she jumps, and she and Violet and Charlie will be jumping into *this*, this dream world.

The usual worries begin to creep back in, though. What if Jeremy goes ape-shit? What if he tries to get full custody of the twins? What if he makes things really, really nasty and the tension traumatises the kids for life? What if he tries to turn them against her? People can't still cite adultery during a divorce, can they?

And what if Violet just doesn't like Alex—what if she blames him for splitting up her family? She adores her father. Charlie might not be happy either. He loved meeting Alex, thought he was amazing, but that's not the same thing as accepting him as his new stepfather. A sick feeling hits her. She is doing this. And because poor Charlie and Violet are eleven, they have no rights at all and they have to come along for the ride. There's no way this won't mess them up, at least to some degree.

Finally, she has no idea how long this whole messy, awful transition period will take. If she had her way, she'd move them all in tomorrow, but of course she can't do that.

She needs to give the twins time. But she can't stay in that house anymore, not once she's told Jeremy. And the worst bit of all: they're supposed to be going skiing in under two weeks! They're obviously not going now—that decision is made for her—but it'll crucify the kids, and it'll crucify Jeremy. Clara's the only one who hasn't been counting down the weeks to this trip.

Alex tightens his grip on her, but pulls his head back. 'Spill, Fiori. What are you stressing about, angel?'

She swallows. 'It's fine, honestly.'

'It's not fine. You're about to make a huge, huge leap, and I know you far too well to think you're not stressing about your kids, because you're an amazing mum. So *spill*. Everything. That's what I'm here for. You are not alone in this.'

Thank God for this man. She takes him at his word and vomits out every worry that's been turning her brain into a washing machine. They're a different set of worries from the ones that were cycling through her consciousness up until last night, because she has Alex in her future now. But they're still valid.

He lets her vomit and holds her tight. Then he starts to talk, and his words are exactly what she needs to hear.

'It's going to be difficult, babe; no two ways about it. I know it is. But he's not going to try to get full custody. You've been a stay-at-home mum for years, right? It's black and white. And we'll get you an amazing lawyer to fight for you, okay?

'And there is no rush on this. I'll wait for you forever. Charlie and Violet are the priority. We go at their pace. I'll clear my schedule and spend as much time with them as they're willing to spend, and we'll have fun, and get to know one another, y'know? And we have to hope your husband is a decent enough father not to be a dick about this. But if you can't stay in that house, and the kids aren't ready to move in here, then we'll find you somewhere else for the time being. Somewhere nice for the next few months.

'And as for the ski trip—do you think Jeremy will want to take them by himself? If so, I'll whisk you off somewhere, just the two of us. If he doesn't, I can take you and the kids skiing. All these things are tricky, but we'll get over all of them. I promise you.'

'Okay.' She releases a shuddery breath and feels her entire body collapse into him as she allows herself to surrender her worries. 'Thank you. I needed to hear that.'

'We'll get there. I don't suppose your kids are open to hard bribery, are they?'

'Definitely. They're shameful. Like all eleven-year-olds.'

'I might have to give Jackson a call then, get Charlie on-side.'

'Oh my God.' She clamps her hand over her mouth. 'He'd die. You don't know Taylor Swift, by any chance?'

'Afraid not. But I have trained a couple of the *Strictly* pros. Maybe I can call in some favours for Violet.'

'She'll love you forever if you can get her a ticket to *Strictly* this winter. I promise you.'

'I don't know about that. But they're your flesh and blood, angel. I'd already do anything for them.'

'What made you change your mind about everything? You seemed pretty determined, the last few times we spoke. You mentioned Seb?'

His fingers trace the discs of her spine. 'I love your skin so much. Um—some good advice, really, from people far wiser than me. Seb, yeah, and Mum. Mum gave me her blessing, really. Told me Dad was useless even when he was around, and we couldn't blame everything that had gone wrong in our lives on him leaving. She told me that if I was going to let you do this, I'd damn well better be there every step of the way to hold your hand.

'And Seb told me the worst crime he'd committed by not coming out earlier was keeping Evelyn in the dark. He said that by not being straight with her, he'd basically called all the shots. And he pointed out that I'd done the same to you once already, by refusing to let you see me when I was inside and not taking your needs into consideration at all, and he told me in no uncertain terms that I'd be a fucking idiot if I made the same mistake twice.'

She smiles. She tried to make the same point to him, but it's amazing how some people need to hear it from a third party for it to sink in. She'll give Seb a very big hug next time she sees him.

'Sensible guy.'

'Yeah. It hit me then, that it doesn't really matter whether I think I'm worthy of being with you. All that matters is your happiness, because I've put you through enough, y'know? I just want you to be happy every day for the rest of your life. And if it means being with me—well, I'm here to serve. Forever.'

He snuggles into her and presses the sweetest of kisses to her lips. This is it. She knew, the first time he kissed her behind Casa Valentina, that this man would hold her heart in his hands. And he has, for over two decades, and they've both bled, and suffered. For years. Enough is enough. All the promise they've ever held as a couple has come streaming and rushing into reality. The pain was then, and the joy begins now.

FOUR MONTHS LATER

Alex and her dad are arguing. Rather, her dad is yelling at Alex, and he's taking it like a man who's so in love with Vincenzo's daughter that he doesn't dare argue back. It seems Dad's not happy with the super-swanky top of the range pizza oven Alex bought for the garden, and he's particularly unhappy that it's not reaching the right temperature for pizza.

'How do you expect me to make pizza when you have a shitty little oven?' he yells. 'I cannot create masterpieces with this shitty piece of crap!'

Alex grins at him. It's water off a duck's back.

Mum pauses from swigging her third Aperol of the day to scream at Dad in Italian. Alex can't understand what she's saying, but she's telling him that Alex is far too handsome and famous and rich to take this kind of shit from the likes of him.

Everyone else just ignores Dad. She and Maria are used to him, and the kids are far too busy in the pool with their cousins and at least nine or ten inflatables.

Clara puts her arms around Alex's bare shoulders from behind and, standing on tiptoe, whispers in his ear.

'He just feels too much pressure, cooking pizza for you. Ever since you told him his pizza was all you dreamt about in prison, he wants every one he cooks you to be perfection.'

Alex groans and pats his perfect washboard stomach. 'My life would be far easier if he didn't make such good pizza. The Fioris are going to destroy my wellness brand.'

He's wearing fitted Orlebar Brown trunks in a pale, sea foam green, and the combination of them against his skin is pure poetry. He looks so hot, in fact, she wishes she could push him onto a sun lounger, and unzip them, and go down on him there and then. Later. She contents herself with sliding a hand around to his stomach and giving it a little slap to confirm what she already knows: it's rock hard.

'You look pretty well to me. You're perfect. Eat the pizza. Make Dad happy. And if you want to work it off with some push-ups later, I'll keep count. And maybe help by licking the sweat off your back.'

He turns and slides his hands around the waist of her swimming costume. It's red, obviously. His mouth moves to her ear. 'You're a very supportive fiancée. Do you know that?'

'Get a room, for fuck's sake,' Maria groans from the nearest sun lounger. 'You guys are sickening.'

She drags her head around to look at Maria, and Alex's mouth moves to her hair. But her sister is grinning at her in a way that suggests she thinks they're pretty cute.

'Leave my sister alone and go help Peter on the barbecue.' Maria jerks her head to her husband, who's gamely manning Alex's barbecue across the terrace.

'It's so emasculating, being a Fiori man.' Alex's tone is grumbling, but his enormous smile tells her he's thrilled at being at the centre of the Fiori banter. He kisses her hair and turns, his fingers trailing reluctantly away from her waist.

'You love it!' Maria calls after him. 'You've waited your whole life to be abused like this!' When he's escaped over to Peter, she turns to Clara. 'He's literally perfect. You lucky bitch.'

It's been four months since she told Jeremy she wanted a divorce.

It's been three months since she and the kids moved in.

Jeremy reacted badly. He was completely blindsided, and hugely pissed off at being cuckolded by Alex Molloy, of all people. It would be like knowing your husband had cheated on you with someone as hot and high profile as Cheryl Cole, she figured. Absolutely gutting. Nor was he impressed that she'd kept her and Alex's past a secret from him. He accused her of being a secretive little bitch, and of whoring with her 'fucking thug' of an ex.

'I should have put two and two together,' he said. 'I knew he was a piece of fucking scum.'

Through her tears of guilt and fear and disgust, she noticed that Jeremy wasn't heartbroken. He was angry and mortified, but he didn't seem in the slightest bit heartbroken that she was planning on leaving him. She suspected he was more worried about what his mates down at the golf club would say. That made it easier. That, and every nasty word that left his mouth about her and Alex. It drove home that she'd chosen the better man.

That initial conversation was hideous and overly emotional on both sides, but a couple of days later, after she'd spent two tense and wakeful nights in the spare room bed, they sat down again on a Saturday morning when the kids were at tennis camp and Jeremy had graciously put off his game of golf. He was cold and unpleasant and level-headed. Told her that if she was going off with that rich fucker, he'd fight her for every penny she tried to take. That she'd better get a good lawyer, because he had one already, and he was rumoured to be excellent. That she'd be sorry because it would never last with this guy. But that he wouldn't fight her for the kids. She could have primary custody. And the only reason he wasn't kicking her out of the house *right now* was because of Charlie and Violet.

He didn't even fight for his own kids. That was what made her saddest of all.

The following Monday, he buggered off. He packed a suitcase and told her he'd be staying in one of his firm's corporate apartments in Butler's Wharf. He cancelled the ski trip, said there was no way he was taking the kids by himself. What an idiot. What a selfish prick. He threw away the opportunity to have a week of special bonding time with Charlie and Violet over a sport they all loved.

In the end, it couldn't have worked out better. Alex cancelled his entire schedule for a week and whisked them off to Val d'Isère, where he procured a stunning chalet. How much money he had to spend to get something like that, at such short notice, Clara shuddered to think. It gave him time to get to know her kids in neutral (and very fancy) territory, and it played into his strengths.

Seeing him laughing and messing around with Charlie and Violet, and doing stunts with them, and letting them stuff snowballs down his neck, and seemingly having even more fun than they did, was truly life affirming. It was made even more so by her suspicion that he hadn't had too many of these light-hearted experiences as a kid. It's always been one of her favourite things about parenthood—the fact that having children allows you to re-experience the wonder of seeing the world through their eyes. It teaches you how to play again, how to live in the moment and rediscover the power of *fun*.

Her beautiful children are teaching Alex how to have fun. She hasn't considered this: she's thought so much about what kind of father-figure he'll be to them, and he's made it clear that he expects having her kids in his life will bring him great joy, but seeing him with them allows her to believe, for the first time, that they may help him to heal. The three of them will help him to heal.

She introduced him to Zoe, too. They had coffee with her in the Oast House, and Zoe shared her experiences and her perspectives on death. Alex told her afterwards that it had helped. He was never going to relinquish responsibility for taking Lindsay's life, but he said he couldn't help but be soothed by Zoe's own serenity and her suggestion that the machinations of the universe and the longevity of our souls all surpass our human capacity for understanding. People pass, and we never fully understand why. People from our past come back into our now to change our future, and we never fully understand why. We must just accept what is.

Afterwards, he got a new tattoo on his inner forearm.

Rien n'arrive par hasard.

Everything happens for a reason.

It hasn't been all smooth. She can't believe how much she's had to ask Charlie and Violet to take on: Mummy and Daddy are splitting up; Daddy's moved out; Mummy's in love with this famous guy who, it turns out, is her secret ex-boyfriend; Alex wants them all to move in with him, eventually. Having the kids break up for Easter right after she dropped the bombshell has helped; it gave them all time to get to know each other.

Charlie has acclimatised more easily than Violet. Even at the tender age of eleven, he's had differences of opinion with Jeremy and has always been more likely to call him out when their values conflicted. He was also a big fan of Alex's, having already met him, and he was predisposed to be swept up in the glamour and excitement of Mum shacking up with someone so famous. He's already been dining out on his newfound celebrity status at school. As his teacher put it, when Clara filled her in on their home situation: *Short term helpful; long term concerning.* But she couldn't deny that it smoothed the path for them to build a more profound relationship.

Violet's been tougher to convince. She didn't melt down or throw her toys, but she cried a lot of quiet tears, and she was very worried about Daddy. She's always adored Jeremy and is very protective of him. How would Daddy feed himself when he wasn't a good cook, she wondered. And wouldn't he be lonely without their hugs every evening? It felt as though she was taking on a good deal of the burden that should be Clara's, and it broke Clara's heart.

But when she first introduced Violet to Alex, and she saw the look on his face, it broke her heart even more. His eyes welled up as he said hello to her. She'd warned him Violet was suffering, and whereas he was matey and teasing with Charlie, he was quiet and careful with Violet. He told her he would never, ever try to replace her daddy, but that he loved her mummy very, very much and wanted to make them all happy.

After that first meeting, he told Clara, 'She reminds me so much of you. I already want to make sure no fucker like me gets anywhere near her.'

After a week of skiing, when he'd done his best ballerina impressions on the ice rink and bonded with them over their mutual love of raclette fondue, Violet slowly, carefully let her guard down. And when she successfully stuffed a snowball down the collar of Alex's Prada ski suit, and guffawed in delight at his manufactured girly squeals, she turned to Clara and said, 'Daddy would never let us do that.'

Clara opted not to comment on Jeremy's inability to be a good sport and instead said, 'Alex has a lot of fun with you guys. I can tell he loves hanging out with you. You don't treat him like he's famous, and you're all very silly together, and he likes that.'

'He's just Alex, when he's with us.' Violet nodded sagely.

Indeed.

They're now openly together, to the endless fascination of the paps. Someone has leaked parts of their backstory and the press is desperate to get the first exclusive shoot and interview of them as a couple. *Ok!* pitches them relentlessly.

'I'd rather die,' Clara groans.

'I know. I'll deal with it. I've talked about you so many times in the past, and I want to shout it from the rooftops that we're finally together. But I won't inflict it on you. And it won't be with *Ok!* But I'm never doing another red carpet appearance without you by my side. Just warning you.'

'No more skeletal models on your arm?'

'Amen to that.'

They've done a couple of red carpet events so far, and she's survived. They've made the front page of the tabloids each time, and Alex used a sweet, smiley red carpet shot of both of them to announce on his Instagram feed that he was back with his childhood sweetheart, the love of his life. This has prompted headlines from 'Who is Clara Winters?' (*Grazia*) to 'Molloy, she's Married!' (*The Mirror*).

He joins her for school drop off and pick up as often as his schedule allows, and this has caused consternation. Not only has the school had to put security on the gates to keep the paps off the property, but Clara is inundated with overtures from mothers she hardly knows, whether Alex is with her or not. But particularly when Alex is with her. His baseball cap is no protection at all. That first time he accompanied her to pick the kids up, their walk across the carpark was thrilling and terrifying in equal measure. The looks. The pointed fingers. The whispers. But he'd held her hand through it all.

'Most of them are beside themselves,' Abi tells her. Abi can always be relied upon for the unvarnished truth. 'Some are judging you for leaving Jeremy. Some are competing for Jeremy already.'

This is amusing and reassuring in equal measure. He won't be alone for long; she'd put money on it.

'Some are saying you're not thin enough for Alex to stay interested in you.'

'Naturally.' Whether Alex loves her body is right at the bottom of things she needs to worry about. He reassures her on that front every single night.

'And the vast majority are just mad with jealousy. You're shagging one of the most shaggable blokes in England.'

'Indeed I am!'

There have been lots of lovely comments, too. Many people have taken the news at face value: Clara's bagged herself a hot celebrity, and she's been told many times how great it is to see the tables turned; how refreshing that she's the one who's gone after what she wants, and not the husband. But others have picked up their history in the press, including the trauma of their forced separation, and are enamoured with the idea that she's finally back with her childhood sweetheart. Turns out, far more people are closet romantics than she'd have expected.

In the end, it was logistics that accelerated their move into Alex's house. In a fit of romantic spontaneity, he named it Skuytercliff, in honour of the cottage from *The Age of Innocence,* where Ellen Olenska said she could imagine being perfectly happy (yes, she made him read it. And watch the movie. And yes, he loved them both. Especially Daniel Day Lewis). It'll cause plenty of headaches for poor Royal Mail, but she couldn't think of a better name for their home.

In any case, Jeremy wanted to put their house on the market as soon as possible to capitalise on the spring buying boom and the flurry of all sorts of blossom in their garden, and she agreed. It went to sealed bids within a fortnight (lovely Sevenoaks homes like theirs, in gated developments, were always snapped up) and the buyers were in a hurry to exchange and complete.

Clara was concerned that making her kids shack up with their mother's new lover so soon would be putting an unfair burden on them, but she reckoned without a couple of factors. First, the skiing trip had quickly acclimatised them not only to Alex but to the idea of their mum sharing a bed with him, which was convenient. Second, she massively underestimated her children's ability to be bought with incentives shamelessly bordering on bribery.

As soon as they saw Skuytercliff, they were beside themselves, Charlie in particular. They adored their attic, with its grown up vibe, its privacy and toys (Alex had installed an enormous TV, a Playstation and a fridge. Clara rolled her eyes when she saw them). They were obsessed by the pool, and Alex told Violet she could have private ballet lessons in the stunning studio. He walked her through the mood-lighting options, one of which bathed the whole space in lilac light. And finally, he promised them as many sleepovers and playdates as they wanted. Clara rolled her eyes again—he had no idea what he was letting himself in for. Since then, there's been a steady stream of kids through the house, most of them undoubtedly egged on by their mothers.

His tactics may have been dubious, but she has to hand it to Alex: the novelty factor of a beautiful new home, awash with gadgets and their own dedicated space, as well as access to a grown-up who spends hours of his time with them and behaves suspiciously like Tom Hanks in *Big* when he does so, has worked wonders in smoothing what could have been a bumpy few months for them all.

It's now July, and they're all relaxed enough in their new home that the Roche Bobois sofa in the attic has an impressive number of battle scars (now hidden under machine-washable throws) and Alex and the kids are comfortable enough for him to bollock them when needed, and for them to answer back. It couldn't be better. She's already putting her 'Clara room' through its paces. She's completed a whole year's worth of footage for Zoe's cook book. That project is nearly over. With Alex and Connor's enthusiastic support, she's already talking to a number of brands about using photography to tell their stories.

The pizzas are ready, thanks to Dad. And whatever he said about the pizza oven, they're definitely Casa Valentina standard. The meat is ready too: Alex and Peter have done a great job. Five soaking kids and six adults sit around the table on Skuytercliff's terrace, in front of the gleaming slate pool. Aperol has made way for Rock Angel, and Alex stands up, glass in one hand, Clara's hand in the other.

'Fiori family. Thank you for welcoming me with open arms for a second time. I plan to make it far more worth your while this time around.'

'No more prison, please, eh?' her dad yells, and Clara glares at him, but Charlie and Violet are guffawing at this outrageous social faux pas. Alex takes it in his stride and laughs.

'No more prison, definitely. I love your daughter, and I can't wait to marry her. I love her kids, too. I've always wanted to be a proper member of your wonderful family. I've wanted nothing else for over twenty years. Thank you for giving me a second chance. *Salute.*'

He bends down and kisses her, and her world slows down. This life. This man. This happiness. Forever.

THE END

If you enjoyed When Then Becomes Now, I'd REALLY appreciate you leaving a **quick review on Amazon or Goodreads.** Reviews are everything for independently published authors! Thank you so much

ABOUT ME

I like to change things up! I spent my 20s as a banker and my 30s bringing up small children and running my own fashion brand (Madderson London).

I started writing aged 41, and I wonder why I didn't do it sooner.

I've always loved writing. My daughter Tilly has an old notebook of mine filled with half-finished stories and accompanying drawings. I've read for as long as I can remember, guzzling up books so quickly that my mum always protested that I couldn't be reading them properly.

I published my first book, *Metamorphosis*, in February 2020, right before lockdown happened. It's a non-fiction book about escaping from our cocoons and living as a butterfly. As lockdown progressed, I found escapism in devouring lots of delicious chick-lit (for want of a better title) and I realised I had a few novels in me too. I have loved every single minute of writing them.

I've published my books independently, and I love the freedom it provides. The world of independent publishing is fascinating and so empowering--I'm delighted to share more of my experiences of self-publishing if you're interested.

I'd love to hear from you with feedback, suggestions and requests! My email is sara@saramadderson.com.

MY BOOKS!

FICTION

Sorrel Farm Series

Food for Thought (1st)

Heaven on Earth (2nd)

When Then Becomes Now (3rd)

Standalone

Parents and Teachers

The Winter's Fail

NON-FICTION

Metamorphosis

Printed in Great Britain
by Amazon

67240702R00173